SYNCHED

A HARD-WIRED NOVEL

DEANNA BROWNE

CELTIC
MOON
PRESS

Copyright © 2019 by Celtic Moon Press
All rights reserved.
Synched - Hard-Wired - Book 2
Celtic Moon Press
ISBN-13: 978-1-948884-26-6 (e-book)
ISBN-13: 978-1-948884-27-3 (paperback)

Cover Art: Copyright © 2019 Bukovero

*To my family for their love and support.
This book wouldn't be here without it.*

ACKNOWLEDGMENTS_

I'm so grateful for my writing tribe: Dave Bennemen, Jami Gray, Tom Hansen, and Betsy Love. They help me hone my craft and keep me sane when the voices threaten to take over. Thank you!

Also, a big thanks to my early readers that gave valuable feedback to make this a better story including Tom Hansen, Betsy Love, Eleanor Bowers, and Lorelei Mote. I'm also grateful for a brilliant editor, Tyson Pink, and wonderful cover artist, Bukovero.

Also, a never-ending thank you for my family, especially Spencer, Eleanor, and Kathy. They are my biggest cheerleaders and help me manage my chaos, watch kiddos, and keep me on track. This book wouldn't have made it out into the world without their influence and support.

CHAPTER ONE_

Ari ducked to avoid the oncoming strike and spun away from her opponent, only it wasn't enough. The staff hit her in the stomach, her breath escaping with a grunt. Thankfully, her suit absorbed most of the hit, and she carried the momentum though into a backward roll, her own staff still in hand.

"Faster." Niomi drove Ari off the mat and into the sand.

Spinning the staff, she drove it towards Niomi, but Ari was a second behind. Again. Niomi countered, striking out at Ari. This time she blocked the attack with a mirroring forward cut, but Niomi kept coming at her, stronger and faster than Ari ever hoped to be.

Ari retreated.

"Think offensively. Make a plan," Niomi ordered, with a steely determination in her eyes.

My plan is to avoid using my healing kit again. Ari couldn't manage a response between her jagged breaths. Her arms burned with exhaustion, but she struck out. At the last second, she switched directions, hoping to catch Niomi off guard—like that was even possible.

Ducking low, Niomi avoided the hit and countered. That's all it took. Before Ari knew it, Niomi had her staff in the back of Ari's neck and a foot on her lower back.

Spitting out a mouthful of sand, Ari managed to speak. "Give."

Niomi let go of her immediately and stepped back on the mat. "You can't give an opponent that big of an opening."

Ari pushed up on her hands and knees, struggling to catch her breath. Lifting her gaze, she squinted into the partly cloudy sky. "What opponent? You act like I'm going to be a gladiator in the VR programs. Remember, I was hired to program, not fight. I don't need this."

Since she joined VisionTech six months ago, she found the training was nothing as she imagined. Hired as a warper, she thought she'd be focused on programing inside the virtual reality world. Warpers were about as rare as conjoined twins. Why waste time on this? Ari still hadn't figured out why the need for the intense cardio and martial arts training.

Niomi's bright red lips sucked on her hydro pack. She said she was in her forties, but Ari didn't see it with Niomi's muscular body and fierce features. Niomi's hair was shaved all around except for a strip of long blond hair on top of her head, currently wrapped in a bun.

Done drinking, she focused on Ari. "You also need to step up your cardio. You shouldn't get so winded this easily."

Sitting up in the sand, Ari laughed, not even trying to make it back to the mat. She took in the exercise area set up in the middle of this island paradise. Hell in the middle of heaven, she called it. "I think jogging five miles a day is plenty."

Niomi offered Ari a hand and pulled her up. "Being in top physical and mental health will aid you in your abilities inside the program."

"But I haven't even spent that much time in the program." Ari had been doing classes on logics, problem solving, world history and politics, in addition to her combat and physical training.

Niomi narrowed her eyes, her dark tattooed eyeliner knife sharp, matching the intricate tattoo on her ear.

"Okay, okay." Ari raised a hand in defeat and reached for her own hydro pack.

"Finish your strength exercises and meet me in my room by one. We have something new to go over." Without another word, Niomi took off at a jog towards their section of the Wave.

Mind turning with what Niomi meant by 'new', Ari was tempted to skip the exercises, but Niomi would know. Her required uniform, a sleek navy Fit Suit worth more than her old apartment, constantly read her vitals and reported everything back to Niomi. Heading towards the weight set, she re-braided her long brown hair. She may have the tanned skin of an islander, but her already wavy hair turned into a fizzy mess with the humidity on the island.

Nothing she could do about it now, unless she wanted to shave it off like Niomi. She wiped off the sweat with a nearby towel and went to work. By the end of the next hour every muscle ached with fatigue. Instead of running, Ari slowly walked, wishing she would have brought a board for the ride back. Maybe with enough boards she could just float black in a sublime position. She'd have to work on that.

Sweat continued to drip down her neck as she headed towards her secluded rooms in the Wave. Small monkeys chirped in the trees as they jumped from branch to branch with ease, as if almost mocking her. Niomi said working outdoors made training more realistic. Ari loved the view but hated the air. It made her feel like a human sponge, always damp. Watching the sky, it looked to her as if another storm was going to pass through tonight.

The Wave appeared in front of her, the main building of VisionTech. Constructed out of a crystalline photoelectric material that curved and rose like a ribbon waving in the wind, it could project a variety of images to blend in with the surroundings, though from the inside it was clear. It melded a perfect balance of nature and technology.

Her rooms were on the west end of the building, a small annex of sorts. An annex with high security clearance. The doors opened on command, a gush of air greeting her and cooling the sweat on her brow.

"Welcome, Ariana Mendez," her AI said as she entered the building.

"Hey, Henry," she answered her ever-present assistant. Having a computer track her every step didn't sit right with her. She not only had her uniform, but the implant in the base of her neck, right below her VR port, tracking her physical location too. She understood the reason: she was expensive to obtain and worth a lot more. The threat of her being taken by another company or government was real, but it never felt natural.

Ari headed down the silent hall, past the empty communal kitchen, coffee shop, and theater area. It took a while to get used to the isolation, especially when she knew there were hundreds, probably thousands of people working on this island. These rooms, actually the whole wing, were reserved for warpers, but she was the only one. Niomi also had rooms nearby but usually kept to herself.

On entering her own suite, the lights flicked on, and her

playlist blared through the halls. Mostly electro songs, they seemed to fit the sterile environment, but every now and then she'd listen to some old Latin tunes to remind her of home.

Walking into her bathroom, she stripped down and jumped into the shower cubicle. Warm water massaged her muscles, and she had to fight the urge not to linger. Today, Niomi had something new for her and Ari still couldn't guess what it was.

With a command, Ari shut off the water and turned on the full body, floor-to-ceiling dryer. Like a silver doorway, it warmed her up and dried her off in no time. Once her hair was mostly dry, she dressed in a clean Fit Suit. Ari didn't always wear these electronic suits, but Niomi preferred them for work, especially if she was going under, so they could monitor their vitals. Fingering the expensive material, she wondered how much these suits helped while in the VR.

If her father had one, would he have still gone into a coma? Probably. His VR coma was of his own making. Not wanting to face reality, his subconscious chose to never wake up. But they could maybe help her brother, Marco, who had the same tendencies.

Thinking of home, she wished she could call Reed, but he worked until five. Her boyfriend was the one thing she was able to bring with her. VisionTech gave Reed a job and opportunities that he couldn't find back at home, opportunities that kept him just as busy as Ari. Pushing aside her distracting thoughts, she headed out to find Niomi.

The hall shone with its pristine white floors and large floor-to-ceiling windows leading out to a view of lush jungle life making the beauty feel alive. A colorful bird soared down into the dense foliage. Surreal.

Ari continued down the hall as a knock sounded from her suit. With her hands tangled in her hair she was unable to see who was calling. "Answer," she said. "This is Ari. Who's this?"

"Only your most brilliant friend that you will adore and worship forever." Ari recognized his voice of her technical liaison.

"So, why are you so brilliant today?"

"I finished your personalized modification for your VR suit. You'll be flying through your program."

"Flying, huh? Pretty sure humans conquered that in the 1800s."

"Not like this. Trust me, you'll love it."

A grin stretched wide on her face. Vinh's job was to assist with her gear and anything else she needed. In the past months, he quickly grew into a friend. A quirky friend with no people skills, who loved to socialize.

"Is that part of what Niomi wanted to do today? Try out my gear?"

"Think so. Not sure. Aren't you cutting it close to meet her? I don't want to hear you complaining about Niomi busting your butt in training."

Ari checked the time on the HUB built into the forearm of the suit and realized she was late. "Flip. I better go." She rushed down the hall.

The annoying AI called out. "Remember your meeting with Niomi in room—"

"Yeah, yeah. Hold your horses, Henry." Her artificial personal assistant's name changed weekly, sometimes daily, depending on Ari's mood. Henry was the name of Ari's first pet, a pissy old cat. And it fit, today.

Ari hurried down the hall. If she was a minute late, Niomi would require her to run some serious mileage with her tomorrow. And Niomi could run for miles on end. As it was, Ari had never been so fit in her life and never wanted to be. It's her luck to be stuck with a full-time trainer that thinks muscles outside a virtual are just as important as in.

"You have thirty seconds to—"

"Shut up, Henry." She quieted her AI as she sprinted around the corner, her feet sliding on the floor.

Metal doors appeared, and Ari hurried to her usual training room, sliding to a stop. While the door read her chip and scanned her cornea for clearance, she tried to slow her breath. Then, she walked into an empty training room.

Once inside the room, her breath caught in her throat as she took in the bloody face before her.

Two men fought on the screen in some type of office. The fight was shown from the point of view of a of man wearing a black suit of some kind. He was attacking another man dressed in long cream robes. The man in black obviously had the advantage as he pressed forward, striking repeated blows with his fists. Ari cringed as she watched blood drip off the robed man's chin. His dark skin couldn't hide the crimson color staining his face and dripping onto his beige robes.

She had seen violent movies and games, even played a few herself. But with this oversized screen, she didn't hear a soundtrack in the background, only the dull thud of hit after hit punctuated with the moans of pain. It not only looked real, but felt real, like she was the attacker. The Suit spun around, using his elbow to strike at the man's jaw. A sickening crack echoed through the room as the robed man fell back; Ari turned from the screen unable to stomach any more.

She noticed Niomi standing further in the room with

the director at her side. Ari had only met him one other time, when she first signed her contract. She remembered how generic and perfect his looks were, with dark hair, pristine pearl skin, and purposeful brown eyes. Now, with the dim light of the room, Ari thought her first impression was right—attractive yet nondescript.

Niomi glanced over her shoulder. Narrowing her eyes, she motioned for Ari to watch the screen, her lips pursed together with a firm silence. Ari didn't dare speak and turned back to the screen.

The suit straddled the robed figure, whose fight appeared to finally die out. The robed figure spoke with the accent of an elite, "I don't have the answers you seek. Killing me won't help."

"Oh, I don't plan on killing you." The suit slowly bent forward and grabbed the man's forehead.

The screen blanked out, replaced by lines and lines of code in teal stripes. Code flew by faster than Ari could read it, and she had been practicing. After a moment, things slowed, and she caught bits and pieces. What was this, and where was this coming from? It looked like they were scanning a drive of some kind, but if so, that meant the suit was in a virtual world.

She had hundreds of questions, though with a quick glance at Niomi, Ari knew better than to ask. Whoever was running this, it appeared they were looking for something. They followed certain trails of code, then abandoned the trail and began with another. The lines slowed down. When Ari could finally read what he was after, she thought she'd be sick. Small children... couriers for information... She couldn't figure out all the details, but there was something about them going insane and there was a slaughter...

"What the hell?" She reached for a nearby table, not trusting her legs to do their job at the moment.

"Pause feed," the director spoke to the screen and then turned to Niomi, his condescending tone evident in every syllable. "You sure she is ready for this?"

Niomi watched Ari closely, as if accessing her reaction. The reaction beyond what the smart suit recorded. She turned back to the director. "No, but I'm sick of hearing her complaining. And we don't have time for it."

Ari snapped her head towards Niomi. "I don't complain." Okay, that maybe wasn't technically true, but she did all Niomi asked.

"Let's not get into that now." Niomi's dark red lips pulled up into a smile. "The director wants you pulled into your next level of training."

"I didn't think beating up politicians or clergy would be part of training. With as much money as you guys have, I would have thought you could hire some thugs for that."

The director walked towards Ari, seemingly unbothered by her accusations, like they were too beneath him to address. His pressed white uniform held a small silver clip on the pocket. It didn't say a name or anything as mundane as that, but Ari was sure it held something a lot more important. "Arianna, we don't expect you'll fight anyone. Your training for Niomi is merely for your health and protection in and out of the virtual. But we need to make sure you are ready for whatever gets thrown at you."

"If I didn't watch that guy get beat to a pulp, I'd feel better about it."

"That agent was always a bloodthirsty type," Niomi said.

Niomi must have trained him.

"We soon plan to introduce you to VLEX and want you prepared."

"VLEX?" Ari took a seat at the nearby silver table that she often worked at with Niomi. After her workout, her body couldn't take any more hits.

"I'm sure you've heard about it. Even whispers in your school?"

Ari shook her head.

"It's the elite virtual world created for diplomatic meetings and international business cooperation," the director explained like a lecturer on circuit.

"I assumed those types of worlds existed, but never heard of the name."

"VisionTech has quite an investment and active participation in VLEX."

"I see." Ari couldn't get the bloody image out of her mind.

"VLEX is nothing like what you just saw. That event didn't transpire inside VLEX and that agent wasn't ours. Someone released it to expose people. We just needed you to see what type of people are out there and what could happen if you're not careful."

People that obviously need to be tried for their crimes.

"If I had my way, it would have been a lot bloodier," Niomi said.

"I was hired to program, not fight or be some cyber spy." Ari pressed on her temple, wondering why they ever thought to hire her. "Ask Niomi, I'm a horrible fighter."

"I don't want a fighter," the director said. "I want a smart mind that can gather information and protect itself against digital manipulations."

Ari almost laughed. "And here I thought I'd be stuck writing virtual-in-virtuals for pervy old guys." She'd learned about programs where one could go so deep in the virtual world that they would forget they were in there. Rich people often wanted to retire like that.

"The powers you have to manipulate the virtual environment are a lot more important than that."

"So, what's next? Going into VLEX?" Ari asked.

With a voice command, Niomi turned on a smaller monitor in front of Ari. "Soon, but time in the VLEX is very expensive. You'll watch, learn, and train first."

The screen flicked on to a picture of a grandiose city, streets lined in stone, and buildings rising up to reach the sky. People moved around the city like ants scurrying around on an expensive table. The sky was a perfect shade of blue, the clouds scattered around on a sunny day. The perfection traveled to another level; even the weather knew better than to destroy the image.

"Can anyone watch this?" She wondered why she'd never seen this before in her schooling. Granted, her schooling usually only dealt with their own history of wars and innovation.

"It costs to have eyes on the city and even this view is limited, but we keep a constant eye on things. We are a global company that has important business throughout the world. We need you to help protect our interests inside VLEX." The director stood, one eyebrow raised as if expecting an answer.

Did she really have a choice? She signed her contract and if she didn't have to hurt anyone, she'd do what she could. And being here, she could do more for her family financially than anywhere else.

"I want to see my family again," she said, changing the subject.

"Of course." The director said with a smile. He had an

air about him, like he was God himself. Turning to Niomi, the almighty commanded, "See that it happens." Without another word he left.

Ari let her breath go and relaxed in the chair.

"Do you know how much work and money it takes to contact your family?" Niomi asked. "It would better to focus on your training."

Ari shrugged. She knew but didn't care. "So, bill me."

Niomi shook her head in disappointment and headed towards the screen, pulling up the command key in the corner. "While I get your request in order, I want you to start memorizing these skins."

"What are skins?" Ari turned in her chair to study the screen. A pale girl, with red hair and freckles appeared on the screen.

"People you will be in the VLEX. You need to memorize their back stories, their co-workers, drink preference, what they wear and other appearances down to the freckle. You will be required to become these people when necessary."

"Where do they come from? Am I taking over their jobs? Won't someone notice?"

"Don't worry about that part. You work on being a chameleon. You'll never show your true self in the VLEX and may have to change appearances in a second's notice. Changing code from within will alert the authorities but you'll be long gone before they find you."

"Anytime people say 'don't worry', somehow it makes me worry more."

Niomi left the girl on the screen and took a seat next to Ari. "Do you trust me?"

Pulling back slightly, Ari considered the question. She had worked with Niomi for the past six months. Hell, they had sort of bonded over hours of martial arts videos—the old school ones from before computer manipulation ruined film. Niomi was hard, yet fair. But what did Ari really know about her?

Niomi sensed her hesitation. "I've always been honest with you. Ask me and I'll tell you."

"I can't beat someone to a pulp like in that video. I can't kill anyone."

"We aren't asking you to. This isn't real. And your training is more for the mental and physical benefits. But you're telling me you've never played games, killing orcs or whatever the hell kids are playing nowadays?"

Ari rubbed an invisible spot on the desk. "That just looked so real."

"Never forget where you are or who you are." Niomi's voice hit a stern intensity usually saved for training. "There are great differences between these two worlds, but the person is the same. There are several ways to handle a situation in the VR, as you know. Your other tools are a lot more powerful than your fists."

"What did the agent do to that man's mind?" The image of blood and then the massive amount of code unsettled her. Invading someone secrets, their beliefs, felt wrong. Despite her natural aptitude, she loathed the idea of VRs to begin with.

"That tactic is only used in serious circumstances, where information is vital. The information will be taken to the authorities. Think of it as interrogation without real or lasting pain. Society has spent years painfully torturing others to get information and a lot of the time that information would be forced or false. That age is passed, at least with warpers." Niomi placed a hand on Ari's shoulder. Even though they touched all the time as they fought, this felt important. Her steel eyes held a softness to them. "Warpers are a blessing."

The verdict was still out for Ari. When she was first called to study virtual reality programming, she thought it a curse. As she came to accept her position in society, she realized the power she had, and the price tag placed on her new ability. Yes, warpers had gifts others dreamed of, but did they really help society or just push it farther down the electronic rabbit hole?

"You'll see soon enough." Niomi broke the tension between them and headed to the screen. After a couple clicks, she turned back. "I sent you the files. You can check them out this afternoon, then take a break tonight. Why don't you watch an old movie while you eat? You could probably use a break."

"Are you sure I heard you right? Did you just say I could use a break?"

Niomi rolled her eyes. "Don't make me regret it, newbie," she replied, pushing Ari out the door.

"Guess that means I'll order the sushi?" Ari said to the door. Since they lived on an island, Niomi pushed fish along with fresh fruit and veggies more than anything. Raw fish was hard to swallow at first, literally, but now sushi was one of Ari's favorites. Now sea urchins were disgusting; Ari had to draw the line somewhere.

Back in her room, Ari called Reed, and he appeared on her huge screen.

"What are you smiling about?" He sat at his desk, working on an art table in front of him. Island life agreed with him. His skin tanned to a nice light brown while his hair had sandy blond highlights.

"Every time I see your face two feet tall, I can't help but smile." She never tired of looking at him.

"I'm pretty jealous of your screen too, but we can't all be spoiled." His soft lips pulled up into a grin.

"Free tonight for a movie?"

"Sorry. I have homework." He motioned to the tablet in front of him. "Rain check?"

"Of course."

"Call me when it's over, so I can say goodnight."

"Deal." She clicked off the screen and checked with her only other friend on the island, Vinh.

Since he was busy as well, it was only Niomi and Ari for the movie that evening. It wasn't as relaxing as a real movie should be with Niomi constantly critiquing every action section. They did have a large plate of sushi and fruit delivered to accompany the old Asian movie. The translation was a bit spotty as the actors' lips didn't quite coordinate with their words. But, since most of the movie was fighting, it didn't matter.

As the movie ended, Ari turned to Niomi on the other side of the couch. "How did you get into fighting so much?"

Niomi startled a bit at the question, and it wasn't easy to surprise Niomi.

Ari continued, "Come on. How can one person want to constantly eat so healthy, fight with weapons, and run like someone is always chasing her?"

Niomi turned towards the screen and turned it off with a command. Her blonde hair fell to one side of her head. With her profile to Ari, she could see the vulnerability in Niomi that was usually covered by a strength and fierceness. After six months, it surprised Ari as much as the next words.

"Growing up, I was hurt... bad. I swore I'd never play the victim again, and I haven't." Niomi turned, her shoulders tightening, and eyes narrowing back to their normal position. "You want to know why I'm hard on you? It's because I never want you to have to live through something like that. So maybe next time you can quit your whining and trust me."

Unsure of what to say to that personal confession, it took Ari a moment to reply. "I trust you, but it doesn't mean I won't complain when you torture me."

Niomi threw her napkin at her. "If you're going to complain, you might as well get clean up duty. Don't forget you have homework tonight. Get started on the skins."

"Thanks," she said sarcastically. Ari grabbed the left-over plates, her thoughts on Niomi. That was the most she had shared with Ari in six months. It didn't mean they were going to start to do each other's hair, but it was something.

Since Ari's abilities were worth so much, they didn't want her with the rest of the population. The more people that knew about her, the more chances the outside world would too. Granted, she had her boyfriend, Reed, but he was working like crazy to catch up with their tech program and started a design program at night. That left Vinh, and Ari's maid, Jewels, who only came around if Ari called her.

She messaged Reed to make sure they were still on for tomorrow morning and then headed to her rooms. Dressed in pajamas and tucked into her soft bed, Ari flipped on her large screen and starred at the red-headed woman. With a finger, Ari enlarged the picture of the woman to view the 3D image closer, not only to study, but to memorize it.

This woman must be important enough to impersonate. Who knew, maybe she wasn't even a real person? She pushed aside those thoughts, she couldn't do anything about them now.

Ari continued to flick through the pictures of men, woman, dark, light, tall and short. They kept coming and a sickening sensation grew in Ari's chest. Not because of all the work this entailed; growing up poor, she wasn't afraid of hard work. She worried as her life shrunk to these small rooms and her only life was wearing others' skins, what would be left of her when she was done?

CHAPTER THREE_

The next morning, Ari's legs burned as she sprinted bare-
foot through the sand. Damp sand flung behind her as
strands of sweaty hair clung to her neck. The ocean blue
stretched as far as she could see. Beauty taunting her in her
misery. Her legs felt like rubber and she thought she better
stop before she ended up face down in the sand.

She reached out to Reed next to her. "I give."

They slowed down, but Reed kept walking. "Come on.
You'll get a cramp if you stop."

"If I cramp, just throw me out to sea," she said between
pants of air. She pulled out her pony tail, letting her wavy
dark hair fall past her shoulders.

The HUB on her wrist, beeped. "You've completed
2.75 miles in twenty-five minutes. A quarter of a mile
farther yesterday, but an overall lower speed by 2.4
percent."

She moaned and dropped into the sand. Her breath
coming out in ragged gasps. Ari stared out at the aquama-
rine water. It didn't matter how many times she looked out
at this never-ending expanse in the last six months, she

never got tired of it. As the ocean breeze cooled the sweat on her skin, she breathed in deep.

Reed sat down next to her in the sand, running a hand over his short sandy brown hair. "We went farther. Niomi can't give you that hard of a time." His silver Fit Suit clung tight to his body. He looked comfortable, whereas on Ari the suit felt constricting.

"We'll see. If I don't keep improving, she may not let me run with you anymore." As every VisionTech employee was supposed to get regular exercise, Ari recently convinced Niomi to let her run with Reed in the mornings, so they could spend time together.

Ari sighed at the thought of her upcoming meeting today. She'd fallen asleep memorizing all she could of the first three skins Niomi gave her. And now, with a sleep deprived brain, she doubted she would remember any of it.

Reed nudged her shoulder. "What's distracting you?"

"Work." She leaned onto his shoulder, breathing his warm spicy smell mingled with sweat. "Niomi started a new project for me."

"That bad, huh?"

She sat up. "Have you ever heard of VLEX?"

He furrowed his brow. "Recently we've been reviewing their security measures and how VisionTech has mirrored and improved upon them. What does your project have to do with VLEX?"

Ari lowered her eyes. "Don't think I can say." Per her contract, she wasn't supposed to discuss details of her job with anyone, including Reed. She figured sharing info about VLEX wasn't a big deal, since the whole elite population dealt with it.

"I get it." He wrapped an arm around her. "Your super cool top secret job is beyond lowly me," he joked.

"Trust me. I wish I didn't have it."

His brow furrowed. "Is it that bad?" He leaned towards her, nuzzling into her neck for privacy.

Since their suits had communication devices, they were always aware they didn't have control of who could listen in. And after school last year, they weren't taking any chances.

Ari leaned in, enjoying the closeness. "I'm fine."

"If you say so. Granted, sitting on a private beach with their hot boyfriend, most people would be fine."

"Except that he has an ego larger than the ocean." She gave Reed a friendly shove into the sand.

"It's hard not to. I'm surprised you haven't ravished me yet."

It wasn't for lack of trying. Finding true privacy was a struggle. Yet, with so much change lately, taking things slow was probably a good idea. Maybe it's because he was her brother's best friend and they grew up together. Deep down, Ari knew this was more than some teenage fling.

Digging her feet in the sand, they resumed their spots next to each other, watching the waves crash.

"You're in security," she said. "Do you ever worry that you'll be asked to break into something you shouldn't? Do something you shouldn't?"

His smart hazel eyes searched her face, probably for what she couldn't say. "I don't worry and don't plan to until it happens. When it does, I'll stand my ground and make my own choice. You make your own choices, Ari, and I'll be there to back you no matter what." He took her hand.

A comfort settled deep in her belly. Gratitude and desire in having Reed by her side overwhelmed her, and she leaned forward to kiss him. In her enthusiasm, she pushed him over and ended up in the sand. He held on tight and rolled until he was on top. Kneeling above her, the sun high-lighted gold strands in his hair. He looked like some sea prince.

"Is that how we're going to do this?" he asked with a mischievous grin on his face.

"Oh, shut up and kiss me."

And he did just that. Reed lips were light as feathers at first, teasing her. Wrapping her hands around his neck she pulled him down to show him she meant business. She melted into his kiss, losing herself in the desire of his touch.

She wrapped one leg around his thigh and in a move Niomi would be proud of, flipped him back over. Sand scattered between them, as Ari smiled down on him.

He squirmed under her hold but didn't really try to break it.

"Now you have me? What are you going to do with me?"

Ari savored this picture of him playing with her. His mouth turning up on the sides, struggling not to laugh. His kind eyes rose to the challenge.

"Well..." she leaned down to devour him, but her HUB rang with a call.

Before she could answer it, Niomi sounded. "Hey, love-birds, stop making out and get back here."

"How does she know?" Ari mouthed, surprised.

Niomi answered the question without even hearing it. "It's your suit. Your heart rate is up, but your location isn't really moving. Maybe if you studied more, you'd figure it out."

"Uh. We're heading back." Ari stood up and offered Reed a hand.

"Making out is a legitimate form of exercise," he said to Niomi.

"Not the way you two do it. Move your butt." A small click signaled the end of the conversation.

"Should I be offended?" Reed asked.

Ari laughed, shaking sand out of her hair. "Let's take it more as a challenge for next time."

"Want to race back?"

She rolled her eyes in response. When he looked resigned to walk, he checked the HUB on his suit. She used the distraction and took off. Cheating was necessary if she was going to win.

They finally slowed as they approached VisionTech. Technically, the whole island was VisionTech, but they headed to her rooms in the the Wave. The wilds of the tropical forest surrounded them on their path. VisionTech did a great job at working around the environment.

Reed grasped her hand when they arrived at her door. "Did you ever think we'd end up here? Working in a tropical paradise?"

"It's almost perfect." Almost being the key word. There was a painful spot in her heart where her mother and brother resided, and she knew Reed felt the same way. Their quarterly visits never quite felt like enough. Yet, they did get to spend time together on an island paradise, hand in hand.

"See you tonight for dinner?" she reminded him.

"I actually have to work on my proposal for the Art Department." He looked as disappointed as Ari felt. Reed had been working with the Security Department and staying in their dorms but was given an opportunity to work with the Art Department in his free time. With his love for drawing, he couldn't pass this opportunity up.

"You'll do great. I know it." She raised up on her tiptoes and planted a kiss on his cheek. "Ping me later."

———

While Ari was in the shower, Niomi sent her a ping that they'd set up a meeting with her family. It took a team to arrange, so they would be untraceable. Ari dressed in a pair of dark jeans, comfortable old favorites that reminded her of home, and a blue t-shirt she couldn't figure out how they got so soft.

She didn't want to wear her Fit Suit in this VR to let Niomi monitor every heartbeat and pulse. These VR's were different from normal for her. The program connected to an illegal market, which cost plenty, but let them contact VRs around the world. And breaking through the barriers Ari's government set up wasn't easy either.

"You ready?" Niomi greeted her as Ari entered the VR lab.

"Have been for weeks." This would be only the second time she had spoken to her family in months.

"Get on it." Niomi motioned to the seat. "I'm just finishing the connection. Any setting you want in particular? Better to not use your powers if you can help it."

"How about an island or beach? Like what we have here?" She'd love to show her mom what her view is every day. Even her brother, Marco, might be jealous.

Her trainer shook her head. "I can't do the exact location. Too dangerous, but I'll find something exciting."

Ari rolled her eyes as she sat in the leather seat. Exciting to Niomi could be a volcano or something. Ari leaned back and reached for the cord.

With her hair already in a high pony, Ari slipped the cord in the base of her skull, where her port resided. The metallic click still sent a cold shiver down her spine. She'd never get comfortable with a machine invading her mind, and she never wanted to.

"You have thirty minutes," Niomi said from the computer. "We'll be monitoring for eavesdroppers."

"Thanks." Ari tried to relax, closed her eyes and let herself go.

When she opened her eyes, she stood at the edge of a great canyon. One step forward and there was at least a hundred-foot drop. Her muscles tensed as she stepped away from the edge. Exciting was one way to look at it. Stepping back, Ari took in the landscape. Browns and reds colored the canyon walls, with a clear blue lake carving a path down below. Tall bushes surrounded her and set in the middle was a wood bench.

She sat down and didn't have to wait long before her brother appeared—alone. He wore a black buttoned up shirt and jeans, his hair a bit long and starting to curl around his ears. Every day he looked more and more like their father. Her heart ached at their loss. Last time she saw her father, he was babbling to himself inside a VR program, one which he'd never left for the last seven years.

She shoved those memories aside and rushed to give her brother a hug.

"Good to see you too, Ari." He returned the hug, his arms wrapping around her waist and lifting her in the air. "Putting on some poundage, sis."

Pushing back, she whacked Marco on the shoulder. "Shut up."

"Ouch. Muscles too." He rubbed his arm, over-exaggerating.

"I've been working out, so watch it."

He laughed. "It's good to see you're doing well and can fight off unwanted advances."

She ignored the dig at Reed. "Where's Mom?" She turned, hoping to see her mother join the virtual.

"Couldn't make it." His eyes lowered, a soberness falling on his usually jovial features.

Ari grabbed his arm. "What happened?"

"What didn't? The government tried to put her into a labor camp, saying that she needed to pay back for your education. I was underground at the moment—"

"She can't be at a camp." Ari had constantly worried about the backlash for running away from her schooling, but people reassured her they would be safe. "I'm coming home, now."

"Whoa, slow down and let me finish." He led her over to the bench. "Don't worry. She's not at a camp. I broke her out and she's hiding off-grid with me."

Ari slumped against the bench. "Good. But what does that mean exactly? Why isn't she here?"

"They only told me about this meeting an hour ago, for security reasons they say. I'm out on business and had to find a place to hook into an off-country network. Not the easiest thing to do with an hours' notice. And it's not the most upstanding establishment. Mom would have to clean this machine for an hour before using it."

"Probably." Their mother was a clean freak that hated VRs to begin with. "So how is she doing with everything?"

"Given the alternative, good. I think she's finally come to see the value of the black market."

"Are you getting the money I send you?"

"Yeah. Dave makes sure I get it in cash. It helps Mom's conscience. She looks down on my methods to earn money." He grinned the same naughty smile from when he was eight.

"Good. Is everyone else okay? Reed's mom?"

"Yeah. I give her cash on the side, but she refuses it most the time, saying to save it for Reed. How is he?" Marco had been best friends with Reed since they were kids.

"Good. He's learning a ton and gets to do his art and graphics at night."

"Is he keeping his hands to himself?"

"A bit too much, actually. Could you talk to him about that?"

"Gross, sis." He pushed her slightly. "Also, Tessa wants you to say hi soon. I have a couple messages for you to download off the server when we're done. And that idiot Garrett from school keeps posting on all the gaming boards for you. Saying you owe him or some trash like that."

Her stomach sank at the idea of Garrett. She did owe him a favor but didn't see how to return it here in the middle of the ocean. She'd worry about that later. Maybe Tessa—her old roommate—would have an idea. "What else have I missed?"

Marco continued updating her on all the neighborhood gossip and when done grilled Ari on what she was doing, eating, and playing. Her brother loved gaming as much as anyone. She told him what she could while remaining as vague as possible. The minutes flew by and took her back to the time when they last lived in the same house. They would sneak into each other's rooms and talk until they fell asleep. Except this time neither came close to tired, and Niomi's voice signaled three minutes left.

"That didn't feel like half an hour," Marco said, standing up.

"Not at all."

"So when will we see you next?"

Ari shrugged. "Not sure. I'm starting the next phase of my training soon, not that I'm sure what that entails."

"Well, don't get crazy in there, you'll—"

"Get out now! And cover your tracks." Niomi's voice boomed inside the program. "Now!"

Marco's smile fell, and he nodded. "I'll be fine. Get out." And he quickly vanished.

Only then did Ari pull out of the program.

CHAPTER FOUR

"What the hell?" Niomi shouted as she pulled the cable out of Ari's port. "When I said leave, I meant it."

"I needed to make sure Marco was okay."

"That was really stupid."

Ari ignored the insult. "What happened in there?"

Niomi stormed back to her computer, her fingers flying over the keys. "Someone hacked into our site. Security is looking into it now. You didn't do anything in there did you? Morph the program?"

"No. I was just talking to my brother." Ari pushed up from the chair, slowly curling her fist. "By the way, the government is after my mother. She had to go into hiding. Did you know?"

"I don't follow your mother. My job is you."

Ari slammed her fist onto the table. "You promised they would be taken care of."

"Take it up with HR. I have enough trouble taking care of you."

"Niomi!" Fury raced through her veins. This wasn't something Niomi could just blow off.

Her trainer slowly turned, glancing at Ari's fist on the table. She took a deep breath and exhaled slowly. "You're right. Your family is important. Are they safe and getting the money they need?"

Ari realized her body trembled in fear. Would her family be okay? She forced herself to focus on the here and now. "Marco got my mom out, and they are in hiding. Dave has been getting them the money. But what about now? Will Marco be okay?"

"I'm trying to find that out." Niomi motioned to the screen. "We take every threat seriously and will track down the hack. It could be just a bored troll out there or something more. But given what I read about your brother in your file, I think he'll be okay. After hacking into the Mayor's feed and escaping unscathed, he can make it. He's smart and has connections. And if we have to, we can relocate them if they want."

Sitting down on a nearby stool, the tightness in Ari's chest lessened. "You're right. Marco can take care of himself. And he'd hate for me to pull him out and trap him somewhere in a real job." He told her no more than once when she tried to convince him to come with her.

"We have a team that will assess the situation. They'll let us know as soon as they know. If people don't connect you to them, the safer they will be."

She nodded. "Okay."

"Go grab a drink and calm down. I'll go over things with Security and create an incident report. Vinh will be dropping off your upgraded suit soon as well." Niomi turned back to her computer.

Trying to calm herself, Ari headed down to the kitchen to grab a drink. Since she'd accepted the position at Vision-Tech, she worried whether it was the right decision for her family. If she hadn't, the government would have forced her into another position without ever seeing her family again. Was it selfish to want freedom, even if your family had to pay the cost? Next time, she'd talk her brother into coming here or at least sending her mom.

Sick of being stuck with her own thoughts, she called Vinh. "Are you heading over with my suit?"

"No hello? How are you doing, Vinh? I'm sad at how downhill your manners have gone since you arrived at VisionTech."

Vinh continued rambling. As she turned the corner, she found he stood in the hall with a suit in hand. "I blame Niomi really. This isolation can't be good for a person."

Ignoring his lecture on manners, her lips curled up in a smile at the sight of her new suit. "You finished it."

"You doubted me?" It was a shiny gray material that was clearly expensive.

"Never." She reached for her suit, the soft material lighter than she expected. With the ache and worry of her family still present, she was grateful for the distraction. "Have time for a drink?"

He glanced at the time on his wrist. "Yeah. They won't miss me for a while."

They headed to the kitchen for some hot drinks. Ari thought the coffee machine in the communal kitchen must have authentic beans growing in the walls, along with farmers grounding them by hand. It was better than anything she ever tasted. They each grabbed a latte and sat down to chat. Talking to him about home, the fear faded to the background. Vinh laughed as she relayed some of Marco's old stunts, and he shared some of his own.

Vinh grew up not too far from where they were and was recruited as an engineer. Making his own AI by the age of fourteen, he was brilliant and left his home in Thalasia when he was seventeen. He'd been here only a few months longer than Ari.

"So, did you ask out Tara from Marketing?" She'd been hearing about Tara for weeks now.

He shrugged. "She started dating some idiot from Security. I guess some people are into big muscles and not big brains."

"Sorry."

"Don't be. Glad I found out now and didn't waste any of my brilliance on her." A message pinged on his HUB, and he heaved a sigh as he read it. "I got to head out. Thanks for the coffee."

"Anytime." Ari realized that they didn't even get to talk about her suit, really. Which must have been hard for Vinh. She traced a silver line that caught the light against the black material. Guess the time for moping was done.

———

Ari got to test out the suit sooner than she thought. The next day they went inside a basic VR program. With Vinh's new suit on, Ari stood across from Niomi at what looked like a park of some kind. Cement paths curved around large grassy areas. Large trees were scattered around, providing cool shade as colorful flowers dotted the landscape, adding the perfect amount of color. It would have been a great place to spend the day with Reed, instead Ari stared at Niomi who looked ready to fight someone.

"Do you remember the first profile in the notebook I gave you?"

Ari thought of the strawberry blond woman and nodded.

"Become her."

"Now?" Ari had never assumed another personality, though she'd been taught how.

Niomi looked around, her shoulders raised. "Anything better to do?"

"Okay." Ari closed her eyes, thinking back to the woman, Kari. Most people would consider her attractive with wavy strawberry blond hair and dark blue eyes. Though Kari tried to hide her large forehead with bangs, her full cheeks took up a lot of real estate on her face. Her body was thin, except for a large chest, which Ari didn't look forward to wearing or creating.

Taking a deep breath, she began the writing code. Instead of manually writing code number by number, with Ari's gift, the world morphed around. Her heart picked up with exhilaration as she recreated herself, pulling from Kari's picture. When completed, Ari opened her eyes.

"Look at yourself." Niomi brow slanted in annoyance. "This 'close your eyes' thing has to go."

Looking down, Ari saw the problem. She exaggerated all the physical aspects she remembered. This version of Kari could have passed for a cartoon character. Her chest was double what Ari remembered, while the rest of her thin frame lacked any muscular definition. Her face warmed at the embarrassing rendition. "I guess I need some work."

"You guess?" Niomi cocked a brow, but her mouth twitched as if tapping down a smile. "First rule, keep your eyes open so you can make adjustments along the way."

Ari lifted her arm and focused on the code that laid underneath the image. It took her a few minutes to complete the arm perfectly, and to add the freckles to the right locations. A perfect imitation proved harder than she thought.

With a huff of breath, she dropped her arm. "I can't be expected to do this every time I enter a VR. I can't possibly memorize every freckle and hair for every person you gave me. I may be a warper, but I don't have a photographic memory."

"That's where your suit comes in. It can memorize files you create and recall them for you."

"Really?" Ari chuckled with relief.

"You still have to create them all yourself and learn to do it fast."

Nothing could be easy with Niomi. "Why? Why does everything have to be the hard way with you?"

"What if your suit malfunctions? What if you have to become somebody else to survive?"

"I didn't think about that." Ari swallowed, embarrassed for her overreaction.

"The VLEX is a world unto itself with a whole different set of rules. Imagine sneaking into a top-secret meeting, the punishment for which was life in prison."

"Wait, wait a moment." Ari rose a hand, grateful to find it hers. "What I'm doing could make me end up in prison?"

"If they could catch you or us, yes, but they won't. It is that serious though. They will track you down if they can. Warpers have always been banned from VLEX. Not that it stops all the powerful countries and corporations from sending their spies in."

"Then why am I going there?"

"To find out information about a new bill that has been introduced to the world council. They will not let private corporations in on the dealings, only governments, and we can't trust them to tell us what this bill entails. Information is power and some small message or captured conversation could be worth millions."

Ari paced for a moment inside the program. She knew what she was hired to do couldn't be easy, not for what she made, but the realization of what she had to do was a bit daunting. Steeling her resolve, she lifted her hands and began again, forming the arm into Kari.

Minutes, then hours passed as they worked on perfecting Kari. Ari felt almost embarrassed how intimately she knew this woman's body. When they were complete, they saved the data and worked on the different ways the woman liked to style her hair. She looked forward to someone with a simple short crew cut, maybe a man.

If it ended at looks, maybe Ari could have handled it, but then there were even more things to perfect. The sound of her voice, how she took her coffee, her education, and they even covered her past lovers—which Ari found disturbing. Ari's mind felt like a pile of mush. The thoughts of all the files on her computer overwhelmed her as well. Just when she thought she couldn't do any more, Niomi had one more test for her.

"Kari," Niomi began, she'd been referring to Ari as Kari for some time now. "What would you do if I did this?" Niomi shoved Ari backwards.

Ari stumbled back in surprise. Her training kicked in and she took a defensive stance. Niomi attacked, striking with her fists. Ari blocked, spun under to force Niomi to turn. Her face tightened, her lips pulling down in a scowl. Without warning, Niomi lunged forward, tackling her to the ground. It took mere seconds before Ari was on her stomach pinned to the ground eating grass.

"Give." Ari mumbled from her position. With Niomi's fierce attack, Ari tried to figure out what the hell was Niomi trying to prove here.

"There is no give, here."

"What?"

Niomi dug her knee into Ari's back. She grunted with pain. Ari had seen Niomi pissed before, but not like this.

"If you remember anything, remember this. You are always in character. Kari wouldn't fight back. She'd be scared, startled, probably scream. And if she fought back, it'd be like a girl who had never fought before."

"So, I'm supposed to just take it."

"Yes, you are. You can take pain. Distance yourself in the program if you have to, but take it."

Ari swallowed, still bound by Niomi's tight grasp. Angry tears welled in Ari's eyes as her helpless frustration built. "Then why teach me to fight at all?"

"Because one day you will need it. You won't always be Kari." Niomi leaned close. "Remember you are a warper. You don't have to fight, you can change this program to be whatever you need it to be. You, better than anyone, know this is only a game. Separate yourself and outsmart them. You always have more than one choice."

The next second, Niomi vanished, leaving the program.

Ari lay panting face down in the grass. Sometimes her life felt like a game, whether it be the government or Vision-Tech, she'd constantly be playing by other people's rules in and out of virtual reality programs. One day, she'd love to live her life on her own terms, but that wasn't her reality for now.

CHAPTER FIVE

By the time she got back to her room and showered, Ari only wanted to curl up in front of a show and eat all the ice cream she could get her hands on. Heading down to the kitchen, she found Jewels tidying up. She found some ice cream in the freezer from before. Jewels was one of the few people on the island that had access to Ari's rooms, and she helped clean, launder and do anything that a robot couldn't. Not a busy job, but Ari appreciated having her around.

"How are you doing today?" Ari grabbed two different cartons: mint chip and rocky road.

Jewels motioned to the cartons. "Better than you."

"Do you want some?"

"No, dear. These old bones work better with a light load. Can I get anything for you?" Jewels' eyes sparkled with kindness. Her old age was seen in the silver that lined her hair, or the age lines etched on her face, but those eyes shone.

"No." Looking down, she questioned her choice of food and grabbed a bag of popcorn just in case before heading to her room. "I'll catch you later, Jewels."

"Take care, dear."

Not wanting to see Niomi, who was the only other person to live in their annex of the Wave, Ari kept to her own rooms. She'd opened the bag and dug in by the time she got to her bedroom and curled up on her couch. The familiar ache flared up. Missing home, she called Reed.

He picked up with audio only, "Hey Ari." People spoke in the background.

"Hey, you busy?"

"A bit. I'm meeting with the art club, working on my design project." He had to submit a portfolio to be accepted as an art intern with VisionTech, and right now they liked him a lot more in security. To move divisions wasn't impossible, but not many people did it.

"Okay... I just—"

"Give me a minute guys," Reed spoke to the others in the room.

Instead of quieting down, they got louder. Several cat calls made it through the line to Ari. She felt embarrassed to be bothering Reed when he already had so much on his plate.

"Sorry, Ari. I'm stepping into the bathroom now." The background noise muted quite a bit.

"I know you're busy. I can let you go. I just wanted to say good night." Her stomach sunk, already missing him.

"You sure?" Before she could reply, he continued. "I am swamped over here but can take a break if you need."

"Don't worry about. We can talk tomorrow. Goodnight, Reed."

"Goodnight." The click ending the phone call, echoed through her empty apartment.

She dug into ice cream, angry at herself for being so disappointed. Reed came to VisionTech because of her and to be with her. Wasn't that enough confirmation of his feelings? He was busy chasing his dreams and she needed to be supportive. She usually was, but today was a long day and she just wanted to talk. After a while, these quiet rooms started to get to her.

Halfway through the carton of rocky road, Vinh video called her. Once she answered, he started laughing.

"Really?" She didn't find herself amusing. Self-consciously, she tucked a loose strand of hair behind her ear.

"Sorry," he tried to reign in his jovial expression. "Was my suit that hard on you that you're eating a whole carton of ice cream?"

"I can turn you off," she threatened.

"Come on. Tell me how it went."

Digging into one more big bite just to prove to him that she could, she told him how it went. Vinh was one of the few people she could talk over some of her missions with. He had a high security clearance with the company so that he could improve and work on the gear for virtual reality programs. Despite his sarcasm, or maybe because of it, she relaxed as she vented about how Niomi trashed her in the program.

Their conversation turned to home, a common topic between the two of them. "I'm tired of machine food. I wouldn't think fish would be that hard to cook," Vinh complained. "But I tried it again, and I couldn't make it through the plate."

"Home cooked can't be beat." Ari's stomach tightened at the thought of her mother's food.

"I just have to convince them to let me in the kitchen. Show them a thing or two about the value of fat."

Thinking of home, Ari thought of her family's situation.

"Hey, Vinh, could you possibly help me check up on my family? There was some trouble with my last visit."

His lips pressed into a tight line. He shook his head slightly as he lifted a finger. The screen blinked out and then reappeared a moment later. "Ari, you know better than to talk about certain things on an unsecured line."

"I thought everything was a safe line here on the island." They were completely shut off from the outside world in this little speck of paradise in the middle of the ocean.

"Don't be naive."

She swallowed, realizing what she was asking of him, and felt guilty. They were friends, but they hadn't known each other for long. "I'm sorry, you don't—"

"I'm not saying I won't help." His smile lifted on one side.

"So, you'll help?"

"I can't contact your family without losing my job. It would put both them and you in danger."

Disappointment pulled at her shoulders, then an idea came to her. "What about a friend at a different company?" Her ex-roommate and best friend Tessa should be easy enough to contact through her father. Maybe she could check in on Marco and Ari's mom.

Vinh bit the inside of his lip. "Maybe. I can't promise anything, but I'll get the information later. You'll owe me, you know."

"Agreed. I'll work on wrestling a fish for you on my next run," she joked. She didn't mind owing Vinh.

The next morning, Ari stood outside the wave, waiting for Reed. She took a few steps towards the shore. *Did we say we'd meet at the beach and I forget?* Double checking her

HUB, she didn't see a message. She called him, but it went straight to voice mail.

Before worry set in, she reminded herself he was at one of the safest places in the world. He probably just had a late night and slept in. After sending him a message, she set off on her usual path.

Surprisingly, the run went by quickly. Thoughts of not only Reed but of her family occupied her mind. By the time she returned, Niomi was at the gym warming up.

"I thought maybe we could skip sparring and weights today, since I still have so much to work on." With a pile of twenty or so profiles to learn, Ari needed all the extra time she could get. Not being bruised or sore for a day would also be a side benefit.

Niomi shook her head. "No. We never skip your training. Trust me on this. The healthier you are out here, the better you'll do in there. And soon you'll be in VLEX more than you want. I can quiz you as we fight."

"Oh joy." Ari picked up a staff. She wasn't too disappointed though. The less time inside the better in her book.

They went through their usual physical training session. Then Ari had time for a quick shower and snack before joining Niomi back in the VR. Once in a program, she spent her entire session as Kari in a room full of mirrors.

The odd feeling of being displaced slowly vanished as they worked for hours. Not that she'd ever get used to looking like another person, but it didn't surprise her anymore to look down and see a petite pale arm with perfectly painted rose colored nails. By the time evening rolled around, the voice sounded almost natural.

Once out of the VR, they studied videos of Kari's life. Not that Ari would ever be this person outside of VLEX, but she needed to know every personal detail possible. After watching her eat dinner with her parents, take in a stray cat, and even cry when that cat died, Kari morphed into a real person, someone Ari would probably enjoy meeting.

"What happens to Kari when I impersonate her in the VLEX?" Ari leaned back in the chair, her notes in the screen on the desk in front of her. "Is she told to take a vacation or something?"

"Not sure and it's not our business to care. We focus on our job and doing it perfectly. The rest is up to others."

Ari straighten up. "You're really okay with not knowing?" Her trainer didn't seem to be the type to take orders with such blind faith. But Ari had only known her for six months or so. Maybe she was wrong.

Niomi set down her screen marker. "When you've been in this business for ten years or so, you learn that you don't want to know. We have enough work set out for us. To take on any more isn't good." She stared at the screen for a moment as if contemplating saying more but didn't.

Words left unsaid floated in the air, leaving an uneasy sensation crawling along Ari's arms. She wasn't so easily appeased.

Niomi changed the subject, and they continued analyzing every minute detail of Kari's life.

By the time Niomi called it quits, night had fallen. Soft blue lights illuminated the hallway. The moon hung high outside, shinning down on the night life on the island. Most of the animals slept, but a few nocturnal creatures moved through the trees and if lucky she'd glimpse a bat or long tail.

Her first week or so in the Wave, she found watching the evening wildlife disconcerting with its never-ending darkness. But now she enjoyed it on clear nights. Inside her room, she even programed her walls so she could continue seeing outside.

Too exhausted to even eat, she drank a high calorie shake so Niomi wouldn't harass her. In bed, a call came through. Reed.

She accepted the video call. "Hey, stranger."

His sweet smile and kind eyes filled the video. "I'm so sorry. I met with the art team until late into the night and by the time—"

"Stop." Ari interrupted him. "I'm going to pass out any second and don't want to waste it on apologies. I get it. Tell me how your day was instead."

"Okay." They settled into their usual conversation. Talking much longer than Ari thought she would last. She realized how much she missed him. Even though they weren't that close physically, it was close enough.

The next few days passed in the same fashion. Reed's busy schedule kept him from a lot of morning runs, which Ari hated but supported. Ari spent the day training with Niomi, memorizing more profiles, or skins as Niomi referred to them. Then she spent her evening chatting with Vinh or Reed. The three of them even met for dinner once. Ari cherished her time with both of them. They kept her grounded and reminded her of who she was as she spent the day learning to be someone else.

CHAPTER SIX_

Dusting on a fine layer of powder, Ari finished getting ready for her date. She never considered herself one of those fancy girls that spent hours in front of the mirror, but tonight promised to be special. After getting permission from Niomi, Reed asked her out to a restaurant. A real restaurant filled with other people.

Ari would meet other employees or even islanders. Currently she could count on one hand how many people she'd met, most being paid to be there for her. She never considered herself a social creature, but being stuck in isolation, even if a tropical paradise, changed that.

Niomi wouldn't tell her why it was now okay for her to eat and see the other workers. Of course, no one could know that she was a warper—she had a fake identity and a position in administration to a higher up—at least she got to keep her first name.

Her HUB beeped letting her know Reed was waiting outside, and she headed out front. As she walked out the doors, Reed let out a long whistle.

She smiled, appreciating the compliment. "Guess it's better than me sweating in a smart suit."

"I like you sweaty too. But it's not every day you wear a dress."

"Thanks." She smoothed down the dark floral material. The sleeveless dress fit the island attire and was more comfortable than even jeans. Her hair remained wavy, like usual, and she had pulled up the top half to keep out of her face.

Stepping forward, he tucked a strand of hair behind her ear. "You look beautiful."

Nervous energy tingled down her neck from where his touch lingered. "Thank you. You look great yourself."

He wore tan pants and a blue button-down shirt. His hair looked recently cut, but it still held a slight wave on top. She clasped her hand tight to keep from reaching out and touching it. If they started that, they might never make it out.

"Ready for dinner?" He cocked a brow.

"Definitely."

He moved to the side and motioned to the vehicle behind him.

"Where did you get a car?"

"I requisitioned one... I may have mentioned to Niomi that it would be safer to transport you."

"Amazing." She hurried towards it, checking out the built-in electric panels and polarized plates underneath. Yes, she might be nerding out, but she'd only seen this once before when she first came to the island and she was too much in shock to appreciate it.

"All the guys in my dorm checked it out too. The acceleration is pretty nice as well." He clicked the doors open.

She climbed inside, eying the panels. They spent their

trip talking about the car's AI and flipping every switch and option the car had to offer. Her favorite was the massage chairs so far, but they still had the ride back to explore more options.

He pulled up near the beach, a lit canopy in the distance. Hurrying around, he helped her out of the car. Since the restaurant was outside in the sand, they kicked off their shoes in the car and strolled in the sand up to the hostess. He had made reservations. With the restaurant full, there had to be about fifty or so people, but no one bothered Ari.

They sat across from each other with the waves crashing in the distance as their backdrop. Tiki torches lit the night. They devoured grilled meats with tropical fruits and veggies stuck on bamboo sticks.

"Can you believe this is all real?"

"This is as real as it gets." He reached forward and lightly touched her hand. "But I know what you mean. If you would have asked me last year when we started school where I'd be, never in a million years would I say an island in the middle of nowhere with my best friend's sister."

"Ditto." She placed a hand on the side of her face. "My face hurts from smiling."

"Good. Maybe some dessert will help with that."

After scrolling through their choices, they selected their desserts from the tabletop screen. She picked pineapple sorbet, and he went with a coconut and date cake. He reached for her hands clasped on the tabletop while they waited. She couldn't help but get lost in his hazel eyes.

"I get to see my mom again next week." Reed said.

Ari snapped out of her reverie. "That's great. I hope everything is alright since my mom left."

"Me too. I've been asking about having her come work here, as a receptionist or even a maid."

"Is that an option?"

"They will consider it when there is an opening." He released her hands and reached for a drink. "There are so many islanders here for the basic jobs though, so we'll see."

Guilt pricked on her conscious. She was the reason he was here and his mom wasn't. Maybe she should talk to Niomi about getting both of their families here. Before she could offer, his HUB rang with a message.

His brow tightened as he scrolled through it. "They have to be kidding me."

"What?"

"My art team. We're putting a presentation together for a new game on Monday, but there was a problem with the storyboard and they need some new designs right away."

Ari's stomach sank. "They can't do—"

"They can, and they did. Kimmy, the director of my team, tried to work around it, but couldn't. I have to go in right away." Lifting his gaze, regret colored those beautiful eyes.

"You have to go. I understand." She bit down on her lip to prevent her from saying anything else. She'd supported him in finding a place here, because she brought him here.

Sighing, his shoulders dropped. "This sucks."

"We had a great night."

"I hoped for more. I don't get to see you as much as I'd like."

"I know."

Standing, he leaned forward, brushing a light kiss on her lips. One that had her cursing Kimmy. Warmth rushed to her face and he stepped away.

"You better leave before I tell Kimmy where to go," she warned.

He smiled. "Take the car back. I'll call for a ride, and I will be there for our run Tuesday morning after my presentation."

"Okay."

He left just as the two desserts arrived at the table. The hurt of being alone burned as she stared at the food. Logically she understood that he was busy and supported him, but emotionally... well... good thing she had two desserts to work through.

She grabbed her fork and dug in. After all the work it took to get here, she wasn't in a hurry to leave. Given enough time, she finished both desserts while watching the moon over the dark waves. Maybe life wasn't how she envisioned it, but it could be a hell of a lot worse.

———

The next day, Sunday, Ari was in the midst of studying when Vinh surprised her with a call. "Hey, can we meet up for lunch? At the beach?"

"At the beach?" Ari asked. There had never been anything romantic between Vinh and Ari, yet he'd never asked her out to lunch either.

His gaze narrowed on the screen in her room. "Get over yourself and be ready. Okay?"

"Okay." Ari could use a break.

Still in comfy gray pants and a tank, she headed outside and found Vinh parked with his hoverboard. More casual than usual, he wore shorts and shirt. They kicked off their shoes and headed to the beach on foot.

"You going to tell me what this is about? You don't have any food on you?" She motioned to his thin bag.

"Trust much?"

"Just curious."

"Your curiosity can wait. It's my butt I'm more worried about."

Ari bit back a retort about his back side and continued in silence. She trusted Vinh. He headed straight for the ocean and stopped in front of the water's edge.

Sitting down, he pulled out a small box. He flipped a switch and a green light flashed in the corner. "That's so we can talk or go online without any ghosts."

"Okay?" Then she remembered her request last week. "Is this so we can contact my family?"

"Did you really think I was asking you out on a date?" Sarcasm was spread on thicker than necessary.

"I didn't know what you were up to. But thanks for that." She gently shoved his shoulder.

"Let's see if this works." He popped open a computer as well. "We can't contact your family directly, but I thought we could troll any groups or sites they may frequent."

Ari tried to think of the best way to reach Marco. He wasn't a regular in any sites or groups. Maybe games, but Ari wasn't sure which ones he frequented these days. Games. Now Tessa was a regular, because she created her own.

"How about Neptune?"

"I may have heard of that before. Let's check it out."

A nervous itch crept along her spine. "Are you going to get fired for this? I don't want you to get in trouble."

He rolled his eyes. "I won't get fired, maybe suspended. A lot of the guys around here sneak in to check gaming stats or look up old friends. Let's just not get caught, okay?"

They found Tessa's game and Vinh already had a fake profile to contact her. "What do you want to say? And remember it can't say much."

"Don't be easy or anything." Ari racked her brain to think of a way to let Tessa know it was her. "Okay. Tell her it's Oya, Goddess of the sky, wanting to reconnect and check on my family."

Oya was from a VR game she played with Tessa last year at school.

Vinh finished the message and then shut down his equipment. "I'll check now and again for a reply and let you know."

"Thanks." Ari extended her legs in the sand and stared out into the never-ending expanse of water. "You know, I never even visited the ocean until last year in the VR? I grew up in a desert."

"Really? You know I grew up staring at this same ocean, just a different side?" He set down his bag and leaned back on his hands. "You are lucky to have such a secluded spot. I get sick of watching guys attempting to surf. There's a reason we work here."

"True." Most people spent their time plugged in and the real ocean wasn't as forgiving.

He glanced at her direction. "Have they scheduled your first mission?"

"Not yet, but soon." She picked at her pants, pushing away the churning in her stomach.

"Nervous?"

A chuckle escaped her lips. "Yeah, guess so. It's weird to study a person I never met before. Like really study, their family, co-workers, past lovers. Just weird."

"I think weird has only just started. Wait until you get inside."

"Have you been inside VLEX before?"

"No. I've just heard some rumors since I've been here." He dug through the sand, picking up a seashell.

"Like what?"

"Just how different it is. People with no sense of morality except how it pads their wallet. You might be able to contact Tessa from there."

She sat upright, turning to stare at him. The idea excited her. "Really? How?"

"You're connected to everything in there, and I mean everything. Just be careful who is watching. There is more that goes on then anyone knows or is willing to talk about."

"I will." A tumult of emotions swirled around, excitement and nerves vied for the top spot. Not able to sit still, she stood and offered a hand to Vinh. "Ready to head back. If I'm out here too long, Niomi will wonder why I'm not exercising."

He took her hand. "We don't want that. You can probably take me down as it is."

"Maybe."

He did have a husky frame. "Don't piss me off or I'll shrink your suit."

She raised her arms. "You win."

"See, it's not all about muscles."

They headed back towards the Wave. "I agree with you. Now if you could convince Niomi of that."

CHAPTER SEVEN

As the next few weeks passed, Ari immersed herself into her work, trying to keep her thoughts off missing her family back home. Vinh did get word back to her that Tessa reported everything was okay. He even found out she was working for her father's company and had some back channels to contact her. Ari didn't want to press her luck though or jeopardize Vinh's position.

So instead she focused on her job and worked harder than ever with Niomi. Even though they covered the basics of several different skins, they always came back to Kari. Kari was to be Ari's first job. A job that approached faster than Ari realized.

She had memorized Kari's work contacts, her favorite drinks—yes even in VR people met for drinks—and everything else she could. Finally, on a Saturday morning, Niomi informed Ari that she was ready. Monday, they would skip their morning exercises and go into VLEX.

Even though Ari was ready—she knew more about Kari than even her closest acquaintances—there was something unsettling about the mission. Feigning to be someone else, constantly lying for hours on end, worried her. It felt like there was some invisible line she was about to cross, and once crossed, it would change her forever.

That Saturday evening, Reed and Ari went on another date. They realized early on that the small island only provided so much entertainment. Of course, there was a plethora of VR stimulations to experience, but they both decided they liked to spend time in person. Besides going out to eat, there were only a handful of outdoor activities available to the employees and residents of the island.

"Did you decide where we're going?" Ari asked when he picked her up in a car. The car door hissed shut behind her. She shook out her hair, wet from the light rain.

"I did." His smile curled up, distracting her.

"Are you going to share?"

"You'll see." He focused on the road, despite not actually driving the car at all. He was recently shaved, his short dirty blond hair styled to perfection. He wore a button-up shirt and shorts, his attire giving away nothing as to their date.

She tugged at the edge of her blue sundress, hoping she was adequately dressed. "You know I hate surprises?"

He cocked an eyebrow in her direction. "Really?"

"Really." She stared at him, raindrops lightly hitting the car window.

He leaned towards her, lightly kissing her. He pulled back a fraction of an inch, their lips almost touching. "How about that surprise?"

"Brat." She leaned forward, meeting his lips with a fervor.

By the time the car announced they arrived at their destination, they both were a little out of breath.

"I told you, you like surprises," he pulled back, lips slightly swollen.

"Maybe I just like *your* surprises." Heat flushed her face, the warmth feeling good.

"I'll take it."

They exited the car, and Ari got her first good look around. They were deep in the jungle, only a light mist from the rain hit them. Tall trees rose all around, green covering everything in sight. A few other cars and scooters littered the dirt parking lot. A small path lead into the forest. Through the foliage, she spied a brown staircase leading up and around a tree.

Her stomach flipped a bit, with nerves or maybe excitement. "Are we going up there?"

"After our adventure on the rooftop, I thought you were fine with heights."

"I am."

He reached for her hand. "Good."

The brown staircase was built out of metal but shaped to look like weathered wood. As they rose higher on the automated steps, the rain sprinkled on them, making Ari's wavy hair curl even more.

"Sorry about the rain." Reed stood behind her. "I'd already made the reservations."

"Don't worry about it." The rain was unpredictable and constant on the island, unlike the desert she was raised in. The warm and humid weather made the rain a welcome relief.

At the top, a couple workers stood ready to escort them into a small cart which must have been made from the same see-through material that was used on the Wave. The cart perched on top of a thin track. Reed placed his hand on the scanner for them to accept his reservation. Inside the cart, the clear plastic-type material surrounded them, giving them a 360-degree view of the jungle.

Anticipation bubbled inside of her as she turned to Reed. "I like this kind of surprise too."

"Good."

The attendant stepped back and pressed a button. "Enjoy."

With a whoosh, they slipped into the jungle, held up only by the wire. At first, only quiet permeated the jungle, but as the cart crawled along, the wildlife came alive around them. Small monkeys jumped from tree to tree, speaking in their high-pitched voices.

"Look." Reed pointed to a snake wrapped around a branch.

"Amazing." She didn't want to miss a thing.

They continued pointing out all the different animals or plants for the next thirty minutes as the cart rose and fell under the canopy of trees. When the car slowed to a stop, she didn't think it could get any better, but it did. They climbed out onto a deck around a large tree. A network of platforms and bridges connected a mass of trees. It resembled a tree house beyond her wildest dreams.

They were directed to another tree, which held a table, two chairs, and a candlelit dinner. She laughed as they took their seats. "I didn't even know this existed. Where is the book that tells you about all this stuff?"

"It's on the directory." He picked up his napkin.

"I need to look at that directory again." She spread the napkin on her lap, looking at all the sparkling lights that surrounded them. "I'm surprised it's not busier. This place is beyond anything I've seen before."

"Well, it's not as packed at the VRs, but VisionTech

wanted a few things outside for people to do. Want to order?" He motioned to the screen in front of them.

She pulled her attention back to the menu on their table. "Yes, food."

They ordered dinner, both hamburgers, hers with grilled pineapple, his with cheese and onions. An attendant quickly delivered their meal, and they dug in. The mixture of flavors flooded her taste buds. She never got tired of how good the food tasted.

"Do you ever think how odd it is that we're eating a cow on an island in the middle of the jungle?"

"I'm usually too busy enjoying the food to think of where it comes from." He took another big bite of his burger.

"True. Why waste time with questions?" She joked and took another bite.

After they'd emptied their plates, Reed leaned back in his chair. The falling sun peeked through the clouds, pulling out the golden strands in his hair. "So how is work going?"

Ari was pulled out of her animal watching. "Yeah, work." She set down the fry she was holding and reached for a drink, unsure of how to answer. "Well, Niomi seems happy with my progress as she's not complaining as much as usual."

"That's a good sign."

Nervous, Ari played with a napkin. "I guess... things are just changing."

He leaned forward. "Good change or bad change?"

She shrugged, the knot in her shoulders tightening. "I won't know until it happens."

"No use to stress until it happens, right? Then if it's not working out, you can talk to Niomi."

Ari bit her bottom lip. Yes, she could talk to Niomi, but it didn't mean Ari's job would change. She'd committed to VisionTech for five years. Her contract didn't leave a lot of wiggle room when it came to her role in the company. She didn't want to worry Reed though. "You're right, why worry about something that hasn't happened yet?"

"True." He pulled a long thin box from his pocket and pushed it towards Ari. "I made something for you."

"Really?" She reached for the box, intrigued. Since Reed was an artist, it could be anything. She opened the box and found a necklace with a beautiful light blue stone, wrapped in silver wire. The silver hugged it, swirling artistically around it. "It's amazing."

"You like it?"

"I love it." She pulled it out to put it around her neck.

"There is a surprise with it as well. Here let me." He reached for the necklace and turned it over. "It's made from a lace blue agate stone, and in the back I put a small drive."

"A drive?"

He pulled the drive from the back, it was smaller than her pinky nail. "I know you've been missing home and your friends. So, I put all your pictures from home on it. Your brother helped with this too. This way you can keep the memories close to your heart."

Emotions tightened her throat, making it difficult to speak. "Thank you. I can't think of anything more perfect."

He put the drive back in and helped her put the necklace on, the cold stone comforting on her chest. She stood, wrapping him in a hug. She was so grateful for his thoughtfulness. "How can I ever repay you?"

"You don't have to."

She pulled back ignoring the happy tears pooling in her

eyes. "I can pay for dessert," she offered, joking as it wasn't anything close to what he did for her.

He smiled. "Did I ever tell you how much I love you?"

"Not lately."

He leaned forward and brushed a kiss on her lips, soft and sweet. "Let's see what you order for dessert before I tell you," his eyes held a light sarcasm.

"You doubt my judgment?" She narrowed her eyes.

"Never. You did pick me after all." His cheesy smile warmed her soul.

CHAPTER EIGHT

Sunday rushed past in a blur of emotions as she spent several hours poring over the pictures Reed gave her. Cherishing every memory also brought on a bout of homesickness. One that even living in paradise couldn't cure.

Monday appeared before Ari could straighten out her concerns about the mission. Since Kari went into work 8am VLEX time which was 3am Ari's time, she skipped her normal routine and headed to her VR lab first. She didn't bother with breakfast as she didn't think it would stay down. She tugged on her new suit as she entered the lab, her necklace laying on top.

"Glad to see you early for once." Niomi didn't bother turning around, remaining focused on her screen.

"Good morning to you too," Ari replied.

"Take a seat. I'm waiting for the green light to send you in." Niomi glanced her way. "Nice necklace. Reed's doing?"

"Yes." Ari lowered herself in the chair and leaned back but didn't want Niomi to sidetrack her with mention of jewelry. "What do you mean by green light?"

"That's Kari's access to the VLEX and will be open for us to use. You remember everything? Her passwords?"

Ari tried to believe that Kari gave VisionTech her passwords. "And Kari will be where?"

"Think of it as a vacation day."

"Won't she notice when she comes back to work the next day?" Ari didn't like the way Niomi was being vague.

"Look, Ari." Her trainer turned to stare down at her. "I don't know the specifics, that's not my department. Most likely, she'll be transferred to a different VR that mirrors her real life. Or maybe she really will be sick. I just do my job and ask that you do the same."

Biting her lip, Ari clicked the cable into place in the bottom of her neck. She pushed away the worry that maybe she made the wrong decision all those months ago. Her stomach churned as she thought about the real Kari.

No, I can do this. Ari was ready. Niomi had pushed her hard to make sure she was ready. While waiting for Niomi, the silence ate at her calm facade. Every dark thought of what could happen flashed through her mind. By the time Niomi turned around, Ari's hands were clenched against the arm rests.

"Okay. Ready?" Niomi glanced down at her hands. "You'll be fine in there."

Ari nodded.

"Remember your training. If you must manipulate the code, move quickly afterward. Don't blow the cover. You're Kari, no matter what."

Ari closed her eyes, the darkness welcoming her. It took effort for her to open them, entering a whole other world. Squinting against the bright light, she tried to get her bearings. She sat behind Kari's desk. The dark brown walls made the room appear small. One wall held a moving picture, a lighthouse during a storm. The smell of fresh-cut flowers permeated the office. Lilacs, Kari's favorite flower, were arranged in a vase near the desk. Large clear panels blinked in front of her. One side held a scroll of announcements while the other had a bulleted list of things for Kari to do.

"Glad to see you early this morning." A dark-skinned man with silver hair and a heavy accent stepped through the office. He was dressed impeccably in a navy suit and red tie. "It's a busy day. Get out the morning memos. I also have the 1070A bill that needs to get out before noon."

"Will do, sir." Ari recognized the man as Kari's boss, President Higgins from the Icelandic States.

He stopped mid-step, turning to stare at Kari.

Ari kept her nerves buried and turned. "What is it, sir?"

A small smile crept on his face. "Nothing. Keep up the good work, Ms. Trenton."

"Of course." She turned back to the screen and began scanning the tasks set out for her today. Ari had worked on a similar process to prepare for this, but she knew she couldn't possibly do them as quickly as someone who had worked here for years.

The morning was filled with scheduling meetings, returning correspondence, and other menial tasks. Most authorities didn't conduct business outside of the VR because outside everything was traceable. Traceable meant hackable, and both meant possible to track down and assassinate. In the VLEX, hacking was significantly more difficult. Ari didn't want to contemplate the hoops VisionTech had to jump through to get her there.

Once President Higgins headed off for his mid-morning meetings, Kari could finally breathe for a moment and do her real job. She pulled up the bill 1070A. They had security protocols in place to detect unauthorized file transfers back to the real world. This is where her skills came in handy. This was all one big program.

As she re-focused her vision, lines of codes appeared before her. Reading it like a blue print or recipe card, she manipulated the program to give herself the clearance to send the file. Changing which office it came from, she sent it off to an untraceable account Niomi gave her.

Before she closed the program, she scanned the bill. The political jargon made it hard to follow, but words like studies and virtual reality caught her attention. They were doing experiments of some kind to study the effects of certain drugs.

The monitor beeped, and she flinched back from the screen. *Calm down. I'm not a kid caught in the cookie jar.* Checking the monitor, she realized she had a lunch at Milano's with a representative from President Tremblay's office. The meeting said it had to do with sharing notes from the latest energy crisis meeting, but Ari couldn't figure out why they didn't just meet over video feed.

Either way, she gathered the small purse Kari kept in her top drawer and headed out. Kari's office was on the thirtieth floor of a sleek building. Once outside, she recognized some of the buildings around her from the limited photos VisionTech had of the VLEX. A variety of buildings with different architectural styles circled around a town square.

Ari had studied maps of the VLEX but, experiencing it first hand, it all felt different. On a perfectly paved cobblestone street, she walked to the center town square, which appeared to have been built with every single country wanting their say. A hodgepodge of restaurants flashed a variety of food, most Ari had never heard of. She passed a fountain with a very large naked statue of a man holding a spear of some shape in his upheld hand.

Ari also knew that once inside a store they could go on for miles. A cool magic trick written into code. So, while it only took fifteen minutes to walk through the town center, one could spend many more hours exploring all the space. When she took a minute to look beyond the illusion to the code involved, a web of characters appeared that were so complex even Ari couldn't unravel it easily. She blinked a few times to focus on the program again.

Another few minutes and Milano's appeared up ahead. When she entered the restaurant, a wave of garlic and other spices she couldn't identify flooded her senses. Even though she knew the food wasn't real, her mouth watered in desire.

"How can I help you?" A beautiful hostess greeted her.

"I'm meeting with Antoine." Ari scanned the crowd for a familiar face even though Antoine wasn't a name she remembered from training.

After the hostess glanced at a screen, her gaze lifted. "This way." The women wove through a maze of tables and alcoves of people deep in conversation. They headed to a very secluded table in the back.

A gentleman stood up catching Ari's, really Kari's, gaze. His warm smile and beautiful features made Ari smile back instinctively, despite not recognizing him at all. When she went to greet Antoine, before she could reach out her hand for him to shake, he pulled her into a strong hug.

A very small and undignified squeak escaped Ari's lips, as he lifted her briefly into the air.

"It has been too long," he mumbled into her neck.

Ari stiffened realizing Niomi's information wasn't completely up to date. Kari must have found a recent boyfriend given this dark secluded table not that many people knew about it. Recovering from her shock and surprise, Ari tried to soften against his hold. "It's good to see you too."

He kissed her neck briefly then stepped back and offered her a seat. Despite the uneasiness crawling along her skin, she forced a smile and sat down, smoothing out the beige skirt she wore. She had only kissed two guys in her life, one only in the VR, so having this strange man kiss her neck sent shivers up her spine—no matter how attractive he was.

He had a foreign look to him with dark heavy brows, a sharp nose, and a chiseled jaw. His dark hair had a wave to it, as if the wind happened to blow it naturally perfect. There was no way this man looked this good in person. He had to have some upgrade to his program skin to make him look like a model. Changing clothes was one thing inside a virtual, but skins were trickier and usually required extra programs and costs ahead of time—unless one is a warper like Ari.

"So how has your day been? Higgins still on your back."

Ari tried to look for the answer he wanted and give it to him. "Of course. The work never stops."

He reached across and grabbed her hands before she could stop him. *Man, this guy was fast.* "If you're not feeling particularly hungry, I scheduled a back room for us." He kissed her top knuckle.

She jerked back, holding her hand against his chest.

"What's wrong?"

Crap. Niomi hadn't prepared Ari for anything like this. She remembered her words though. *I am Kari. So how would Kari get out of this?*

He leaned back in his chair, the lines in his brow deepening. "You seem off today, Kari. What's going on?"

Ari closed her eyes for a second. She'd never been an actress, never wanted to, but now she had to sell this lie better than anything before. "Sorry, Antoine." This time she reached for his hand. Ignoring what this meant, she held his hand tight.

"Higgins has been riding me hard. I barely got away today and in fact I have to get back right away." She glanced at the HUB on her wrist. "I sneaked away, because I just had to see you for a moment. I'm so sorry."

Slowly the lines on his face smoothed and the same softness and desire in his eyes returned. "I can't wait until we need to meet outside this program."

"Me too." Unsure of what was happening, she hoped that wasn't possible. Representing different countries, she went on the assumption they lived thousands of miles away.

"I know. This is enough for now, but you need to find extra time inside before then."

Extra time inside VLEX was expensive, which paid for the program. Any other similar programs were just as expensive. But Ari didn't want to force him to be suspicious. "I'll do my best, but I really need to go now."

Pushing out of the chair she turned to leave. Before she made it a step, he grabbed her shoulder, turning her around and gathering her into a hug. "You must be in a hurry if you forget to kiss me good bye."

Ari tried to step back and figure out an excuse, but he leaned forward pressing his lips against hers. It was over as quickly as it began, but it was intense.

"I'll see you soon." His dark eyes shone with the promise of tomorrow, and Ari's insides twisted.

Speechless, she nodded and then hurried out of the restaurant. After she broke free of the town center, she slowed and caught her breath. Guilt gnawed at her conscience. She'd kissed another man, and not any man, but a freaking gorgeous man. She didn't want to. Antoine was probably an overweight bald man who cooked numbers for his country. She shook out the feeling of him on her body and rubbed at her lips. Even if it was a VR, it felt very real and very much like a betrayal to Reed. But it really wasn't her choice. Or was it?

She'd talk to Niomi when she got back. For now, she'd finish her day, and hope no other surprises jumped out at her.

CHAPTER NINE

Ari awoke from the VR with a gasp. Something pulled at her arm. A patch pinned into her flesh with a clear tube connected. She reached to tear it off.

"Just wait a sec," Niomi said from her computer station nearby.

"Why did you patch me?" Ari had seen plenty of those while visiting her dad in the hospital.

"You've been under for eight hours. You needed fluids."

Slumping against the chair, Ari realized she was right. The working day flew by so quickly that she forgot about the real world. Anxiety gripped her throat. She'd never been inside the program for so long. How long was too long before she forgot completely about reality like her father?

Once unhooked from the wires, Ari stood and stretched out her limbs, trying to soothe her nerves as well as her muscles. "Kari has a new boyfriend. It was a nightmare."

Niomi pushed a stool towards her. "Write down everything you did and everything you can remember."

"What? I sent the needed documents. Don't you have cameras there?"

"No. They are banned and do regular sweeps for monitoring devices. If all the information can come back so easily, then it would be easier to steal." Niomi turned away from the screen. "Just finish your reports, we'll get a twenty-minute workout in, and then you can call it a day."

Ari checked the time, and her shoulders slumped. In the VR for over eight hours, then more paperwork and exercising? The idea made her want to crawl into bed. Her stomach grumbled at the lack of substantial food.

"Okay. At least Kari will have to deal with her own handsy boyfriend tomorrow." She pushed her hair out of her face and pulled the stool towards the desk.

"Sorry, that's you again, Ari."

"What?" She stopped. "He's going to figure it out. And what will happen when she returns?"

"Let us deal with Kari. You deal with the boyfriend." Niomi had gone back to working at her station, her eyes glued to the screen. "It's part of the job, sweetheart. And trust me, it's not bad in comparison."

An unsettling sensation resided in her neck and she rubbed her port. Maybe she was just tired. Exhaustion pulled at her limbs, and she headed towards the door.

"Where are you going?" Niomi's sharp words carried a threat.

"I'm going to grab some food if that's something I'm *allowed to handle*." She didn't even bother to keep the sarcasm out of her voice.

"Don't be long."

Ari stormed down the hall, every step echoing through the empty corridors.

"Can I help get some food started for you?" the AI said from the communications panel in her suit.

"No."

"Okay. I'd recommend a meal high in protein since your patch mainly covered fluids—"

"Shut up." She slapped at the panel on her forearm.

Since she didn't give it the correct command to silence itself, it kept rambling. "Your pulse and blood pressure are rising. Try slow deep breaths to lower your—"

"I said, shut up!" She tore at the panel.

Her fingers were useless against the tough flexible fabric. Her nail tore on the panel's lining. Frustration boiled in her veins as she started to take off her suit. The button near the neck panel released the suit. Yanking off the arms, she didn't realize she had nothing else to wear until she stood in her bra, the suit hanging on her waist.

Granted, being alone in this section of building she didn't worry about modesty. Out of the suit, she finally could take a deep breath. The AI continued to ramble on health tips.

"Silence."

The machine quieted.

"New name: Antoine." Her lips tightened. She could practice new evasive tricks on her AI and pretend it was Kari's boyfriend.

She made her way into the kitchen, as it was closer than her room, and ordered a pizza and soda. Halfway through the pizza, she realized Reed would be on his lunch break. This VLEX time was already throwing her. She should talk to him now because she'd be passed out by the time he was done with the day.

After several rings he picked it up. "Hey, Ari."

"Man, it's good to hear your voice."

"Rough day?"

"Definitely. How about you?"

"Good but busy. They have me running scans on their

firewalls, trying to break them. I haven't gotten through yet, but I hit a few weak points. That always impresses the boss." He sounded happy, and Ari couldn't help but imagine cuddling against his chest.

"And your art?"

"Ehh. I'm loving it, but not good enough to join the team full-time." He paused for a moment. "It sounds like you're avoiding talking about your day."

"There is only so much I can say. I was in a program for eight hours, and now I have to head back for paperwork and a workout. Niomi is her normal pleasant self."

"I understand. Ming rides my butt, too, most days. I think that's just part of being a manager."

Silence permeated the connection as Ari sagged back against the chair. She ached to tell him what really happened in her day. The boyfriend and the espionage were only the start. Constantly acting like another person, being careful with every word and action, was exhausting. He didn't need or probably want to hear all her whining though.

He spoke next. "I miss you. Want to video chat?"

She glanced down, still in her sports bra, fingers covered in pizza sauce, and she could only guess how bad her hair and face looked. "Not right now. I have to head back. We'll talk soon."

"Okay. Want to call me tonight?"

"I'll try, but since I've been up since three and have to wake up that early tomorrow, I'm not sure I'll make it."

"True."

"Bye, Reed. Love you." She ended the connection. Folding two pieces on top of each other, she picked up her double slice and started back down the hall. She pulled her suit back on with one hand while eating with the other. Her thoughts traveled to Reed, and she wondered what he'd say if he knew the whole truth—that she is stealing another person's life and kissing a different boyfriend.

––––––

The next day started in the VR while it was still dark outside. Niomi insisted she eat a good-sized breakfast before she plugged in. Once inside VLEX, the same office materialized. This morning her work went a touch more smoothly. Finding an additional file requested by Niomi, she sent it to a different electronic address. Hopefully nothing out of the ordinary when people reviewed her actions. Ari had a list of files she needed to find before closing this case.

As the day sped by, Ari watched the clock with dread. Already finding her lunch date with Antoine on the schedule, a myriad of thoughts ran through her mind of how to put him off. Niomi said just to break it off. Then they would let Kari believe Antoine broke it off with her. That might be the simplest way, but not the kindest.

Ari had a hard enough time taking over Kari's life, she didn't want to ruin it as well, and hoped Kari would be back rather sooner than later. So, when the clock struck noon VLEX time, Ari messaged Antoine. *Busy at work today, probably won't make it. Can we do tomorrow?*

It didn't take long for Antoine to reply.

No worries. I'm running behind, too. I can make it by 1. Does that work?

She rolled her eyes, wondering how to gently let him down.

I can try, no promises.

If you have to, remind your boss that by VLEX regula-

tions you're allowed a 30 min break for every 4 hours worked, inside or outside of the VR.

Great, she thought. Instead she replied: *Will do.* An odd sensation still crept down her spine every time she saw a picture of Kari as herself, but it was a good reminder. Acting like her old self was too easy. It took work to remember what she was doing here.

When it hit one, she headed outside to the market not quite sure how to handle Antoine. She did have one other option, but it wasn't something she had mastered very well inside the program. Inside the same restaurant with the delicious smells made her stomach grumble. Antoine sat at the same table with two meals and glasses of wine at the table.

His dark almond eyes lit up when he noticed her. Ari wondered what he looked like in real life, but could only read the program, not his mind. Standing to greet her, she stepped forward slightly and then focused on the code around them. She attempted to separate her consciousness from the image of Kari she projected. It helped when all she saw were numbers and letters, not images.

Ari manipulated the code to have Kari hug Antoine and then when he leaned down for a kiss, Ari didn't even flinch. She felt sick, lying to this man and to her own boyfriend. Trying not to think about what was happening, she was grateful it didn't last long.

"I can't stay, but I ordered you your favorite." The edges of his lips pulled down in a pout. "I'm expected back but had to see you briefly if I could. I can't wait until our vacation together."

"Vacation?" Her initial surprise pulled her back into the images, wrapped in his arms with thoughts of how bad this could be.

"Yes. Remind your boss of your time off next month,

okay? No excuses. It is the slow season for him, and you earned this time. I can't wait to see you and show you my home."

"Me too." She lied, and prayed she'd be long gone before that happened.

"Have a good weekend, and we'll catch up on Monday. You okay?" One of his perfectly shaped brows arched in question.

"Yeah. Just stressed." She wasn't as quick as she needed to be with the coding.

"Don't worry. The season will slow down soon." He leaned down for a kiss.

Just focus on the code, just focus on the code.

After a quick kiss, he headed off. Looking down at the table, she realized he had finished his plate, and left a plate of ravioli for her. Even though she knew her body didn't need the food, it felt weird not to eat all day and it smelled amazing. Biting into the ravioli, she realized it was mushroom. Nasty.

She glanced around the nook of the restaurant. The low lighting and spaced out tables gave quite a bit of privacy. A young woman sat nearby with her nose in a book.

Ari turned back to her meal. With a few minor alterations, spaghetti filled the plate. She reached for some bread and dove into the pasta. She ignored Niomi's advice that food was a waste of time and enjoyed herself.

Even though it was all fake, she savored her plate and tried to finish it off with the glass of wine. Except wine wasn't for her. Changing it to cola, she finished it off as the girl from the table next approached.

"Thought you may want some company. I'm Hailey." The girl gave a timid smile.

Ari froze for a brief second with uncertainty but didn't

want to cause a scene. "Sure, have a seat. I'm Kari. I don't have long before I head back to work though."

"Me too." Hailey tucked a stray piece of caramel colored hair behind her ear. "Where do you work at?"

Ari didn't think it would hurt to tell her, since Kari would probably do the same. "I'm the Presidential Aide over with the Icelandic States."

"You work with Higgins?"

Ari nodded and took another drink. "Where are you at?"

"I'm with the European Union."

"That must be big."

Hailey shrugged. "I guess. I'm holed up doing data transfers and security."

"Sounds..." Ari searched for the word.

"Boring?"

She laughed. "Sorry, I didn't want to sound rude."

"No worries. Most of the time it's boring, but sometimes it's fun to chase after the off-world hackers."

Ari wasn't sure who off-world hackers were exactly but didn't want to sound ignorant.

Hailey put her elbows on the table and leaned forward, her voice barely above a whisper. "I belong to a group you may be interested in joining."

"What kind?"

"Well, let's just say its members don't have to eat ravioli and wine if they don't want to, either."

Panic tightened Ari's chest, making it hard to breathe. "I don't know what you're talking about."

Haley placed a hand on Ari's wine glass, and the liquid turned clear. "You're not as alone as you think you are."

Ari couldn't find the words or air to speak.

Hailey stood, her purse over her shoulder. "Don't worry. I'll be in touch." She left as quick as she came.

Ari glanced around, wondering if anyone else saw that. No one was close, and those she could see were engrossed in conversation. Gripping the glass, a tingling sensation traveled up her arm. She always knew she wasn't the only warper in the world, but to actually meet someone like her. Someone she could talk to, someone she could ask questions to? She stared at the glass, thoughts spinning wildly through her mind, before heading back to work.

CHAPTER TEN

By the time, Ari left VLEX she wasn't sure what she was going to say to Niomi. They went through the process of unhooking her from the machine and taking out her health patch for fluids. Black dots danced in front of Ari as she stood. Not eating real food all day took its toll.

"Are you ready for notes or do you need to eat something?" Niomi's kind voice surprised Ari.

"No. I just want to get it over with."

Niomi watched her with a careful gaze. "Anything go wrong in there?"

"No. Just had to watch the code of Kari making out with her boyfriend. Did you get my files?"

"Yes." Niomi turned back to her computer. "I told you to dump the boyfriend."

"Didn't seem fair to Kari."

"I forget just how young you are."

"I have a relationship. I'd hate for someone to ruin things with Reed."

Niomi shrugged but didn't reply. It was hard to fight with someone who was silent, so Ari turned to her report.

Her fingers danced over the keyboard. She skipped over changing the food and meeting Hailey, unsure how Vision-Tech would feel about it. Ari wanted answers first, to figure things out on her own before having to deal with Niomi about it. Niomi kept plenty of things to herself. Finishing her report, Ari's thoughts went to home. Her heart ached as she thought of Marco and her mother. Even though she still resented her father, she missed him too. Not that she liked to visit him inside his virtual coma, but having the option was nice.

When Ari sent off her report, she turned to Niomi. "When do I get to visit my family again?"

"You know how expensive it is—"

"I don't care. Take it out of my paycheck." Her account had been growing substantially even with her transferring money to Marco.

Niomi shut off her screen. "Truth is, we can't locate them at the moment."

It took Ari a moment to process this. They didn't know where Marco was. What if her mother got captured? "You lost them?"

"Good thing is if we can't find them, then the government can't find them either."

"Unless they found them first." A chasm of fear threatened to overwhelm her.

"With our most recent intelligence, we have no reason to believe that. Marco probably took your mother underground."

"We need to pull them out. They needed to leave as soon as my mother lost her work." Ari stormed over to Niomi's computer and tapped it on. "Contact Security. I'll go back if I need to. I know some of Marco's old joints."

Niomi stepped towards Ari, gently pushing her to the side. "You can't go back. It's too dangerous."

"If it's too dangerous for me, it's too dangerous for them." She faced her trainer.

About the same height, they stood less than a foot apart. Heat flooded Ari's face and body, like if she didn't do something right now, she would explode. Niomi's gaze gave nothing away as it bore into Ari.

"I don't think I feel well enough to exercise today." Without giving Niomi a chance to respond, Ari stormed out of the room. She kept going until she made it outside, passing the hoverboards and bikes, knowing she didn't have the patience for them and ran.

She headed away from the ocean and towards the center of the complex. The ocean held peace for her, and she didn't want peace but answers. Though her heart thrummed with every step, she didn't feel a thing. A numbing fear or rage took over. Niomi needed to learn that until Ari found her family, she wouldn't work for them. Not ever.

Checking her watch, she realized Reed was still working. He wouldn't be able to break for a couple hours. She didn't want to cause trouble for him. Maybe Vinh.

Unsure of the last name she gave her AI, she pressed the button on her suit instead. "Call Vinh."

"Calling Vinh."

After a moment he picked up. "Hey, Ari. What's going on?"

"I need to talk to you."

"I thought we were talking right now."

"No, in person. I'm in front of the center community of the Wave, but not sure where you live, or work, or whatever it is you do right now." She paced in front of the doors as several other workers flowed in and out. Talking without an earpiece she probably looked crazy.

"Are you alright?"

"Yes. No. I'm really not sure right now. I just need to talk to you."

"Stay where you are. I'll be down in a minute."

She picked at a seam on her Fit Suit and realized Niomi knew exactly where she was and was probably monitoring her blood pressure or something insane. "Hey, can you also bring me some clothes?"

"I don't even want to ask." He ended the connection.

She ran a hand through her hair and ended up pulling out the tie and redoing the whole braid. By the time Vinh made it out, she had worn a good path in the dirt with her pacing.

"Hey, want to go bowling?"

"I'm not in the mood for bowling."

"They have bathrooms to change in and so much noise and chaos that we'll blend right in." He cocked an eyebrow the best that he could and ended up with an odd face looking like he was trying to wink at her.

Thinking past his odd face, she realized the noise might give them the privacy they need. "Okay."

Ari changed into an old gray shirt that said something in a foreign language, with crossbones behind it. It fit well, though she had to roll the cotton pants a couple times. Her necklace rested again on her skin, a comforting reminder she wasn't alone. She couldn't throw out her smart suit— Vinh would kill her. She remembered lockers nearby and stored it inside.

Looking around, she realized the bowling she remembered from old games and movies was nothing like the bowling they had here. There were anti-gravity vacuums where people flew across to knock down some sort of rings that hung in space. People cheered loudly after a girl flipped into several rings, scattering them. Even though the normal workday wasn't over, everyone had different shifts, and the room was littered with people drinking and playing different games.

She quickly found the bar, where Vinh sat in front of a drink. "Thanks for the clothes. I'm just not in the mood for Niomi, you know."

"She can still find where you are," he said, referring to the chip in the back of her neck.

"I try not to think about that. At least she can't check my heart rate and perspiration levels."

"So, what's going on?"

Ari briefly closed her eyes, trying to rein in her emotions. "Niomi can't find my brother or mom. Which means they haven't been getting money either."

"Dear God, I'm so sorry, Ari." He placed a hand on her arm. "It doesn't mean that anything bad has happened to them though."

"It sure can't mean anything good."

"Don't panic until they find out."

She flung her hands in frustration. "I'm not going to wait around for them. I need to find them myself. And I need your help."

Vinh pulled back slightly. "What are you talking about? I signed a similar contract as you did when they hired me. Everyone did."

Ari leaned forward, resting a hand on his forearm. Anyone watching may think it was romantic how she whispered into his ear. "If my government finds them before me, there is no hope. They'll keep both to get to me. They won't be safe. You know that." She bit down for a moment, pushing back the tears in her eyes. "I refuse to work until I find them. Your job is to help me work. Help me, please."

After a long moment, he nodded. "I don't know if I can help, but I can try."

She leaned back in her chair, taking a deep breath. "I'll take all I can get. I thought about starting with Tessa."

He looked around him and scooted to the edge of his seat, closing the distance between them. "We can go for a walk on the beach if you want, or maybe we could meet for a late-night bite to eat in my rooms?" His words were formal, his gaze intent as if trying to say more than he could.

"I want to talk to her directly." She kept her voice soft but strong.

"Let's plan on tonight then. 11:30 in my rooms. I can get a guest pass for personal reasons."

"Of course." Ari didn't care what the company thought of why they were meeting.

He checked the HUB on his wrist. "I better get back to work."

"One more thing. Where is your room?"

He pointed behind her to a huge information screen. "That will give you directions to the campus. Please don't get into too much trouble before I see you next time. You don't want Niomi calling Security on you."

"I don't think she wants that either," Ari mumbled under her breath.

As Vinh took off, Ari realized she had quite a bit of time until 11:30 and had no desire to head back to the lonely rooms she was assigned to. She tried to reason why Niomi tried to keep her from the other employees on the island. Niomi said it was because if the others found out what Ari really was then she'd be in danger. But if they trusted Ari to go inside VLEX and lie all day, couldn't she be trusted to do it here?

She ordered a large ice coffee and was determined to stay awake and avoid Niomi. Grabbing her drink to go, she headed over to the information desk to find where not only Vinh's room was, but also Reed's workplace and sleeping quarters. He had a break in thirty minutes, and she wanted to surprise him.

Meandering through the rest of the community center, she got to check out the variety of restaurants and recreational sites, including some intense VR gaming. She saw the ranking on a huge scoreboard along with a couple guys betting on the outcomes. After the chaos got to her, she stepped outside and took the path to the apartments on the inner island.

An afternoon shower rolled in and starting raining down, so she hurried inside. She realized how she must look, like a wet dog in oversized clothes, and a shirt she worried may be from an Asian death cult. Searching the room, she continued down the hallway, and Reed's office door stood out down the hall with glass lining either side. She glimpsed the rows of desks and little boxes geared up to be offices.

An attractive young woman stood outside the door. Her strawberry-blonde hair was pulled into a high bun, and her face accented with bright makeup. Ari stayed back, a bit self-conscious of her own appearance.

People began filing out the door, speaking to each other. Reed emerged after a handful or so people. Once the pretty girl spotted him, she headed over to give him a hug. He stepped back after the hug but continued talking to her. He didn't even notice Ari and continued their conversation to the woman as they walked down the hall.

"I loved the color in that one though." The woman briefly touched her shoulder.

Ari smothered any jealously remembering just how Vinh and her must have looked in the community center. Looks can be deceiving. Instead she stepped out into the center of the hall.

Reed glanced up and stopped, surprise freezing him in place. "Ari? What are you doing here?"

She shrugged, not wanting to go into it with the woman nearby.

He hurried towards Ari. "Where's your suit? What happened?" He wrapped her into a tight hug, and Ari could breathe for the first time in hours despite his grip.

"I'll tell you later." She whispered in his ear.

When they separated, the pretty woman watched them, waiting for something.

"Oh, Kimmy, this is my girlfriend, Ari. Ari, this is Kimmy. She's my adviser in my art internship."

A brief look of confusion crossed Kimmy's face before, her bright pink lips curled up in a fabricated smile. "Here I thought you were making your girlfriend up."

"Nope. Here I am in the flesh." Ari offered a hand.

They quickly shook hands. Kimmy's long nails were each painted with a united scene. Ari might have found them fascinating if those same claws weren't just touching her boyfriend. Okay, maybe she couldn't bury all her jealousy.

After a moment of awkward silence, both girls looked to Reed.

"Kimmy, can we meet later to talk about my project?" He motioned to Ari.

"Yes, of course. We'll talk later tonight." She walked past Reed, that same plastic smile glued to her face.

"Let's go outside," Ari suggested.

"Okay. I have ten minutes or so." He led her to a nearby door, which opened for them. They headed towards a bench with a large umbrella to block out the slow drizzle of rain. He kept her hand and sat down next to her. There were only a couple of people across the courtyard.

"Where did your suit go to?

"These are from a teenager with angst issues, Vinh."

"What?" His brows lowered in confusion.

"Sorry, I better start at the beginning." She told the story, and her fury and frustration built.

"Do you think it's safe?" he asked about Vinh helping her. "I could go with you?"

"That would look odd, since our cover is a romantic guest in his room that late."

"Romantic? Should I be worried?"

"No. I'm not his type. He's told me more than once." She leaned a head on his shoulder, his strong frame comforting. "I'm more worried about what Marco is up to. My mom has to be okay."

"Marco knows how to land on his feet. I'm sure they're alright." He traced little circles on the back of her hand. "Maybe you should just wait for Niomi. They would have more resources to find them."

"I can't. This is too important to trust them. They should have never lost them."

Reed's hub beeped. "Crap. I gotta go. Keep me posted and message me later."

"I'll call you when I get home." Ari lifted her wrist to show she didn't have a HUB on. Hers was embedded in the suit crammed in a bowling locker.

"I can grab you an old one, if you stick around until I'm done with work."

"It's okay. It's nice to be free for a bit."

He leaned over and kissed her goodbye. It may have been sweet, but it was enough to warm Ari's insides. When he tried to pull away, she wrapped a hand around his neck and pulled him closer. He tasted a bit like his favorite mint coffee, and she loved it.

"I really..." he spoke in between kisses, "don't want... to go... but have... to."

She hated letting go. Somehow, with Reed by her side, everything felt like it was going to be okay, like her crazy plan would work. "I'll call you tonight."

"Be safe." He placed one more kiss on her head before leaving.

Ari remained on the bench, watching the end of the rain trickle down and hoped she and Vinh could pull this off.

CHAPTER ELEVEN

An evening rain shower kept things dark and wet, so Ari stayed inside. The evening passed in a blur of greasy foods and hot drinks. More than once, she wondered if Niomi would show up and drag her back to her rooms. Granted, she probably had cameras watching Ari now.

As the center and nearby restaurants filled up when the five o'clock shift let out, she found herself drawn to the gaming counter. Anti-gravity bowling wasn't for her, but betting on it was much more entertaining. The cheers and moans as people wiped out helped her push aside the worry that she couldn't do anything about.

"Are you going to watch the game all night or bet on it?" a short islander asked. Her pretty, petite features were overshadowed by the woman's brisk manner. "Huh?"

Feeling like she could do just as well as the semi-drunk people around her, she said, "Sure?"

The woman placed Ari's hand on the scanner. It beeped with a green reading.

"Yes. Good credit. What do you want to bet?"

Ari scanned the board looking at the upcoming matches, realizing she had no idea what to do.

"Come on. I don't have all day."

"Yes, you do, Oliana. It's our job." A man stepped up to Ari's side. "I'm Tamar. Forgive my sister. She's used to dealing with the belligerent all night and forgets we have other customers too. Do you want a recommendation?"

"It would help. I'm new to all of this."

"Number forty-five's breath reeked of alcohol when he registered. I think the only reason he's competing is because he's tired of fighting against gravity. He's one drink away from falling over."

"Thanks for the tip." She placed her bet with Oliana and a few minutes later was ecstatic to find she won.

She people-watched the rest of the night. Measuring up the contestants' build and guessing on how they will do. She even placed some bets on the VR gaming going on. People could watch inside the game and place bets as the game went on. After watching Tessa's game for hours at school, Ari knew what to look for and made out pretty well with that. Most people left her alone, only Oliana and Tamar make the rounds to offer her drinks and congratulate her.

At eleven o'clock she called it.

"No more? Come on, the next one will be a big one." Oliana said.

"Sorry, I have to meet a friend."

"Like that?" The woman looked Ari's outfit up and down like a disgruntled mother.

"Yes, I don't have much else right now."

"There's a shop down the street. You don't want a man to think you are cheap and easy." With a dismissive wave of her hand, she moved on to another customer.

Maybe the woman was right. As a romantic guest, she

sure didn't look the part. Jumping into the store, she picked up a pair of jeans and a dark blue shirt. It didn't scream date, but it was practical, so Ari could always wear it later. She usually chose her clothes from a screen, so picking them out in person was a nice change of pace.

A few minutes later, she entered Vinh's apartment corridor. Sleek gray tile, highlighted in soft lights, gave it a nice calming atmosphere. Unlike Ari's rooms though, these had no view. Just gray walls with different panels highlighting community events. She pressed her hand on the panel to the left of the door to let him know she arrived. Soon the door opened, and she stepped through.

She didn't know what she expected Vinh's room to look like. Maybe a high-tech automated room where he didn't even have to brush his own teeth? Instead cartoon graphics covered the walls, and the rest was covered with... junk. Maybe not junk, she found a computer drive on one counter next to a bowl.

"In here," he hollered from the next room.

She headed into his bedroom, where the surfaces were just as cluttered. "Don't they have a cleaning bot you can use? Or maybe a closet I can put these clothes in." She held up the clothes he lent her.

"Not one I trust. The chute is in there." He pointed to the hole in the wall partially covered by a shirt. "Last time they cleaned, I couldn't find stuff for a month."

Ari doubted that but didn't want to criticize him as he was about to put his neck on the line for her. "How can we talk to Tessa from here? I thought—"

He spun around. "Every night at 11:30 they send a backup of the daily files to the mainland. I have a friend who works in the backup department. He's willing to dump our records between 11:30 and midnight for a price."

"And what would that price be?"

"It should only cost a week of work for you."

"Of course. But aren't they going to trace where my money went to?" Money didn't matter to her right now, but she didn't want to get Vinh in trouble if she could help it.

"He can run it through the center under gaming or something. And this way, you can have a conversation instead of a message."

Ari grabbed a nearby chair, and after moving the pile of junk on it to the nearby table, pulled it up next to Vinh. "How are we going to reach her?"

"Through her game. She's on it nightly. Just ask for a private room."

After adjusting the headset, she put in an extra pair of gaming contacts he had and wrist sensors. He planned on joining the game too with his own gear.

"Are you familiar with the game? It's a basic RPG."

"Yeah, I've played before." She turned on the game and her world changed around her. Tessa's game wasn't as immersive as a VR, but with excellent graphics, it was the closest thing to it.

Ari and Vinh dropped in the game atop of a cliff. Below them, a battle raged on: above them, a dark icy mountain with mysterious challenges. The choices were clear: prove oneself in battle or fight your fears of the unknown in the mountains above. Each of them were an elf type species with basic armor they could only upgrade after they earn enough points. They picked the elves because they were simple characters to create with decent speed and fighting ability.

Vinh, looking particularly tall and muscular, turned in her direction. "Hurry and request the audience with the King."

"Of course." She tapped her wrist on the table in front of her to access her menu. She sent a message to Tessa, or King Vega, requesting an audience. The subject held the word Oya in all caps. Hundreds of people requested an audience; she just hoped Tessa saw hers before midnight.

When she returned to the game, Vinh's sword was drawn as he faced the mountain. "Some people decided against the mountain and are on their way back down to battle."

Three Fae creatures hurried down the slope. One looked like a tree sprite, the other two's green skin had Ari guessing earth sprites. She didn't play the game enough to know for sure what happened if she died in here. They just had to survive until Tessa got their message. Ari didn't have time to wait for re-entrance to the game and send a new message from a whole new character if she died.

Vinh took point and obviously had enough hours gaming to handle himself. The tree sprite ducked left and headed straight for Ari. Sword out, she cut towards him. While slicing off one of his limbs, another branch reached out and cut her from behind. *Stupid.*

She stepped out of range and held a more defensive position. This time she saw the extra limb as she feigned then changed direction. Unfortunately, the tree sprite stepped out of range. Before it could strike again, it fell in a pile of ash at Ari's feet, along with the Fae that Vinh was fighting.

"What the—"

Vinh couldn't finish his sentence before they were both sucked into a meeting with his Highness, or hers, really. Ari wondered why Tessa had picked the title of King, but it didn't matter. Her androgynous character sat upon the throne with long purple hair tied in a braid on her shoulder.

Her sharp, oversized features looked masculine, but the long eyelashes and gold nails that matched her crown held a feminine touch.

"What brings you to my realm, dear Oya?" Tessa continued to use Ari's old gamer name, which made her believe this game may not be secure. Ari could play along.

"My family is missing."

"Are you sure?"

"At least from my end they are."

Tessa stood and came down from her throne, a tall golden staff in hand. A slight sparkling illusion surrounded her body. Sick of the illusions, Ari wished to talk to Tessa face to face, just like she had for hours on end when they were roommates at school. "Can you cut these out?" Ari motioned to her costume.

"Sorry. This is a program, not a VR. I have not coded your real body and I don't care to do mine."

"I don't mind," Vinh said, sitting in a nearby velvet chair.

"Of course you like it, you look like a porn star." Ari rolled her eyes.

"Back at you."

"Whatever." Ari turned to Tessa. "Have you been in contact with my brother?"

"Not recently. A week ago, when I talked to him, he was going into deep hiding. Maybe out of the country. I gave him some money."

The pressure on Ari's chest lightened. "Really?"

"Yes. He offered to work it off in romantic favors, but I declined."

"Sounds like Marco." Ari took a seat in a nearby chair, some of the stress and worry melting off her shoulders.

Maybe VisionTech was right. If they can't find him, then neither could anyone else.

"He usually checks in every couple weeks or so. Want me to pass anything along?"

"I'll forward you some money. Just tell him to stay out of trouble."

"Don't think that's Marco's style."

"True." Ari chuckled thinking of all the trouble Marco got in as a child. She turned to Tessa, grateful for all she had done. "Thanks for your help. You work for your dad now?"

"After I was kicked out of school, I focused on my brand. After my dad saw my sales, he offered me my own division." She rolled her eyes as she absently spun her staff. "Now it's one of the most profitable divisions. Wife Number Four is hating me right now. It's great."

"Not to interrupt, but we need to go," Vinh said. "I don't want to push our luck."

"Alright." Ari turned back to Tessa. "What's the best way to stay in touch with you? I can't make this a regular thing, staying in Vinh's room this late."

Tessa stared at the engravings on her gold staff. "Do you have access to an elite VR?"

Ari glanced at Vinh, unsure of what she was allowed to say to Tessa. Granted, she was already breaking a million rules of her contract today. "Do you mean VLEX?"

"That's one of them. I don't go in myself, but my father has an office in there for messages, meetings and whatever. Look up the CEO of Ryope Industries, a subsidiary of my father's corporation. I'll get your message."

Ari could somehow manage that. "I'll be in touch then. You don't know what this means to me."

"Don't worry. I'm even trying to get Marco to work for me and finally put his shady skills to honest work."

"Thanks again." Ari reached out to hug Tessa.

Even though Tessa wasn't known for her touchy feely behavior, she returned the hug. "Just take care of yourself. That's what your mom would want me to say."

Ari laughed. Tears pooled in the corner of her eyes at the idea of her mother.

"We need to go," Vinh said.

"Okay. Give them my love, Tessa."

"I will."

Pulling out of the game was hard. It was only a game, Ari reminded herself. Tessa didn't even look like herself, but still... it was Tessa. Ari took off the gear, missing her old roommate.

"You alright?" Vinh leaned over and touched her arm. "You know I don't do crying girls very well."

Realizing her cheeks were wet, she wiped at her eyes. "I'm good. Thanks for this. I hope I don't get you in trouble."

"What's a little trouble when it comes to a friend?"

CHAPTER TWELVE

The next morning, Ari pulled herself out of bed and wondered if they made a patch with straight caffeine. Since she forgot to collect her uniform from the center lockers, she wore an older model Fit Suit, brushed her teeth, and ignored the messy hair. She refused to apologize for yesterday. She did what she had to do. They kept her trapped like a lab rat, isolated and alone. When she reached Niomi's lab, she steadied her resolve as she marched inside.

Niomi's steely gaze focused on Ari. "Did you enjoy your temper tantrum yesterday?"

"Really?" Ari wished she'd had another cup of coffee before she dealt with this. She stopped and started again. "So anytime I escape my cage, you're going to call it a temper tantrum? My family is missing."

"Your cage?" Niomi motioned to the window in the back of her room. "The ocean at your doorstep, your boyfriend at your call. Is this what you call a cage?"

"Yes, if I can't leave unescorted? You trust me in the VR but not in the community center."

"We were just limiting your exposure not banning it.

Your work now is so much more important than gambling on games."

"So, I'm bound to never have friends?"

Ari bristled at the idea that Niomi tracked her, even if limited.

Her trainer didn't notice though and continued the lecture. "Oh, by the looks of your late-night tryst, it seems you became better friends with Vinh."

"We're just friends."

"If you pull that again, Vinh will be re-assigned. Romances are forbidden with personal designers. If you want to keep Vinh as your tech liaison, keep it to one boy."

Ari bit her lip to keep her initial retort in. She didn't want Niomi to think it was anything else. "Are we done? Or do we not have to work at this ungodly hour?"

"It's not my fault you only got two hours of sleep." Niomi turned to her console, and with a flick of her wrist, her screen displayed a man. "You have a new assignment today. We've got a short window of opportunity to sit in on a vote. You'll be Representative Tao."

"Tao?" She didn't think he was one of the main profiles she'd memorized, though after focusing so hard on Kari the other twenty-five tended to blur together.

"Yes. I wish we had more time to work on this, but we don't. You'll only be in for a couple of hours today. He's an older man so move slow. We have a program to help with his accent." Niomi handed her a small screen with a picture of him. "Here is his file. Look over it. If anyone asks you something you don't know, feign not feeling well, mention heartburn."

Ari scanned his file. Two children, one boy and one girl. He had three grandchildren. Wife of 30 years. Worked in the state department for most of his life and recently assigned as a representative. She didn't have the time to memorize co-workers or acquaintances but studied their faces so she'd recognize them. "You said something about a vote? Are you sure I'm ready for this?"

"You have an assistant who will direct you to the meeting. Tao rarely goes in VLEX and is only there for the vote. Your vote will be 'Yes' as we expect Tao's would be. It's important to see the other votes. Remember any 'No' votes and any conversations you overhear."

Ari felt overwhelmed and underprepared, but Niomi didn't seem to care. She directed Ari to the chair. At least they didn't need a patch since she wouldn't be as long.

"Tao wouldn't take notes, but if you need to, then do so. You can transfer them out if you need. We need the details of the bill and the votes. Good luck." Niomi plugged her in.

Ari took a deep breath and plunged herself into the VR. She found herself sitting at a sleek black desk. It was bare except for a single screen set off to the side.

An Asian man entered the room, in a simple black suit. "Glad to see you made it alright, sir."

From the movement of the man's lips, Ari knew the translator Niomi sent her with was working. She nodded and scanned the screen in front of her for any news or information she would need but found only messages from other representatives discussing their worry about the Roman and Middle Eastern votes.

"Are you ready, sir?" The man, presumably Tao's assistant, stood with the door open.

Ari stood with a slow precise movement, hoping this man didn't know Tao too well. Tao took the lead, which could be a problem as Ari wasn't familiar with this office. Gratefully, the elevator was within sight. They headed downstairs. Niomi had made Ari memorize everything she could about VLEX, so she was comfortable leading the way to the United Nations building that held the political forums and votes.

People escorted her inside, her assistant—she found out his name was Chi from overhearing another person—remained by her side. Inside the large building the sleek silver design shone on every surface. People of every race moved with purpose, only conversing in hushed tones.

Ari stopped for a minute in surprise. Next to an older woman was Hailey with her brown hair wrapped in a bun. Hailey glanced her way but didn't appear to recognize Ari. Before her staring became awkward, Ari continued forward, grateful Chi didn't ask any questions.

In his personal voting room, there were drinks and a small sitting area sectioned off containing one chair, obviously for Tao. Stepping inside, she realized the room opened to a large arena. It was more of a private suite where everyone could see each other.

A single podium stood in the center with a dark-skinned fellow. Once in her chair, she viewed the screen to her right. Unfortunately, the wording was in a different language. She traced a finger down the screen and realized she'd have to look at the code to decipher it.

Chi stood behind her. "Are you alright, sir? Can I get you anything?"

She froze for a moment, not realizing Chi was so near. Remembering Niomi's advice she rubbed a spot on her chest and stared forward. "A drink will do."

As she sipped some sort of tea, she read through the information on the screen. The bill that was up for a vote dealt with new virtual reality research that the Russian States were accused of. There weren't specific details on what they were researching. The wording was filled with so much legalese it was hard to read.

Ari was grateful that once the proceedings started Chi went into the back room, as it gave her time to copy the files discreetly. As the man in the center of the arena spoke, the bill appeared on the screen. He called on the author of the bill to speak. Ari focused more on copying the transcript as it came through on her screen.

People were worried about the Russian's research threatening national security. The Russian representative was adamant that the research was purely academic, concerned about people's wellbeing inside the virtual. When it came time to vote on whether to send a team to investigate, she was so caught up in the discussion that she almost forgot to enter Tao's vote.

With a click of a button, she entered her yes vote. Sitting back in her chair, the enormity of what she just did hit her. She wasn't just getting information for VisionTech. Impersonating a country's representative and forging a vote must be illegal in all countries in so many ways. Prison didn't begin to describe how much trouble she would be in. How did she let Niomi talk her into this? It felt so simple in the beginning.

The man in the middle, President of the Union, Ari realized, concluded the meeting, and she rushed to copy a vote of the bill. The data, invisible to everyone but a warper, remained in her pocket for when she could transfer it alone.

The walk back to her office, Chi continued behind her, his gaze burning the back of her head. He watched with a careful eye which put Ari on edge. When they entered the office, Ari kept walking to her private office.

"I'll see you on the other side, sir," Chi said.

Ari sat down at her desk staring at her hands. What did

she do? If she wasn't here where would Tao be? Or Kari for that matter? What was Kari thinking being back at work, if she even was back at work, that is. *Stop it. Finish the job and get out of here. You can question all you want on the other side.*

She quickly sent off the data to the temporary address. Then, with a silent prayer that Tao was alright, she pulled out of VLEX.

CHAPTER THIRTEEN

Ari's head pounded as she returned to reality. Ignoring the headache, she unplugged herself and checked on her files.

"We got the data you sent. I wasn't sure you could translate that quickly and copy the data. Good job," Niomi said.

Getting a 'good job' was rare from Niomi. Its equivalent was jumping up and down for joy from normal people. Niomi was so pleased, she gave Ari the afternoon off. Granted, in Niomi's words it came as, "You need some rest before I have to deal with more teenage tantrums." At least she was smiling as she said it.

The insult didn't even hit Ari. She didn't have many notes because of the short day, and she copied all the meeting's proceedings as fast as she could. A numbness poured over Ari as she headed to her room, thinking about what she had done and her role with VisionTech. She hated the nagging feeling in the back of her mind that maybe she made the wrong choice coming here.

As she entered her bedroom, her maid was making her bed. Ari didn't see Jewels often, as she normally worked when Ari worked.

"Sorry to bother you," the older islander said with a heavy accent. Her black hair, laced with silver, was wound into a large bun on top of her head. "I thought you'd be working."

"Me too." Ari shrugged, kicked off her shoes and plopped down on a sofa on the opposite side of the room, her head still throbbing. "Don't leave on my account. I won't bother you."

Jewels finished tucking in the sheets and turned to dusting. Ari couldn't see any dust, but the woman kept wiping at the corners. "These robots think they can do everything. Press a shirt, vacuum a floor, but phooey. They don't get the details that show it's really clean."

Ari couldn't help but smile. She'd never heard anyone use the word phooey before.

Jewels turned. "What's wrong with you? Why are you not working today?"

"I did a good job, so they gave me the afternoon off."

"Then why aren't you happy?"

Ari picked at the hem on her suit, unable to answer that question. The maid didn't push the issue, but with a humph, continued cleaning. Lost in her thoughts, Ari wondered about her contract again. She knew it was a five-year contract, but with a no-compete clause and whatnot, she didn't know where to go next. Maybe she could talk to Tessa and work for her? There had to be something else. Maybe tell Niomi she refused these assignments. There had to be different work someone with her abilities could do.

"Jewels, can I ask you a question?"

The woman continued cleaning. "Does your mouth work?"

"How long have you been working for VisionTech?"

Jewels paused for a minute. "Four rainy seasons now. I

didn't want to work at first. Hated VisionTech for taking over our island. I stayed home and watched my grand babies."

"They took it over?"

"Yes. They gave big money to our chief, and that man had only eyes for gold. He gave up almost all our land. Now we work for them. Slaves so we can play their fancy computers and games." She spit on the ground to show her displeasure.

A small machine came out from under the coffee table to clean it up. Then she spit on that too. When it parked, she reached down to clean it off.

"Do you like working for VisionTech?" Guilt simmered for not keeping her room cleaner and making Jewels work.

"Yeah. I'm used to taking care of babies, kids, and my husband when he was alive. Work is good. Work keeps you alive." Jewels gave Ari a sideways glance. "So does eating, you know? You are getting thinner. Eat more. Maybe I will cook for you, not this garbage computer food. You need pig fat. It will fill you out in no time."

Ari couldn't contain her laughter. "I'm sure pig fat will do that." Instead of getting straight lard though, she grabbed an apple from the bowl in front of her. Maybe her headache was due to lack of real food. The patch can't be that good for you. She bit into the apple and continued to listen to Jewels tell stories of the island when she was a child.

———

The next morning it was back to Kari's life again. Ari did catch up on her sleep yesterday, but she still felt the lingering effects of her headache, like she was hungover or something. She sat down in the chair ready to go.

"I almost forgot. How were you feeling yesterday?" Niomi turned from the computer.

"Fine, I guess. A bit of a headache."

"Good to know. We'll take the rest of the week out of the VR and work on your training to mix things up."

"If training is the alternative, I feel great." Ari pulled up her hair to make way for the cord, but something caught her. "Is the VR why I had my headache?" She didn't remember getting them at school.

"More just being inactive. That's why we workout so much. Your body would deteriorate if you were plugged in all day getting your nutrients from a patch."

"Makes sense."

"Also, everyone was very excited over the information you gathered. They approved a visit with Tessa since we still haven't found your family." The way Niomi said it made Ari think Niomi knew something of her previous visit.

"Sounds great." She wasn't about to get Vinh in trouble. If VisionTech couldn't find them, maybe that was for the best. Ari rubbed the base of her neck, which was sore from laying down in this chair so much. "See you on the flip side."

Kari's day dragged on. Replying to emails and scheduling meetings made Ari realize she never wanted to be a secretary. Maybe it was how active she had been with Niomi that ruined her for a boring desk job. There were a couple memos from the aftermath of the vote which Ari carefully forwarded on to Niomi.

When lunch came around, she forgot about Antoine, but hadn't heard anything from him either. At this point she didn't think blowing Kari's boyfriend off for one day would hurt, but Ari wanted to go back to the restaurant and see if

Hailey was there. After contemplating the pros and cons all morning, Ari decided the more she knew the better. Then she could decide whether to include Hailey in her report.

Ari strode through the market, watching people visit and talk. The sound of foreign accents transported her all over the world in mere seconds. Walking into the restaurant, she spotted Hailey in the back reading again. Ari headed towards her.

"About time you showed up?" Antoine's voice traveled through the large room.

Turning, Ari found Antoine at the bar, and her face warmed as all eyes turned on her.

He stormed across the room. "First you don't answer my calls yesterday. Then you blow me off. Today you show up and didn't even notice me."

Alcohol wafted from his breath. Ari wanted to shake him, tell him to pull it together. The booze wasn't even real, but that didn't matter, his brain thought it was.

Instead Ari tried to explain. "It was—"

"Don't even say it."

She reached out and grabbed his hand. "I'm sorry. I didn't mean to hurt you."

She didn't have time to blink before she was enveloped in a hug. Antoine leaning down to smell her hair. Ari really wondered what Antoine's and Kari's relationship was based on.

Ari pulled back, wanting distance. "I have a work meeting today, so I can't stay and talk, but I hoped to see you."

He lifted his dejected face. "So, you're not breaking up with me?"

Placing a hand on his face, she struggled to keep the facade of romance together. "Of course not. The session ends soon. Then we'll go on vacation and make up for lost time. Alright?"

Leaning forward, he kissed her, sloppy and wet. At least it was short. She had to pull back to distance herself from the uncomfortable kiss.

"See you soon, Love." He left with a smile on his face.

Ari sagged with relief. Noticing people nearby staring, she turned and hurried to the back. Hailey's large grin said she'd seen the whole scene.

"You may need to start going to other places to eat. People will talk," Hailey said.

"Funny." Ari placed a hand on the chair. "Do you mind if I join you?"

"Sure. I figured you'd be back."

"How's that?"

"You're greener than most. Not as well seasoned as most, so you must be full of questions."

Ari brushed aside the menu on the table and met Hailey's gaze. "What do you mean *than most?*"

She leaned forward arms out in front of her. "You know what we are."

Nodding, Ari couldn't deny that out loud. "Yes, and what do you do here? What do you want?"

"It's what do *you* want." Hailey pointed a finger at Ari. "Do you like being a tool? Let me guess, are they helping you? Saving you from a life of enslavement?"

"What if that was true?"

"I'm sure it is true. That's how most of us started, but they never tell you the real cost. They never tell you there is a life out there where you are your own boss."

"There is?" Ari asked. "If so, what are you still doing here?"

"Stopping *them* from taking over the world." Hailey stood.

"How can I find you?"

"I work in the European Union. Hailey Keller. By the way, next time let's meet at Ricco's down the way. The food is better."

She left Ari staring at Hailey's empty glass of wine, wondering what the hell that all meant.

CHAPTER FOURTEEN

Niomi was true to her word and didn't schedule Ari for any missions in the VLEX for the rest of the week. After their two-hour morning workout, the rest of the day she had off. If that wasn't enough, Niomi even gave her a car to use to go the community center if she wanted. A week ago, Ari would have jumped at that offer. Now, she didn't want the crowd. She wanted to think. To decide if Hailey was for real or just trying to con her. Either way, Ari was keeping it out of her report until she knew.

The only way to know for sure would be back in VLEX and she had a few more days until then. Niomi pulled some strings to get Reed a half day at work and he surprised her with a date at the beach. They tried surfing, which they both were horrible at, and ended up just riding the waves in on their stomach. They ate sandwiches while watching the sun set. If someone could paint the perfect date, this would be it.

Except Ari's stomach felt heavy with everything she hadn't told him but didn't know how. Given they were swimming, her smart suit was off but they both had HUBs.

Devices she wasn't sure she trusted. She slipped hers off and then reached for Reed's.

"What—"

She silenced him with a finger to her lips. Nodding, he allowed her to take both bracelets. She buried them up in the pile of clothes they wore over their suits. Returning she sat next to him, his sandy shoulder brushing against hers.

For a moment, she said nothing. She wanted to enjoy the peace she felt. The contentment of being here at the beach on a perfect date with a perfect boyfriend.

He nudged her with his shoulder. "Want to tell me what that was about? If you're thinking of getting down and dirty in this sand, Marco just might kill me."

This took Ari by surprise. "What? You thought this was about sex?"

He looked down for a moment. "Maybe. I don't know."

They hadn't talked about sex before. Many couples their age usually had sex in the VR. All the romance without any of the nasty consequences. But Ari didn't want that. The way she read code, it felt like porn or something. But real sex... no one did that until they were older and wanted kids.

"It's not like I haven't thought about it, but I think we should wait until you're older," Reed said.

"I agree. I'm barely seventeen, and the eighteen months you have on me isn't a lot older either." They'd celebrated her birthday a few weeks after arriving to the island. "Did you want to try it in the VR?" The hesitation strained her voice.

"Not in a million years. I know how you feel." His kind expression turned devious, a look that he usually only pulled around her brother. "I think I have a better plan."

He trailed one finger down her bare arm, and a rise of

goosebumps gave way.

"What's that?"

He leaned towards her and placed a very light kiss along her collar bone. "I will continue to torture you." Another kiss closer to her neck. "Until you're over eighteen." Another kiss below her jawbone. "Then you'll have no choice but to marry me."

Kissing her lips, he pulled her down on top of him. Shock flitted through her body. Marriage? At seventeen the thought hadn't crossed her mind. Not that she wouldn't want to marry Reed, one day. The more he kissed her, the more she saw that reality.

Abruptly, she pulled back. "You really think that I'm that easy? That I'll marry someone just because he is a good kisser?"

One side of his mouth pulled up in a crocked grin, his eyes sparkling in the falling sun. "Challenge accepted."

He quickly rolled her over in the sand and spent a considerable length of time showing her what a good kisser could accomplish.

Feeling as if she was going to burst with desire, she pushed him off. "Mercy, please."

He laid back in the sand, arms behind his head, looking pleased. At least he was breathing as hard as Ari. His muscular chest rose and fell rapidly as she admired what she saw.

"That isn't fair," she told him.

"What?"

"First, you don't want to get married, right?"

He shrugged. "Maybe not right now. But I like the idea of us getting married."

"Second, you distracted me."

He leaned back on his elbows. "I would say that I'm

sorry, but I'm not." His swollen lip curved up into a big smile to prove just that.

Ari couldn't help but lean into him. He laid back again, one hand under his head and one around her as she laid on his warm chest.

"So, what did you want to tell me?" He traced a finger on her arm.

"You know how I'm not supposed to talk about what I'm doing to anyone outside our team."

"Yeah." His arms tightened around her. "Has that rule changed?"

She swallowed a lump in her throat. "No. But things are happening inside."

"Did you talk to Tessa again?"

Ari had told Reed what happened with Tessa and how she was helping her family. "I see her tomorrow, but it's more than that."

"Okay." Reed was never the type to really push Ari and his silence confirmed that.

"You remember me telling you about VLEX? The community made available only to the governments and the wealthy?"

"Yeah. Everyone knows about them here, but no one's willing to elaborate. So, it's mostly rumors."

"It's not just rumors to me, it's my job. And the things they have me doing in there..."

His grip tightened around her waist. "If they're asking you to do things you don't want to, you just need to say so."

"It's not that clean cut. You know it isn't." She had responsibilities to her family and Reed.

"Nothing ever is."

His heart continued to beat out a steady rhythm as the waves climbed up to splash at their feet.

"Things will be okay. We made things work before and we can again."

In between heart beats, she heard everything he didn't say. How he enjoyed his work, loved his art internship even more. They both had been given opportunities they may not find anywhere else. But at what cost?

———

The next day after lunch, Ari headed to the lab to visit Tessa. Niomi stood at the ready, the private room already scheduled. As Ari looked at the screen, it reminded her that Niomi would be able to see everything as it transpired.

The setting Niomi picked this time was at a coffee shop. The quaint shop had outdoor seating overlooking a park. Birds flew in a scheduled pattern, something her old teachers would find abhorrent.

"Hey, friend."

Ari turned away from the birds to find Tessa sitting on the other side of the table. "Glad to see you."

"What's going on?" Tessa currently had dark blue hair wrapped in a bun on top of her head, the bottom half shaved. Numerous piercings filled her ears, and a jewel in her nose.

In excitement, Ari hurried forward and wrapped her in a hug.

"Ugg," Tessa tensed. "I guess we're doing hugs now."

Pulling back, Ari tried to stir some of the same worry she had last week when she first learned her family was missing. Ari didn't know what Niomi knew but thought it best to keep up pretenses. "We lost Marco and my mom. Have you heard anything from them at all?"

Tessa paused for a moment before she realized the situation Ari was in, then relaxed into her chair. "Not recently, but he checked in last week. They had to go underground a little bit more to get off people's radar."

Releasing a big sigh, she leaned on the table. "Thank God. Are they getting the money I sent you?"

"Yeah. They're doing okay and wanted me to send their love." She sipped the small cup in front of her.

"Thank you." Ari knew Niomi was watching this interaction, so she had to be very careful what she said. She needed to ask about Kari, but how? "Can I ask one more favor?"

Tessa cocked a brow. "Like a stray cat, I'm unable to tell you no, so go ahead."

"Great. I'm a cat now." Unsure how to go about doing it, Ari raised her hand for a drink. How could she hide from Niomi in here?

Tessa must have sensed her hesitation. "Remember when Professor Coleman used to go on and on about how talented you were?"

Not remembering any time Coleman complemented her, she was hesitant to reply. "What?"

"Yeah. I never saw it myself. Maybe that's because you sucked at my game, especially when you never changed weapons. I thought you were really dense."

Was Tessa telling her to use her power? Maybe how she pulled back when making out with Antoine, she could layer what Niomi saw in the VR. People go layers deep in the VR. Just because she hadn't done that yet, didn't mean she couldn't. The thing was, writing a whole other conversation while talking to Tessa would be tricky, maybe impossible.

While Tessa continued rambling on about school, and friends. Ari focused her vision to the code. A rush went through her as the world around changed to letters and numbers spinning in a perfect orchestra. She kept the world Niomi sent her to and created a simple scripted play between the two girls that involved drinking a lot of coffee to keep her trainer occupied.

Then she created a second layer with no visuals, just a black screen. Niomi would only be able to see this if she pored through the code, which would take a normal person hours. Ari's fingers tingled as she finished the work and pulled Tessa inside her blank world.

"It took you long enough to catch on," Tessa said when the surroundings changed.

"We don't have much time," Ari said.

"What's going on?"

"Can you have your lawyer see if there is any way to get out of my contract? Leave a message in your game for me if so. My friend will get it."

"Why do you want out?"

"I don't know if I do yet. It's just inside VLEX..." Ari fisted her hand unable to put in words her concerns. She didn't know what really happened to Kari and President Higgins. "I'd rather work for you."

"I'd love to have you, but if anyone caught wind of you, then it would be over. I don't trust my dad with what he'd use you for. It's harder to hide than you think and I'm not sure you'd be safe here."

"Just look into it for me okay? Also, can you check out a Kari Trenton for me? She works for the Icelandic States in VLEX."

Tessa's face tightened in worry, her lip ring pulling to the side. "I will. We better go back before anyone catches on."

They went back to the coffee shop and said their good-byes. Ari left not knowing whether she felt better or worse.

CHAPTER FIFTEEN

Monday, Ari returned to the VLEX as Kari, business as usual. Except for the pit in Ari's stomach as she thought about the real Kari. She hated the glimpses of the pretty woman's reflection she accidentally picked up now and again.

When Hailey emailed her asking about lunch, a spark of interest surfaced. Ricco's at noon. There was nothing unusual about making a friend with other workers in the VLEX. If anything, it was encouraged. Networking and lobbying were the only reason for lunch or drinks inside the VLEX.

When it hit noon, Ari headed down to the town center. She followed the path, the small red door to Ricco's snuggled in the crowded market. The small entrance gave away nothing. When she opened the door, the flavors of her hometown, peppers and lime, greeted her.

Hailey waved from the bar and stood to welcome her. "Glad you could make it."

Ari nodded, waves of nervous energy rolling around in her stomach.

"I have a table in the back." Hailey led the way down a colorful corridor.

Music wafted down the halls, an old Spanish number. Something Ari's grandmother would listen to with tears in her eyes. Soon they found the source. In the corner a bronze and black machine twirled around playing music. A couple danced in the middle of the floor. The woman wore a bright red dress, cut high in the hip. One hand on her skirt, she whipped it around as the gentleman twirled her.

Ari looked at Hailey and mouthed the words, "What is this?"

Hailey didn't answer but turned back to the couple. They moved with a grace only a skilled dancer could accomplish. When the final chord struck, the man tilted the woman back leaning close to her neck. As he placed a light kiss on her collarbone, she vanished.

Hailey clapped, applauding the man. Straightening up, he ran a hand through his hair, short and dark with a hint of silver. It may be to show his age, but no one ever knew in here. His red tie stood out against his black suit, a perfect match to the woman's dress.

"This must be Kari." He took Ari's hand and kissed the knuckles. "Pleasure to meet you. You may call me Emil."

She had to reminder herself to stay in character but noticed how he phrased that with a curl of his lips—*pleasure*.

"Hailey tells me you have some gifts."

Ari spared Hailey a quick look. "I guess that's a matter of opinion."

A light laughter filled the air, almost as musical as the dance. The musical perfection of his laugh couldn't have been natural, but only something a warper could do. "Glad you have a sense of humor."

Nerves on edge, Ari got straight to the point. "How many people like you are in here?"

His smile remained in place. "You mean warpers like you?"

Biting her lower lip, she nodded. She wasn't ready to admit to anyone her abilities, but this man had abilities of his own. "That's not an answer." Ari didn't want to play games anymore. Could no one be straight? She turned to leave, and a wall appeared in front of her where the hall used to be. Turning around, she realized there was no longer an exit in the room. Yes, she could have moved it, but she didn't want to use her powers unless necessary. As she turned, she narrowed her gaze.

He held a hand open. "Dance with me?"

"Really?" A laugh escaped her. "I don't know how to dance."

"It doesn't matter."

Before she could reply, he took her hand and spun her into his arms. The smell of spicy cinnamon, presumably his cologne, wafted around her. He kept his hand on her lower back while lifting hers up in a formal position. Soon they spun around the room with an agility and grace Ari didn't possess.

Uncomfortable, she pulled back, resisting, but nothing happened. Her body continued to dance close to his. Her hips twisted as her feet danced steps foreign to her. The Spanish number played out of the music player nearby.

Unnerved, she tried harder to stop dancing. Ari slammed her foot hard into the ground, but nothing happened. She focused on the code, the characters and digits flowing along everything in this world. Her power of manipulation, which normally came as easily as walking, didn't work. She could see the code but couldn't change it. Her body continued dancing against its will.

He leaned towards her, his breath warm on her neck "Don't fight it. You'll only hurt yourself."

Panic clamped down on her chest. Her breaths came in jagged gasps. Helpless in his arms, his touch became repulsive.

"You're more special than anyone wants to tell you. You are more than the tool people want you to be."

Closing her eyes, she tried to pull out of the program. Normally, she only had to will herself back into reality, simple and easy. Instead, she remained in the program with Emil's hands still on her.

Focusing, she changed the world around her. Brightly colored letters and numbers spun around her, but she was powerless to change anything. This was her current reality. She swallowed back the tears and fear that threatened to overwhelm her.

The music continued playing and when she opened her eyes, Emil smiled back at her. "You're the future."

Slowly the music ended, and she spun out of his hands. A wave of dizziness threatened to overtake her. Holding onto a nearby wall, she struggled to slow her breath. "What the hell was that?"

"What I'm capable of, and what you will be capable of one day. Your company claims to save you, protect you from those who would poach us like wild animals. Yet all they want is this power for themselves." He reached out his hand, and Hailey stepped next to him, grasping it. "They probably even claim to keep you safe and healthy, but they don't even know how."

"What are you talking about?" The hundreds of questions Ari had fled as she tried to decipher what he was really saying. A headache began to grow behind her eyes, her mind fuzzy. Trying to manipulate the code hurt her more than she realized.

"Why don't you dig a little deeper into this VisionTech of yours? Instead of being their puppet, consider holding the reins for a while."

With a snap of his fingers, Ari stood outside the restaurant. She spun around looking for any sign of them, but only saw strangers continue down the busy walkway. Nauseated, she leaned against a nearby wall and slowly sunk to the ground. Code blinked in and out of her vision as a sharp pain grew behind her eyes. Trying to escape Emil exhausted her energy, but she didn't figure it would be this bad.

Sitting down, head between her bent knees, she tried to catch her breath. She squeezed her eyes shut, and a rainbow of colored code ran against the back of her eyelids. She fought the migraine that threatened to keep her down.

"Are you okay, Miss?" A middle-aged man stood above her in a dark suit. His face was a blur of flesh and code that hurt to look at.

"Just not feeling well." She turned away and prayed he'd leave her be. People weren't sick inside the VR or if so, it would be hidden back in the real world. If somebody was too ill, then the VR monitors would pull them out.

The man remained nearby, obviously not believing her.

She lifted her chin and forced her face to not show the pain she felt. "Seriously. I just got some bad news from my boyfriend. I'll be okay."

He finally turned to leave, mumbling something about drama.

After several minutes, she used the wall to stand. The world around her spun several times, but slowly straightened out. Unsure of how she would finish her work, she stumbled into a nearby bar and asked for a drink. With a swipe of her hand, Kari paid for it with her employee credits. The taste repelled her, but she finished it. With a gasp, she set the bottle down. Characters danced around the glass, and she realized fake alcohol may not fix this type of headache.

If she pulled out of the VR, it would be obvious something happened. Niomi would demand answers. Was Ari ready to tell her?

No, not yet. Not until she had all the answers about VisionTech. With a hand lifted to block out the fake sun, she shuffled back to work. Gratefully, President Higgins had a meeting that kept him busy most of the afternoon. Ari laid her head on the desk, closed her eyes, and prayed for the pain to stop.

CHAPTER SIXTEEN_

With trembling fingers, Ari typed out her report. Her headache turned to a full-blown migraine. Black spots filled her vision, and she worried how long she would be able to stand.

Niomi grabbed her hand and pulled her into a chair. "What's going on?" She slapped on a medi-cuff. A bright light pierced Ari's vision, and she flinched back in pain.

"It's just a bad headache. Let me lay down and I'll be fine." Ari closed her eyes and rubbed her temples.

"I'll take some blood and then get you to your room."

Ari didn't have the energy to protest, but thought taking blood, when she hadn't eaten real food all day, wasn't the smartest idea. By the time Niomi finished her workups, Ari could barely stand by herself. Her trainer escorted her to her room. Ari crawled into bed, hiding from the light that stabbed sharp daggers in her eyes. Jewels spoke in the distance. Absently, she felt someone take off her shoes and inject something into her arm. The pain that should have registered from the injection was little more than a prick. Finally, the lights dimmed, darkness surrounding her.

"Contact me or your AI if you need anything. Jewels or I will be close by," Niomi said then, with a swish of the door, left.

Minutes or maybe hours passed, and Ari drifted in and out of consciousness. Eventually, the pain lifted, leaving her in a fog of drugs. When she could finally sit up, all the light fixtures in the room were glowing softly. Glancing at her HUB, it was nine at night. Her dry mouth tasted like vomit, though she didn't remember throwing up. Stumbling out of bed, she brushed her teeth and downed a full glass of water.

Refilling it, she took a seat. Her muscles ached like she had ran a marathon. There was an exhaustion she didn't think any sleep would cure. Ordering some soup, she checked her HUB and found it was flashing with new messages. Vinh sent a short note, checking up on her and wanting her to call him.

She flipped on her electronic assistant. "Hey, you annoying piece of crap, your new name is Emil. Call Vinh." Maybe she shouldn't so blatantly use his name, though she doubted it was his real name, anyway. Somehow ordering people around gave her some evil satisfaction. Her pain was because of him.

Vinh picked up right away. "How are you doing?"

"Better than I was. What's up?"

"I'm bringing over your suit tonight. Will you be up for a bit, or should I leave it for you?"

"I'll be up. I need to move and clear my head. I'll be in the kitchen, eating."

Realizing her old smart suit was stiff due to sweat, she peeled out of it and jumped in the shower. The warm water massaged her stiff muscles. Wrapping her hair up into a bun, she put on PJs and headed to the kitchen.

By the time Vinh showed up, she had already finished

off her soup and was halfway through the carton of ice cream. Vinh set the suit on the back of the chair. "Is there enough for me?"

"If you hurry."

He grabbed a spoon and dug out his own bite of chocolate ice cream. "You gave Niomi a real scare today."

"Really?"

"Yeah. She screamed at me for letting you forget your suit in the common lockers. Not that the suit would have helped you, but it would have helped Niomi watch your vitals."

She took another bite, savoring the cold chocolate in her mouth. "I should have gone back for it. Thanks for getting it for me."

"What happened in there?"

He asked the question casually, but it felt off. She watched him until he noticed. "What? Do I have something on my face?"

The medicine must still be in her system. Things felt off; Vinh felt off. She shook off the feeling and tried to answer. "Sorry, I'm still a little foggy from the meds. I just started getting a bad headache and instead of coming back, I pushed through it. It just made things worse."

"You better take care of yourself, and I'm doing my part by eating some of this ice cream for you."

Ari laughed, but then quieted down and thought about his comment of taking care of herself. What wasn't he telling her?

The rest of the evening passed with them talking, opening another tub of ice cream, and watching crappy old movies. Vinh loved adding horrible accents to the villains. She wondered why she even thought something was wrong with him.

CHAPTER SEVENTEEN

Niomi wanted to keep Ari out of VLEX longer, but Kari needed to go back to work. Anxious for her own answers, Ari pushed to go back in as well. Her fortitude faltered slightly when her alarm went off at 2:30 in the morning, but after some caffeine she was ready for work.

"If the headache returns, come back in. Even a slight headache can improve with some rest at your lunch break." This time, Niomi put Ari on the patch before she was plugged in.

"I will." Ari planned to lie low today. No Latin dancing for sure.

"Be careful," Niomi said as she slid the cable in Ari's neck.

Ari leaned back and closed her eyes.

She arrived at Kari's usual desk, not a thing out of place. Her usual in-box was piled with messages, but one stood out to her. It came from Worldwide News Source, a VLEX newspaper that usually held headlines from all over the world, along with design changes and other pertinent information for those inside the VLEX. This message caught her eye with the mention of President Tao, the man she impersonated last week.

Opening the news, she learned President Tao had a heart attack. His picture, stoic and strong emerged in 3D from the screen. Being eighty-three, the attack wasn't a total surprise given his family history, but his last doctor appointment reported the Representative was in good health.

Watching his picture, a heavy feeling settled in her gut. Was there even such a thing as coincidence when dealing with a business as successful and precise as VisionTech? And the fact that Ari currently worked in the office of President Higgins, who co-founded that she just voted, must not be a surprise either.

She didn't have time to panic. Not yet. Not without the facts. Checking President Higgin's schedule, she realized she had an hour before he made it in. Hopefully that would be enough.

Instead of the normal tasks of forwarding emails and scheduling meetings, Ari started searching Kari's computer. Any possible important information had been copied and sent over to VisionTech, but that wasn't what Ari wanted this time.

She began in Kari's personal files and found that on the days Ari had been absent Kari had taken personal days.

Her home country was the Icelandic States, where her parents and younger brother still lived. Kari moved into the city and probably didn't stay in contact much anymore. After the political session was over soon, Kari's schedule inside the VLEX shortened, leaving only a few hours a day to schedule meetings. She didn't have the vacation with Antoine scheduled for a couple weeks.

Some snowy mountain resort, Ari gathered by the notes left in the computer.

Then she found a picture. Ari thought it would be of Antoine, he was handsome enough to keep a few of those on hand, but it was of Kari's family. All pale skinned with scattered freckles. Her father had a strong build with blond hair; her mother had the red hair, like Kari, and was just as pretty. Kari and her brother were younger, maybe in their teens. Instead of the serious pose of their parents, Ari could tell the kids were trying hard not to laugh. Their green eyes lit up the picture, and their mouths were pressed hard into a tight smile.

It reminded Ari of her own family. Not perfect, but family. She had to find out what happened to Kari. Hopefully Tessa would have some answers. Ari owed it to her. It was one thing to be a stand-in worker, but to stand in as a girlfriend was a whole other thing. One Ari still wasn't sure how she felt about.

After closing Kari's personal files, she did a search for VisionTech on Kari's database. It pulled the corporation, with the familiar blue and white logo. Clicking on it, Ari could see the company directory inside VLEX.

VisionTech was listed as an electronic technology and software company residing in the United Asian States. The CEO appeared to be an older man with Asian heritage. It could have been Vinh's grandpa for all Ari knew. Ari recognized the photo below it. It was the Director of Special Projects, no other name listed. He was the director of her division that met with Niomi weeks ago.

Recognizing the director didn't help with the rest of Ari's search. She didn't have access to many other important files. Kari's position forwarded files, but she never got to keep a copy of them. Even half of the messages she forwarded to Higgins were classified and closed to her. Ari couldn't even read the bill that she translated as President Tao. She needed more access, but where?

President Higgins pressed through the doors at the exact moment. "How are you feeling today, Ms. Trenton?"

"Much better, sir, thank you."

"Glad to hear it." He continued into his office.

Higgins' computer had all the information she needed, she just needed him. Between his passwords and facial recognition, it would be hard to break into undetected, even for Ari. But what if Higgins did it for her?

Checking his schedule, she saw that he didn't have a meeting for a couple hours, which meant he'd spend the morning in his office glued to his computer. Quietly she snuck out of the office and rode the elevator. On the first floor, she stepped around the corner to find a space with relative privacy. Not wanting to draw attention to Higgins' office, in case there was some security measure in place to alert people when code changed, she came down stairs and became invisible. It was an easy enough transformation that didn't require too much work.

The elevator on the way back up was the tricky part. It took five minutes to wait for the right floor to be selected. While she was invisible, she was still physically present in the VR. So, walking next to people or through walls didn't prove a problem. She could have just popped into Higgins' office, but again didn't want to set off too many alarms or use her powers too much and get another headache.

When she entered his office, she found Higgins on the phone staring at the screen in front of him. "Yes, I know the vote went the way we wanted, but I still worry that we unearthed something we don't want to and will only give other countries ideas they didn't have before."

Ari moved behind him and realized the bill was on the screen. Taking her time to read it, she realized the supposedly illegal methods the Russians were accused of were Virtual Reality Torture and Forced Incarceration inside the system. As she couldn't scroll down on his screen, her mind sped through the implications of this. This took war to a new level. If you could force someone inside a program and keep them there, you could psychologically withdraw any information you could want.

It reminded her of the first program she walked in on with Niomi and the Director. Did VisionTech already have this technology as well? The idea made her ill. Her father was trapped in a VR coma due to his own addiction, now they wanted to force prisoners or anyone they didn't agree with to be incarcerated inside of one?

"Let's schedule a joint commission meeting to seal the specifics of the findings. I'll have my assistant set it up."

Ari snapped out of her thoughts by these words. She raced down the hall where other offices from the Icelandic States were held. When no one was looking, she reappeared in the program, then headed back to her office.

She walked in as Higgins opened his door.

"Sorry, sir. Just needed some fresh air."

"I need a meeting scheduled. I sent you the details."

She hurried to her desk. "I'll get to it right away."

The rest of the morning she spent getting caught up on Kari's work. Things were busy with this new bill that passed. A committee to investigate VR research was being created. Even Antoine didn't have time to meet. They tentatively planned time for coffee later in the day.

By the time Ari finished Kari's work, she took a late lunch while President Higgins was out at a meeting. She didn't bother with going to the center to eat but headed straight for Ryope Industries. It was a small business compared to the worldwide organizations present inside VLEX.

The building had a basic tall rectangular design, but advertisements covered it completely. Not only for Ryope Industries, but other businesses, products, and vacation services. Unlike some of the more cultural designs for buildings in VLEX, this felt like a hundred-foot tall billboard.

After checking the directory, she traveled up to the tenth floor designated to Ryope. The inside of the building looked similar to the outside. Loud advertisements covered the walls, cheapening the sleek design of the office.

The young man sitting at reception welcomed Ari and informed her that neither Tessa nor her father—Ari had met him once before—were in the office today.

With his manicured hair and nails, along with his pressed bow tie, his perfection appeared robotic. Maybe he was part of the program in here. "Would they have left any files or packages for you?"

"Maybe." Ari remembered Tessa saying they could pass messages through this office.

"Your name?" he asked.

Ari wasn't about to give him her real name. "Oya."

The fact he didn't even react to that name told Ari he was a program. He had the same stiff no nonsense personality as Ari's AI. Functional but not fun.

"Tessa did leave you a file." He glanced up at Ari. "What format do you want it on?"

Ari couldn't take it back to work. "Do you have a reader I could use?"

"Of course. There is a password to open the file." He handed her a small screen.

"Thanks." Internally, Ari cursed Tessa. Now she had to

guess at a password. After a few different tries all involving Tessa's game, Ari finally opened it using a variation of Tessa's gamer name: VegaRules.

"Figures," Ari muttered.

The AI glanced up at Ari.

"I'm good. Thanks."

Tessa left a message at the top of the screen.

Your family is safe. Better than this girl you had me check up on. I hope this isn't your co-worker.

Scrolling down, Ari found information on Kari's current address, phone number, position and title. A picture of Kari's apartment, green and white, rotated on the screen. Next was a picture of a red-haired woman coming out the door. She had a striking similarity to Kari, but for someone who had studied and lived her life, Ari knew it wasn't her.

Tessa's message continued.

Kari has been silent online and not in contact with friends. A neighbor claimed that she works long hours and spends even more time in the VR. There is someone living in her apartment, but it's not her. I picked up a red-haired woman on satellite, but it wasn't a match. Not sure what happened to her, but something doesn't sit right. Stay in touch.

Ari slowly sank against the wall. The reader crashed to the floor just as the safety and innocence of Ari's world did the same. She stared at her hands, Kari's hands, so petite, so perfect, with the nails painted in a light pink color that matched the floral dress Ari put on today. Was this the only place Kari would be alive in again?

She tried to reassure herself that it could mean several things. Maybe Kari was on vacation. There may not be a dead body, but Ari knew deep down something wasn't right. They couldn't have hacked her feed or something. If Kari wasn't dead yet, she probably would be. Just like Representative Tao. So easily replaceable, these people were to VisionTech. Inside virtual reality for an extended period, it was easy to gain a sense of invincibility. But outside this fabricated world, they were human and weak.

"Can I help you, Oya?" The receptionist extended a hand.

Surprised she jolted upright. "I'm fine, really." She picked up the screen, and with trembling fingers she deleted the message and handed the screen back to him. "Thank you for your help."

She clenched her hands as she walked out of the building. She needed to think, not freak out. Her HUB beeped a reminder that she had an appointment to meet Antoine for coffee.

Antoine. Her heart ached for that love-sick fool. How could she break it to him? Should she break it to him?

CHAPTER EIGHTEEN

In a small Parisian cafe, she greeted Antoine with a kiss on each cheek.

"Just like the Parisians do it," he said. His musky smell had become familiar which tore at Ari's heart.

He pulled back, holding her hands. "What's wrong, my love?"

"Nothing, nothing." She turned her head as she wiped away a tear that betrayed her. "Just a stressful day at work."

"Yes," he lifted her chin with a finger. "But only a couple more weeks until vacation. Imagine you and me in front of a fire. Glass in hand. A fur rug under our bare skin. I can't wait to meet you in the flesh."

The excitement on his face rivaled that of a child. She couldn't help but smile at Antoine. He wore his heart on his sleeve along with everything. Ari was beginning to see why Kari would fall for him. He wrapped sunshine, love, and magic up and presented it to Kari with a bow.

To *Kari*, Ari reminded herself. *Not to you. You might be the cause of her death.* She bit down on her lip to push back her emotions while he ordered them both coffees. He carried most of the conversation, which Ari appreciated. She nodded and agreed as he complained about a co-worker and then talked about their plans in the mountains.

"You'll love it there. The air is so clean, the sky so blue. Like VR blue, but real. I can't wait for you to meet my brother there."

"Me either." The smile came easier for Ari now because she wanted to believe.

Kari and Antoine felt like some type of show or romance novel. These two characters who struggled for true love only to be thwarted by forces beyond their control. If Ari could put this off for a little bit longer, maybe somehow she could give them the happy ending they deserved. Ari wanted to believe in happy endings.

"Damn," Antoine said checking his HUB. "I have to get back."

He gave her a deep kiss. Ari felt detached, watching it from a distance. It isn't her body, it isn't her life. She hijacked Kari's world, so at least she could keep those she loved protected.

"Love you." His gaze penetrated past the charade and Ari shuddered.

"Love you too."

She watched him leave. Every decision she made had consequences she couldn't see. She just hoped she made the right one where Antoine was concerned.

―――――

Somewhere along the way, Ari had become a pro at hiding. She hid in Kari's life, even in Tao's. Now, as she emerged from the VR once again to Niomi and her reports, Ari realized she'd been hiding in her own life. The pain and fear of what VisionTech had done was sealed tight. Moving through the motions, she typed the lies easily from her fingers. The correct words flowed effortless from her mouth.

By the time she walked away from Niomi, with a promise to exercise tonight, she felt as fake as the AI in Ryope Industries. Walking through the motions of life, detached from reality.

"What time is it?" she asked her AI, wondering where Reed would be. Ari didn't even find humor in tormenting her personal AI anymore, and recently changed his name to just AI.

"4:30 in the afternoon."

She had stayed late in the VR. Messaging Niomi, Ari told her she was going to visit Reed and workout with him. She stopped asking permission to leave her wing, and Niomi knew better than to bug her about it. She checked out a hoverbike and rode to Reed's work.

It began raining during her ride, but Ari welcomed it. The cleansing coolness of the water gave her hope that she could figure this mess out. She needed Reed, needed to be reminded of home and who she was. Guilt pulled heavy on her shoulders as she remembered Antoine. Would Reed care? She didn't want to hurt Reed, but she needed to be honest. He needed to know everything, no matter what his security clearance. He needed to know the stakes before getting sucked into VisionTech more than he was.

She pushed strands of wet hair out of her face and parked the bike. She elbowed through the crowd of people leaving work for the day. Not finding him in the hall, she searched through the clear doors and spotted him. She picked out his wavy blondish brown hair. It had grown out more lately.

As she approached, she noticed his face lit up. He was

talking with his hands, which he did when he was excited. He radiated joy, something she only glimpsed before coming to the island, and usually with her. Laughing, his body shook, and his eyes sparked to life. One step closer, and Ari found out who he was talking to—Kimmy.

Ari froze, and a realization sunk in. Kimmy was the one who brought joy to Reed. His art, his friends, his life here with VisionTech brought him a happiness. Would Ari be enough to replace all that? She never saw Reed this happy at school. Even with Marco, he always acted a bit reserved.

Reed wanted to do art. He wouldn't be killing people with his art, but inspiring, creating. And this may be the only opportunity he had to do that. Would Ari really take that away?

Could she crush his happiness the same way she would one day crush Antoine's? The guilt of Antoine and her fake promises and declarations of love forced her back. One step then another. Reed could find joy here. Not just with his work, but with Kimmy or someone like her. Ari... well, Ari did a better job stealing people's joy than creating it lately.

After a few steps, she turned and hurried out of the building. Back on the hoverbike she found herself at the outdoor workout facility. Partially covered, it protected Ari from the rain, but not the wind howling through the trees. Howling like Ari wanted to, pushing, fighting forces it couldn't control. She struck out at the dummy, over and over.

If somehow she was stronger, better, then maybe she could figure this out.

CHAPTER NINETEEN

The rest of the week, Ari kept her head down and worked hard. She needed time to figure out her next step. She kept tabs with Antoine inside VLEX searching for the best way to end his relationship with Kari, but never figuring out how to. Blaming President Higgins for keeping her busy, they messaged more than anything.

Staying occupied with work was also the best way to keep her distance from Reed. If she met with him, she may not be able to keep her distance. She wanted what was best for Reed and giving him that was the hardest thing she ever had to do.

So, when Jewels left a note in her room—a real note on stiff paper—inviting Ari to a party, she replied yes. Granted, it was odd that her maid invited her to the party, but Ari wanted to see more of the island and needed a distraction. Ari replied in pink lipstick, the only thing she could find to write with.

Not only did Ari need a reason to avoid Reed that weekend, but she was beyond curious to see where Jewels lived. With Niomi's runs, Ari felt like she had traveled the island, but she never saw any sight of homes or islanders on her section. Ari jumped at the chance to see more of this place.

At first Niomi wouldn't agree for Ari to leave Vision-Tech property even if she had a chip in the back of her neck reporting her location.

"I can take care of myself," Ari told Niomi. "You've taught me that much. And if VisionTech wants me to keep working for them, they can't lock me in a cage for the rest of my life." They probably could, but Ari hoped they wouldn't.

"Let me see who I can get with cleared to go with you." Niomi's anger was evident on her face.

In the end, two security guards were assigned to accompany Ari. Neither one was chatty. Both were way over six feet, with muscles to spare. Their close-cropped hair looked like part of their uniform, which was a navy Fit Suit. Ari had always known VisionTech had to have some type of security or police force on the island. They hid in the shadows though. Now up close, intimidating didn't begin to describe them.

Jewels had sent Tamar, who Ari recognized from her gambling stint. Next to the guards, he stood a good half foot shorter, but it didn't seem to bother him. He wore a simple button shirt with dark baggy shorts, island garb.

"Wonderful to see you again, Arianna."

"No one's called me that in a while. How did you know it's my name?"

He winked at her. "I guessed. In my village, names are long and meaningful. Unlike Bob and Joe here."

The man with darker hair looked down at him. "Not quite."

"But close, eh?" Tamar raised a brow.

"Let's go." Ari thought the less talking the better in this case.

The group filed in a car. The guards sat in front, like adults sitting in a children's toy set. Tamar gave directions through the jungle. Then at the end of a long road, the trail ended with a large tree standing in their way.

"Where now?" The guard called Mike, not Joe, said.

"We walk."

Glad she wore decent shoes, Ari opened the door. The guards clamored out, always staying nearby. They had a couple of flashlights to light the path. Tamar didn't seem to need them though.

He led the way with Ari nearby. "You know if they really want to hide you better, they may want to consider ditching the guards."

"I don't think that will happen." Ari wondered how much Jewels or Tamar knew of her position. The idea that they knew what she did saddened her. Yet her vault of secrets seemed to be bulging at the seams lately.

"Almost there," Tamar announced as they weaved around a large tree.

Ari heard the people first. The chanting and singing traveled through the jungle blending with the wind as if it always belonged there. Then the light from a fire sparked and snapped through the dark leaves. They emerged from the jungle onto the beach.

Islanders gathered around the blaze, dancing and singing. Children ran wild and careless with squeals of delight. They dressed in a variety of styles from jean shorts, to floral dresses and skirts. Most men went topless, while the women wore long beaded necklaces and flowers in their hair.

Tamar pulled off his top, his physique toned. "It's

time to party." He headed off in the throng of people, with a high-pitched cry that traveled far through the forest.

She glanced at the two stiff guards. "You heard him."

Ignoring the nervous looks from the guards, she walked towards the crowd searching for Jewels. The old woman stood in the middle of a circle, dancing to the beat of the drum. The sway of her hips flowed with the foreign words of the song, her long braid swinging behind her. As she turned and noticed Ari, her smile grew.

When the song died down, Jewels pulled in a couple of young men to dance and headed towards Ari.

"I'm glad you made it, dear."

"Thanks for inviting me," Ari said. "You were amazing out there."

"When you're as old as I, you learn a thing or two about how to turn a head." Jewels directed them to a pit in the ground, where some animal turned on a spike, hot coals cooking it from beneath. "Hungry?"

"A bit. What is that?" Ari motioned to the fire.

"Wild boar. It should be done soon, and you won't want to miss it."

"Sounds great." Ari had grown up with a grandmother that would cook all sorts of things. Boar was close enough to pig, right?

Jewels looked around them, searching for something. Her gaze fell on a group of young women in floral print dresses tied more than sewed together. "Oliana," she called, though the rest of the sentence was intelligible.

It took a bit for Ari to recognize the woman that worked with Tamar, urging her to place bets. Her black hair fell in beautiful waves around her shoulders and with the fire nearby, her dark eyes appeared electric. Unlike her previously steely gaze, Oliana's beautiful smile must draw her a lot of attention.

"Take Ari here to dance with you. Show her how the islanders have a good time."

"Yes, Jewels." Oliana gave her a small nod of respect.

Jewels headed over to the pit and Oliana turned to her. "You think you can handle partying with us islanders?"

"I'm here." Ari glanced over to the group of young women dancing. "You may find my dancing only good for a laugh though."

Her face softened as she grabbed Ari's hand. "I could use a good laugh."

Oliana didn't bother with introductions, but had Ari kick off her shoes and taught her the steps to the dance. After a few minutes Ari caught on. She was not as smooth or natural as the others, but they didn't seem to mind. Sweat trickled down her neck as she got lost in the steady beating of the drums. There was something not only peaceful but contemplative to dancing under the night sky. Something relaxing as the women moved in unison, creating beauty in its own right.

With the dinner bell, Ari was jarred out of her trance. Oliana grabbed her hand, her cheeks red with warmth. "Let's eat."

The familiarity the islanders had with one another took a bit to get used too. With hand holding and random touches on the shoulder, even with the men, they appeared as one big family. Being alone, with only seeing Reed occasionally, it felt nice to be included. Even if only for one night.

After being stuffed with food until she thought she might explode, Ari escaped to find a bit of peace and quiet. Of course, her two security guards weren't too far away. She sat in the damp sand, the ocean in front of her, watching the tide disappear into a starry night. Sitting on this island, so far away from the rest of the world, just a speck smaller than the stars themselves, it made her feel small. Not in a bad way, but just as one who realizes how big the whole world is.

It was easy to get caught up in the VLEX, in the fabricated world that dictated rules and regulations to the rest of the others. But the majority of the world wasn't in VLEX. After tonight she glimpsed a whole village of people who didn't rely on VR for fun. Maybe there was hope for their little speck of earth.

"Deep thoughts?" Jewels sat down next to her in the sand. "I've seen what work is doing to you lately. I hoped a party would help you forget your troubles."

"Thanks. I'm just hiding out before someone else offers me food that I can't turn down."

"That might be my fault."

"What? How?"

"You've lost weight lately, so I told everyone you needed some fattening up."

"Not sure I should thank you for caring or curse you for the stomach ache. Two plates were fattening, four plates are just torture. Trust me, I eat when I can."

"Okay." Jewels shrugged. Her silver hair glistened in the moonlight.

"Jewels, have you met any other people like me since you worked here?"

She continued staring out to the water for a moment before replying. "One."

"Who was it? What were they like?"

"He was cocky, arrogant, and good at his job. But he was

sick. I was new to work here, and he was sick soon after I arrived."

"What was wrong?" With her diet, physical training, and resources available to VisionTech, she'd been in the best health of her life.

The older woman tapped on Ari's temple. "Something up there. Something not right."

"Oh..." Ari was hoping for more, but not sure what. Some guide or some person that told her this job got better, that she was on the winning side.

"Doesn't matter. You'll do the job your way and that will be the right way."

"I wish it was that easy." Ari felt responsible for Reed and her family, and worried how fighting with Niomi would affect them.

"It is, if you want it to be."

CHAPTER TWENTY

Ari was unable to avoid Reed all weekend. Sunday afternoon he came over with dessert—and not just any dessert, but a tower of dessert. The bottom contained a variety of small cupcakes, then it proceeded to climb like a pyramid.

"Do you really think we can eat all of that?" She couldn't help the smile that crept up on her.

His brown eyes glimmered with delight as they barely peeked over the chocolate top. "I'm making it a personal goal to see it done. Hope you have an appetite?" He headed down to the kitchen.

She followed him, trying to remember why she didn't want to see him this weekend. *Oh, yeah. He's happy here, and I don't want to destroy his future... again.* The reason got lost in other thoughts as she watched his backside.

He placed the massive tower of baked goods in the center of the table and scrounged around for utensils.

"Let me get some milk." Ari headed to the drink dispenser.

"Good thinking, we'll need something to help get it all down."

She chuckled as she filled the glasses and sat down. He scooted closer and handed her a fork. His spicy scent greeted her, and she fought the urge to lay her head on his shoulder. Maybe she was a selfish creature deep down inside, wanting Reed. Maybe she didn't have to leave. Staying here with him felt right.

"Do I have something on my face?" He rubbed his cheek. "Why are you staring at me? I swear, I only tried a bit of the frosting."

She shook her head. "No. I'm just happy to see you."

"Me too." Leaning over, he placed a light kiss on her lips. He pulled back, a small rolled chocolate piece in his hand. "Now, you have some catching up to do."

She bit down on the candy, her lips brushing against his finger. A warm feeling swirled inside, and she realized just how much she missed him. Not only did she miss his soft lips, but the way his personality could light up a room.

Starting at the top with a caramel chocolate, they worked their way down through the tower. At first with their forks, but when they found something good, they'd always share. Miniature pastries covered in a smooth frosting covered the tower in a variety of shapes but bright corresponding colors, like some type of party or circus.

When Ari picked up one square type cake, the top full of bright red frosting, she couldn't resist temptation. Reed opened his mouth, so trusting. She pushed it into his nose instead.

"Oops." Shrugging her shoulders, she donned her most innocent expression.

He wiped the frosting from his face, a mischievous flicker to his hazel eyes. "Oh, I'll show you oops."

And it was on. They destroyed the last of the tower,

only random pieces ending up in their mouths and mostly by accident. Racing around the kitchen, they managed to have the dessert cover every surface.

Reed wrapped Ari in his arms from behind. "Surrender, and I'll let you go."

Ari hoped he'd never let go. She loved his strong arms and tight grip. But she couldn't tell him that. "Only if you don't make me eat any more sweets."

"Make you?" He turned her in his arms. "And here I thought you enjoyed them."

"I did, until my stomach felt like it would burst." Raising on her tiptoes, she kissed the red frosting still on the tip of his nose. "I enjoyed you more."

He held her tight. "Good."

She leaned her head against his chest, ignoring the sticky sugar covering them. "It's going to take forever to clean this."

"Don't you have a maid or a bot or something?" He wiped her hair and a blob of cake fell on to the ground.

"I'll call out the bots, because I can't make Jewels clean this mess. Not after she invited me to the party." Against her desire, she pushed back and reached for a kitchen towel. Maybe if she got it all in the sink, it could wash down.

"How did that go?" He reached for the second towel. "Did a bunch of islanders hit on you?"

"I mostly danced with the women. It was fun."

"Dancing, huh?" He grabbed her hand, twirled her around, and pulled her into his arms.

Close to him once more, the warmth in her chest grew. Arms wrapped around each other, they swayed to the silence. Their steps small but steady. Reed hummed something simple.

He paused only to ask, "What do you call your AI lately? I'll pick out a nice tune."

"I think it's perfect like this." Unfortunately, in the recesses of Ari's mind, she knew perfect didn't last.

CHAPTER TWENTY-ONE

The following week returned to the normal drudgery of her job. Copying files for Niomi didn't take much extra effort, and even Kari's job slowed as the political season wound down for a break. Unfortunately, that left a lot of time for Ari to wonder if Kari's petite body would now only be alive here, electronically, and to guess how long VisionTech's reach really was.

They didn't seem to be a bad company. Even the islanders didn't complain too much, as VisionTech worked with them to preserve the island and gave islanders work. Vinh, Reed, and hundreds of others enjoyed their work, and it gave them an opportunity they may not get under their government. But did that negate what she was doing? Stealing people's lives for insider trading and political privilege?

Trying to get out of her head, she met Antoine for lunch on Wednesday. Part of her hoped to see Hailey and get some answers about her meeting with Emil. That meeting had been occupying her thoughts constantly, but with no luck at answers. And with no contact, she didn't know where to go next.

Instead of Hailey, she only saw Antoine, which made the guilt-ridden hole in her stomach only grow more. Was she ready to tell him the truth? In doing that she wouldn't ever be able to come back here as Kari.

By the time she walked back to her offices, she decided she needed to do something. Maybe talk to Niomi or even her supervisor. If she laid down the line, they couldn't force her to do anything against her will. They had to have other work for her to do.

Due to the lack of work, President Higgins let Kari go home early. Ari pulled out of the VR. She woke to the lab, bright lights radiating around her.

"You're done early." Niomi turned away from her computer and helped Ari up from the chair.

While Niomi cleaned the cable, Ari walked over to the work station. Niomi usually never left her work open, so Ari took the chance to glance at the screen. It was some type of correspondence.

VP238: How much longer will the assignment be viable?

TR41-A: The team says one week. No one will notice the absence until the session is over.

VP238: Push for more information. We need to know who was behind the final vote?

TR41-A: We are.

"Close screen," Niomi said from behind her and the computer obeyed.

Ari had read enough though to know Tessa was right. If

they hadn't killed Kari, they had restrained her in some way. Ari prayed it was the later.

"I thought you knew better than to pry into things that don't concern you."

Ari had buried her irritation for so long, it bubbled near the surface, ready to explode. "I think it does concern me."

"Really?" Niomi cocked one brow, her tone dismissive.

Ari fisted her trembling hands. "I stole a woman's life. Not to mention Representative Tao. Are you killing them? I didn't sign up for this."

Niomi barked a harsh laugh. "You don't begin to understand how this all works. The information you get changes life, saves lives sometimes. These international laws affect everything, trickling down to every shabby home town. And you're saving your family's life with the money you send them. You have no idea how good you really have it."

"I want out." She blurted out the sentence before she could stop herself.

That stopped Niomi's usually snarky response. Her sharp jaw tightened, and her steely eyes watched Ari. "Have a seat."

She placed a hand on the nearby table. "I'd rather stand." Honestly, she had lost all feeling in her feet but needed to keep strong while it lasted.

"Okay. I will." Niomi pulled up her metal stool. "Maybe I've been too hard on you. My sarcasm has a stronger bite than I intend."

Ari didn't reply.

"You want the truth. I'll do my best." She flipped up the screen, with a couple of movements of her hands she opened to Representative Tao. "He had a heart attack and died in the middle of the night. VisionTech intercepted the call for health services. They had a short window of time to fake that he pulled through, send in a team member to hack his VR feed and get you in. You voted the same way he did to avoid detection, but you got us the information we needed. He was an isolated member, so it was easier to pull it off, but it was far from easy."

Ari let go a breath, glad she wasn't responsible for his death. "What about Kari?"

Niomi closed her screen before turning back. "I'm not exactly sure. They don't tell me details. Representative Tao was in the news thread."

"Not good enough."

"It's all I have. In the past, they have picked loners, people without a lot of friends who are willing to skip town for a bit for a price. Some are sick and would take the payout to let someone else replace them at work for a while."

"Kari didn't seem like that type. Especially with Antoine." Why wouldn't Kari break up with Antoine before she left the VLEX?

"When you're young, love is all encompassing. Kari has had lovers before and will have them again. You are more in love with the idea of them then Kari probably ever was with him."

Ari rubbed a spot on the edge of the desk. Something wasn't setting right. Was she really just young and stupid? Would she really be willing to sacrifice Reed and everything for her family, because she was naive? What about what Tessa found?

"Look," Niomi said. "You only have a week left before session is out. I'll ask for an extended break. It will be good for you."

Good for me? Ari wasn't sure she could even tell what was good for her anymore. But she wasn't about to trust anyone with that either. "I'm not sure I'll ever want to go back. I hate lying about who I am all the time. Stealing other people's lives, even if they are okay with it. Isn't there another division I could work with?"

Niomi let out an exasperated huff. "You don't get how rare you are. You're the sole warper employed by Vision-Tech. If it's getting to be too much, ask for more money, ask for your family to come here. There isn't another division for you. This is it. And life outside of this is a hell of a lot harder. Trust me. You have nowhere else to go. No papers. And your government would be more than happy to find you, charge you for all types of espionage, and haul your ass to forced labor for life. You'll be forced to do the same thing without any of the perks. Do you understand?"

Biting down on her lip, Ari fought to keep her emotions locked down. She gave a curt nod. She understood. She understood that when she first lined up to get her assignment, she was signing her life away. This may be a different cage, but it still was a cage to her. One she'd never be happy living in.

CHAPTER TWENTY-TWO

Ari wanted to wait before she contacted Emil to think things over, but she didn't have time, not if Niomi expected her to take a vacation when the session was out. If she wanted answers, she needed them now.

Friday morning, Ari entered VLEX as Kari. Before she started the day, she reached out to Hailey using her contact info with the European Union. Unfortunately, she didn't reply right away. So, Ari turned to her work for a distraction. Even with a long conversation with President Higgins, she finished before lunch. When she was about to give up and head out to meet Antoine, a message came through from Hailey.

Meet me by the fountain.

After messaging Antoine a lame excuse, she headed out. The sun lit up the fountain in the courtyard, the one of a merman rising up out of the colored stone waves. The statue mirrored those of old, the colored marbles with flecks of gold shimmered in the sun. She approached the fountain and with no sign of Hailey, Ari dipped her hand into the cool water.

"You ready to know the truth?" Hailey spoke behind her.

Ari spun around. "Where did you come from?"

"I asked if you're ready to take off your training wheels."

She couldn't help her eye roll and was more than a bit tired of being treated like an idiot. "I want some answers."

"Do you know the questions?" Hailey's demur look held a lot more of an attitude today with her lips pursed tight.

"Stop playing games or I'm gone." Ari stepped away from her.

"Okay." Hailey reached out a hand to stop her. "It's this way."

Ari followed her down a row of shops. They turned towards a coffee shop, but before they went through the door, Hailey entered a code. When she opened the door, there wasn't anything that resembled a coffee shop in sight.

A long corridor of a shiny black material stretched out towards them. The never-ending hall had no decorations, only black doors with silver door knobs.

Ari glanced at Hailey. "If you're going for a dark ominous bad guy feel, you nailed it."

It was Hailey's turn to roll her eyes as they stepped into a room. "It's to protect our butts, and it keeps the look of the regular code in place for the others."

"Is it like a different dimension?"

"If you want to consider it that." Hailey continued down the hall to the fifth door on the right.

"What do these other doors hold?"

"Nothing but place holders." She knocked once and then entered. "Hey, Emil."

He sat at a desk but when he saw the girls, he waved it away with a wipe of his hand. The desk disappeared, and he stood to greet them. "Good to see both of you. Please have a seat."

Ari sat down in the dark chair and sank back into the smooth interior.

"What I can help you with?"

"What do you know about VisionTech? How do you do what you do? What did you mean when—"

He held up a hand. "One at a time. First, VisionTech. The company you work for is one of many that have a limited role in the government here. I'm not personally familiar with them, but I had Hailey conduct some research." He turned to Hailey.

"As far as blood-sucking corporations go, they aren't the worst." She gave Ari a look like that was supposed to be comforting. "They were one of the first to jump on the VR bandwagon and soon pulled ahead as a major competitor."

"Skip ahead to the essentials." Emil urged with a wave of his hand.

"They have been searching for a warper for some time. You first appeared on their radar when playing online games." Hailey glanced at her. "Not your best move showing off in a public arena."

"I didn't know what I was doing."

"That's obvious." Hailey's lips drew up in a smug smile.

"Continue, Hailey," Emil ordered.

"Since that point, they have monitored all of your family. They have detailed notes, pictures, and information on your mother, your father in the VR coma, even your boyfriend's family."

Ari straightened, remembering the folders VisionTech had on the people for Ari to impersonate. She was just like Kari, her life scrutinized to the last detail. It was no accident when Dave ran into Ari and Reed on their date. They must have been watching her at school. "What about the people I impersonate?"

"That varies. No one has seen Kari personally. So that usually means she's hidden away in some induced coma of some sort."

"Is it possible they paid her to leave?" Ari hoped some of what Niomi said was true.

"Anything's possible," Hailey laughed. "But you're still not asking the right questions."

Ari leaned back and thought for a moment. She wanted to know the truth about VisionTech but that seemed impossible. Not until she talked to Kari herself. That may be impossible now, but maybe one day. She did think of one thing.

"What about your powers? How can you manipulate this world so easily?"

"Closer." Emil answered. "We've been perfecting our abilities for some time. You can learn to do what I do."

"No one is better than Emil though," Hailey interjected.

"But you can learn. Your trainer is not a warper, though. It's like the someone who is colorblind teaching a normal person how to decipher colors. Your trainer can't see the possibilities in front of you."

Ari's mind whipped about what those possibilities were. "How did you hurt me before? How do I protect myself?"

"I didn't hurt you."

"I can still feel that migraine haunting me sometimes." Ari hadn't felt that type of pain before, ever. Emil couldn't pretend that he was any better than VisionTech at this point.

"You did that to yourself. When trying to fight me, you

exhausted yourself. You need to be more careful in the future."

"Maybe you shouldn't restrain people."

"Have you ever felt that before?"

"No..." then she remembered her fight with Williams when she visited her father in the VR world and the confusion after that. "Once, when I got into a fight with an Advisor from school."

"Only twice. That's not a bad start." Emil glanced at Hailey, and something unspoken passed between them.

"What?" Ari asked. "What aren't you telling me? I want to know how to protect myself."

"Okay." Emil leaned forward, his elbows resting on his knees. "Two things. First, if you want to learn more, you need to join us."

"Us?"

"We're an Elite Team that monitors worldwide virtual sites, keeping government officials in line. There are over a hundred people who work with us in different capacities all over the globe."

"In line? You need to be more specific. Because right now you sound like a different version of the same company I'm working for without the benefits."

"We have benefits," Hailey said. "Like not being trapped on some island with limited access. It's called freedom."

"We watch those that have no one watching," Emil said. "At this point that is all I can say, until you prove yourself."

Ari stood, not wanting to even know what *prove yourself* meant. This guy may have answers, but she wasn't willing to play his little games to find out. "Then sorry. I'm out of here." She headed to the door.

"You didn't ask what number two was."

Hand on door, she stopped. Something in her gut told her to stay, just a moment longer. "What?"

"You never asked me why you have headaches?"

Icy tentacle gripped her spine as she forced herself to turn around. "What are you talking about?"

"You're lucky you've only had two episodes. Maybe because you never spent much time in the VR as a child. But warpers have their own special Achilles heel. Ever wonder why VisionTech cares about your health so much?"

Ari's hand stayed frozen on the handle, waiting for him to continue. She questioned that hundreds of times while Niomi was torturing her.

"It's because they don't know how to save your mind. They'll try everything they can to keep their asset around a little longer. Every time you use your power, you slip away a little more." He tapped the side of his temple. "These tools up here may be worth millions to the right companies, but they have a shelf life. Some get five years, some ten or twenty, but everyone slowly slips away to their own little world. We just want to make the biggest impact on this world as we can, before we slip away. And we found a way to hold it off a little bit longer."

Ari glanced at Hailey, and for the first time saw a sadness lurking behind those beautiful eyes. *Could this be real? Or is this just another corporation manipulating her?*

She gave a short laugh. "You really expect me to believe all this. You're the one who caused my headache. Now you want me to prove myself to you guys. How do I know you're not just manipulating me to do your dirty work for you? And you want me to believe you guys oversee all of this for the good of men and not your own benefit?"

"Of course we benefit." Emil stood. "We're not saints. But most of us came from simple means and want to keep these governments and corporations in line. Given your upbringing, I thought you'd be interested. We can help you and your family."

"VisionTech told me the same thing then trapped me on an island."

"We'll give you the money and papers to get out of the country, you do the rest."

She didn't forget the caveat though. "But I have to do something for you first, right?"

"You need to prove yourself. It's different. We need to know you've cut ties to VisionTech and are ready to commit to us."

Commit to someone I didn't know. He was ballsy. "And what would that be?"

"Steal us the project file from your trainer."

Ari pulled back a touch with surprise. "What project file?"

"They'll have a file on you. With your expected longevity, goals they have, and other pertinent information. Feel free to delete your family's information. We have no need of that. But your health history will be helpful to both of us if we're working together in the future."

The words 'expected longevity' struck Ari with a force that took her back a step against the door. Words blurred together and got jammed in her throat. What scared her the most was that maybe he was telling the truth. With that terrifying thought, she left.

CHAPTER TWENTY-THREE

Ari's steps echoed down the dark corridor. Once outside and back in the regular VLEX program, she focused on keeping her breath steady. Niomi would notice any spike in her heart rate. She walked past the shops, past the fountain and up to her office. Gratefully, she was alone. Staring at her blank computer screen, she replayed her conversation with Emil over and over, picking apart what he said and trying to decide if he was being honest.

Her boss startled her when he walked through the door, and she hurried back to her work. She continued to copy his private correspondence and sent it off for VisionTech, though now her conscience nagged her about it. Was she only helping some obscenely rich company rake in more money? Ari needed to figure things out before she took her next step.

She wasn't exactly sure what she was going to do, but ever since Emil mentioned her file, she knew she had to see it for herself. It held the truth, or she hoped it did. Getting her hands on it would be another story.

Niomi greeted Ari as she returned to the lab. Ari

unplugged and wrote her notes, remembering to keep her poker face firmly in place. Lately, it had become easier and easier.

"Hey, I noticed a spike in blood pressure at lunch. What happened?"

"Just Antoine."

"What happened now?"

"Nothing really. Just in the process of breaking up with him, like you said."

Niomi turned towards her, the tattoo in her ear flashing. "You need to make it clean and quick. Just like a bandage. It hurts more at first, but it heals quicker."

Ari nodded. "Yeah. I know. I'm going to head off and get some rest." She didn't feel like getting a lecture on relationships from a drill sergeant.

"Okay. Vinh's on the schedule to run some tests on your suit this afternoon. It would be awesome if you could be in it."

Ari pushed through the doors thinking that a lot of things would be awesome. Despite the bitter feelings she had though, she looked forward to seeing Vinh. He had worked here longer than Ari, maybe he could help.

———

With her mind whirling about, she didn't bother resting, but headed to the gym. After beating the dummy until her arms ached, she made her way to the kitchen for lunch. She read over a message from Reed while she dug into her sandwich. He did well with his art project and would be recommended for a full-time position in the graphics department. She replied:

I knew you could do it. You're going to blow them all out of the water. Congrats!

As she sent it off, she bit her lip. While Ari was genuinely happy for Reed, and wouldn't want it any other way, she knew this meant he had to stay. VisionTech was better than most corporations. But could she stay? That depended on what she found. For once she was grateful her brother didn't want to join her on the island. She couldn't leave everyone she loved.

Her AI announced Vinh at the front door. Allowing him in, she hurried and placed her dirty plate in the sink. She turned around in time to catch Vinh walking down the hall. "In here," she called.

He stopped. "Anything good left?"

She joined him in the hall. "Just finished off my sandwich, sorry."

"It's okay. I better get to these tests."

"What's it for?"

"Just usual upkeep. With any new gear they want regular checkups. We can run it through a basic VR and see how it's doing."

"Great." The sarcasm leaked through her voice as they headed down the hall.

"You can pick the program." He offered, obviously picking up on her mood and trying to be nice.

"It's not that. Just tired of being online." She rubbed the skin under her port.

He shrugged. "Can't say I've had that problem. Sorry."

They entered one of Ari's rooms, which was set up for VR. VisionTech provided it for her to practice or for recreation, but she had never used it. "What do I need to do?"

"I just need you to go through some exercises in there.

I'll be tracking the reports your suit sends and verify them manually."

"You'll be prodding me while I'm unconscious? That doesn't sound creepy at all."

"I only need one arm. I promise no creepiness."

Sitting in the chair, Ari's lunch gurgled in her stomach. Another part of being in the VR she hated was her unconscious form just sitting in reality. It reminded her of her father, sitting in a coma with tubes and machines to take care of him.

Before she plugged in, she wanted to talk to Vinh. "Can you tell me why the company is so interested in my health?"

Vinh busied himself with setting up his med kit. "You're worth a lot. They take care of their assets."

"It has nothing to do with my migraine the other day?"

His hands stilled for a moment too long. He lifted his gaze. "Why do you ask?"

"Just curious if the headaches were common with people like me."

He turned back to his bag. "I've never worked with a warper before."

"There has to be reports or something from previous warpers."

He shrugged.

He didn't answer the question, and Ari struggled to swallow the knot in her throat. Vinh worked for VisionTech with a contract and probable restrictions as well. He may be one of the few people she could really talk to about her job, but could he really talk to her?

"How about tea in some gardens?" Vinh searched available programs on the nearby computer.

"Only if you take out all the characters. I'm not in the mood for their chatter." Tea in the gardens sounded historical, and Ari could only take so much of that. "Or leave them in and I can slowly kill them off one by one." She joked.

"Have a seat. I'll take them out. We don't want to start giving you homicidal tendencies."

She leaned back, plugging herself in, and mumbled, "Yeah, we wouldn't want that."

The VR ran smoothly enough. Vinh could speak to her inside the program and instructed her to do basic calisthenics to measure her response. What weirded her out the most was that he was doing the tests on her unconscious body. She jogged, stretched, jumped off nearby fountains. Laying on her back after a long set of pushups, she stared at the sky and noticed the clouds that weren't quite right. The randomness of nature was hard for programmers to duplicate.

Anxiety crawled up her back, and she found herself constantly picking at her fingers. Vinh obviously was keeping something from her. But what?

Who could she trust? Emil, a stranger she just met, over the people who she now considered friends, almost family? Her gut had been telling her for weeks that something was up with Vinh though.

An idea popped into her head, one that may be stupid, but she didn't care. She sat up in the fake grass. White tables were scattered through the garden. On top were an array of delectable treats, and accompanied by the fresh flowers and roses, it was almost picturesque. Ari didn't feel like picturesque.

With a swipe of her hand, the tables disappeared. Glimpsing the code in the greenery, she amplified it to a neon green. Beautiful roses grew to the size of dinner plates. In a nearby fountain, Ari changed the crystal blue water to black with specks of gold throughout. It looked like the night sky rushing by. She smiled at her creation, and she wasn't done playing.

Instead of bright and sunny, she swirled the colors of a sunset all over the expanse above her head. Even with the drastic changes, the program felt empty to her, so she filled it with the people she had been living with for the last several months.

Kari appeared sitting by the fountain. Her beautiful hair waving around her shoulders. She didn't speak but just trailed a finger through the night sky twirling in the fountain. Ari couldn't muster the heart to fill her voice with fake words.

Guilt and ache grew steadily in her stomach. Ari might not have stolen her life, VisionTech did that, but she wasn't returning it. Her self-loathing was interrupted by Vinh.

He spoke over the coms. "What's going on in there Ari? Your blood pressure is spiking?"

"Nothing. Just playing with the scenery a bit."

"Well cut it out."

A moment is relative right? She took a deep breath, then pushed herself. Remembering Emil and his powers, she didn't hold back. A huge building grew in the distance, like one from school. Then she played with it, changing color and design like a kid with clay. Then she turned back to Kari, all alone.

Ari created people, some profiles she had learned from Niomi and others from her memory: friends from school, her home, Jewels and other islanders. A pain began radiating from behind her eyes and somewhere in the distance Vinh yelled at her. She didn't, no couldn't, stop. The pain and regret burst from within, and she deserved the pain. Her brother appeared next to Kari, pushing a hair behind her ear. He would have loved Kari. Then, their mother next to him.

Finally, right in front of her, she created her father from her childhood memory. He wasn't wide-eyed and crazy from the last time she saw him, but kind and happy. His dark eyes welcomed her, and she lifted his lips in a smile, the smile she had always wanted to see one more time.

Hot tears fell onto her cheeks. "Hey, Dad."

He didn't respond. He couldn't unless she programmed him too. Then without warning, the world blackened around her. Vinh must be manually pulling her out of the program, and she didn't even get to say goodbye.

The bright lights stabbed her eyes, even behind closed lids. "Turn off the lights."

Vinh rushed around the room. Equipment clattered to the floor, mingled with swear words. A patch was pressed onto her arm with a sharp prick.

"What the hell were you thinking?" Vinh asked. "I only needed a couple tests, not a full-blown remodel. Niomi's going to kill me."

"Don't tell her." Ari answered, an arm strewn over her eyes blocking out the light Vinh still hadn't turned off.

"She'll be running in here any minute, I'm sure." Vinh brushed back Ari's hair. "Seriously, why were you doing that?"

"AI, light off." She needed that light off before she could think. The darkness felt like a cool blanket. When she tried to open her eyes, the small lights of nearby equipment had an aura around them. Except the aura ran with code. Squeezing her eyes shut, she tried not to dwell on the consequences of her actions in the program. "I'm trying to figure out what you guys aren't telling me."

He didn't reply. Silence filled the dark room, only the thrum of the machines pumping medicine into her body.

Despite the throbbing pain, she couldn't regret her decisions. She had found her answer. The headaches were a side effect of her powers, just how bad would they get was the question. It must be bad, or everyone wouldn't be lying to her.

Niomi's voiced boomed through Vinh's intercom. "Don't move. I'll be there right away."

"Great," Ari moaned. While she didn't regret her decision, didn't mean she felt like dealing with Niomi while her head throbbed. The patch had turned the knives into small hammers at least.

Vinh let a loud breath go and something clicked nearby. "There are some things I can't say. To anyone. If I do, I worry my contract will be the least of my problems. Do you understand?"

Ari tried to sit up, but the room spun around her.

"Don't. Stay put until she comes." He leaned her back down, and then spoke close to her ear. "Please don't push things too much. Not for me, but for you as well."

"You know how much I care for you, Vinh, but I can't promise that."

CHAPTER TWENTY-FOUR

Niomi stormed in, a bite in her voice. "What the hell happened? And why are we in the dark?"

Before she could tear into Vinh, Ari answered, "To lessen the pounding in my brain."

"Vinh?"

"It wasn't Vinh's fault. AI, low light." While a dim glow bathed the room, Ari sat up, pushing aside Vinh's hand. She couldn't deal with Niomi while laying down.

The tattoo on Niomi's ear, pulsed rapidly with a blue light. "What did you do?"

"Nothing really. Just played around in the program, redecorated a bit and invited some friends over."

"Must have been a hell of a party."

"It was until Vinh pulled me out."

She turned to Vinh. "What are her stats?"

Vinh handed her a screen. "Elevated, but slowly returning to normal."

"Are you guys going to finally tell me the truth?" Ari looked back and forth between them.

Niomi kept her eyes on the screen for a moment before turning back to her. "Did we lie about something?"

Ari gripped the handles on the chair and pushed back the pain in her brain. "Lies of omission are still lies. Somehow this ability of mine creates the migraines. Do they eventually kill me?"

"Of course not."

"But..." Ari knew there was more to this story.

Niomi pulled up a chair. "They are hard on your health, yes. Most brains aren't wired to do what you do. The complexity and mental concentration required taxes your brain. Hence why we do everything we can to keep your heart and mind in the best shape possible.

"Migraines, especially those that affect your vision, are an unfortunate side effect that we can only mute with drugs. Your missions require you to change shape inside the VLEX but we never want to push you with complex manipulations of the code. And for the most part, you haven't had many problems."

Ari thought back to the last time she was half-carried to her room. It happened when she pushed herself and fought back against Emil. Niomi was right about that, for the most part. Most of her problems with the VR were of her own making. Even the code she saw with Advisor Williams was after her battle with him in the VR.

"Why didn't you tell me this before? Then I would know not to push things."

Niomi flashed a glance at Vinh. "In retrospect, I should have. We don't have many warpers around here. I worried that if you knew, you would hold back in training. There isn't a training manual that comes with you. I studied all the information we have on warpers and do the best. Trust me, we want what's best for you. VisionTech has invested a great deal with you and wants to keep you healthy and happy."

"You have information on other warpers?" Being unique, Ari wanted to know as much as she could about herself and her ability. Hence why she reached out to Hailey and Emil in the first place.

"Yes. I can ask for access if you are interested?"

"I am." She paused for a moment, then blurted, "What if I ever change my mind and decide I'm done being a warper?" Ari hated to ask but had to know.

"Again, it would be breach of contract. Which would cost you more than you have earned. Do you have anywhere to go? Really? Why would you even consider that?"

Niomi was right, but Ari wanted to hear it again. Hear what her options were for her and her family. She needed to hear it to help her understand, this was the best place for her, despite what her gut told her.

With a loud exhale, Niomi stood. "If we are done here, you should rest. Maybe a sleep aid will help you heal faster."

"Sure." She had a lot to think about, but with this headache it would have to wait.

Vinh placed a hand under her elbow and helped her to stand. "I kept the patch in. I'd like to keep you on fluids and some supplements while you sleep."

"Okay." She zombie walked down to her room, anxious for oblivion.

———

Saturday, Ari stayed around her rooms. Niomi sent over the files she promised, and Ari dug in. They were far from thorough, mostly snippets of reports and accounts. When

Virtual Reality exploded there was a rush for programs, and thus programmers. Usually programs took six months to write. Then there were rumors about people who could program in weeks, days even.

Most of the industry was baffled. These programmers soon fell off the screen, realizing they could make more money flying solo and selling them to companies for distributions. VisionTech purchased several of their programs from such entities—not that Ari could blame them. They could change or copy the code where needed, and it improved production to a couple months.

In an industry like this, Ari knew from school, months meant millions of dollars. If some program or game became hot, then other companies needed their product out as soon as possible. Hundreds of companies fell, while a handful grew and took over the industry.

None of the files Niomi provided showed any new information for Ari. It looked like they got most of their information from these ghosts, or people programming for themselves. Every now and again, a company would obtain a warper, but no one wanted to share information on such a valuable asset. Unfortunately, their drive for money had warpers turned into tools not humans.

VisionTech had a few warpers over the years, but only for a short time. One warper, an older male, thirty-five years old, worked for VisionTech for several years. A lot of the information was deleted from the file. Maybe to protect his identity or maybe to protect themselves. It didn't say much about health issues though. Only that a healthy diet with regular cardiovascular exercise improved his ability and reduced headaches. No reason was listed for his departure.

Maybe he went solo as well? Ari could only guess. Before she could call Niomi to ask, Reed called her.

"Hey, stranger." His voice echoed in her room.

"Reed." Ari couldn't help the excitement in her voice. She put the call on her big screen while she sat on the couch.

"When are they going to invent teleporting? So I can just jump through this screen to see you."

"I don't think I could ever trust my body floating through the air. It's bad enough with my consciousness meandering the VR."

"True. I just miss you."

"Me too." Her plan of creating distance from Reed to leave him on the island to pursue his dream appeared dumber by the minute. Not that she felt completely satisfied by Niomi's explanation and the secrets they kept from her, but leaving Reed would be too hard. "Where are you at, by the way?"

"Outside your door." His smile lifted on one side, melting Ari's heart. "I got some food and wondered if I could convince you to go to a picnic at the beach."

"You had me at food." She stood, ready to head out. "Let me grab a swimsuit, and I'll be out."

After ending the call, she realized she may need to do more than find a swim suit. She cleaned her teeth, brushed her hair, and threw a sundress over her suit. It wasn't every day she got to spend time with Reed.

After a kiss that was way too short for Ari's preference, they headed down to the beach. He kept her up to date on his new transfer to the Art Department with Kimmy. Swallowing her jealousy of his relationship with Kimmy, she was happy for his joy. It was his dream job. Honestly, she wouldn't even know what her dream job would be anymore. It definitely wouldn't be pretending to be other people, though.

They finished dinner, and Reed turned the conversation back to Ari. "So, I know you are limited with what you can tell me, but how is your work going?"

"It's definitely work." Ari dug her fingers in the sand, not sure how much to say.

"And..." he prodded. "Vinh treating you okay?"

Deciding she didn't want to dampen his happiness, she swallowed her worries. Especially because they weren't concrete. Her migraines were of her own making. "He's good. Just ran tests on a new suit he made me."

"I bet his gear is killer."

"Yeah. They work hard to take care of me."

He reached over and grabbed her hand. "I'm glad. You deserve it."

Sitting on the beach with Reed, Ari's concerns melted away. Maybe Emil was just pushing her buttons for his own agenda. Why risk it all to get her own file? She ignored the voice saying her information shouldn't be secret and enjoyed her time on the beach. Which was much easier when she leaned over and kissed Reed.

CHAPTER TWENTY-FIVE

Ari spent Saturday and Sunday blissed out with Reed, which helped her forget about the files of warpers for her to finish searching. By the time she made it to work Monday before dawn, she still had a smile on her face just remembering Reed's soft touch and warm smell. Unfortunately, Niomi didn't look as happy. Was she still mad about Friday and Ari's stunt in the VR?

"Have a seat." Niomi pulled up one of the tall stools at her desk.

"If this is about Friday, trust me, I won't do it again. I like seeing straight." Ari pulled up a metal stool.

"It's not. I need you to be honest with me for a moment."

"Okay." Ari couldn't fathom what she was talking about.

"How are you feeling? Your data looks good, but I need to hear it from you."

"I'm fine. No headache this morning, and I didn't even have coffee. What's going on?"

Niomi shifted. "They have a new mission for you. It's

slow enough for Kari to take a day off, so they won't miss her."

"You'll have to be more specific."

"I will. First, though, I wanted to make sure you felt well because this assignment will be more difficult and will require you to use your powers. I don't want to push you if you're not at a hundred percent, but this is important. It could mean millions of cryptos and set the industry back a decade."

Ari appreciated Niomi's concern, but she did feel great. And curiosity tugged at her. "I'm fine. Really."

"Alright. Let's get to work." Niomi turned to her computer and pulled up a profile. This wasn't one of the priority ones Ari memorized, but it was in the pile so she recognized his face.

"Rajit Patel, but his friends call him Raj." The man's long face held a sober look. His Indian heritage left him with dark skin, black hair, and intelligent eyes.

"I vaguely remember him, but not enough to really impersonate him."

"It's a short assignment. You won't be in contact with many people." Niomi went through his daily schedule and assignments. "His VLEX connection won't work when he first goes to plug in for work. That buys us thirty minutes. You'll have to hack his system and find the committee nominations for next session. Copy it to a drive then send it out to us from Kari's office."

"Why Kari's?" Ari could manipulate enough of the systems to send it from anywhere.

"They have security measures that we don't even know of. We can't chance alerting the authorities. The repercussions would be catastrophic if it was linked back to VisionTech."

"Where's this at?"

Niomi pulled up a map of the VLEX. "The UN building."

Hailey worked in there. After the last meeting, Ari worried about Hailey recognizing her. "I'm going to steal the list from the busiest building there and hope no one Raj knows sees me?"

"He's not the friendliest guy and keeps to himself. Don't talk to anyone, maybe a nod of acknowledgment when necessary. Just make the copy and get out of there. It'll be the easiest mission you've done."

It may sound simple, but it didn't mean easy. "Okay. Let me skim the file, and I can go under."

"You have three minutes."

"Great," Ari mumbled under her breath. She didn't gather much information in three minutes, and she soon found herself standing outside the UN building in a different skin.

No matter how many times she did this, arriving in a different world, in a different body caused her stomach to flip. Looking down, her long dark hands adjusted the navy tie. She dressed this body in a simple dark suit that she found in his file.

Before she could get used to her surroundings, a woman brushed by next to her. "Morning, Rajit. Something wrong?"

Ari turned to the woman. "No, just about to head in."

The woman tilted her head to the side, her mouth pinching.

Mentally kicking herself, Ari bit down on her huge smile. *Remember, smiling isn't his thing. I can pull off grouchy.*

Without another word, the woman finally turned and

entered the building, Rajit right behind her. The large cream colored building had ancient inspired architecture, engraved columns rising up around them. She didn't spend time looking around, though, just followed behind the woman.

It helped to follow someone in, to copy the little things Ari didn't have time to learn, like standing for a moment on the scanner for clearance, then climbing into the large crowded glass elevator.

Ari clicked on the tenth floor and then faced forward, purposefully avoiding eye contact with anyone. She prayed that Rajit was as big of a recluse as Niomi said he was. They slowly rose, stopping to let others on and off.

On the eighth floor, Ari's stomach dropped as Hailey stepped on board. *What were the odds?* After a quick glance, Ari continued staring forward. Since she was in a different body, maybe Hailey wouldn't recognize her in Rajit's skin. In her bubbly, happy voice, Hailey chatted with another woman in the elevator.

The elevator pinged, announcing its stop on the tenth floor, and Ari quickly stepped into the hall, shoving those long clammy hands into her pockets. She breathed a sigh of relief as she continued down the simple beige hall, only decorated with computerized paintings on the wall. No one questioned her as she made her way through the building. Following Niomi's directions, Ari continued to the end of the hall which opened to a cluster of cubes, and on the left she found a cubicle with the name Patel on the short wall divider.

His co-workers glanced up at him. He gave a short nod, which they mirrored, and then they returned to their work. *I guess Rajit really is a loner, or a real jerk.* She didn't spend time wondering about his personality flaws and hopped on his computer. With a quick glance around to make sure no one was watching, she hacked into his system. With the right scan and the ability to see past the computer and into the codes that created it, it didn't take long for Ari to find the right file.

She copied them down to a drive in her pocket, like a digital piece of paper. Except this piece of paper had to leave the building in a particular fashion to avoid detection. As she stood to leave, none of the neighboring workers even looked up. Maybe Niomi wasn't wrong.

Except nothing was as easy it they say.

As Ari turned around, she found Hailey standing there watching her. Gone was the bubbly, pretty girl. Those large eyes narrowed, burning past the mirage of data.

"You're not going to leave with that."

"What?" Ari pulled back against the desk.

"Don't play dumb with me. You want to sell your soul to the devil, that's your choice. But you won't be taking that to them."

Ari nervously glanced at the others who stared at them with gawking, curious gazes. She wished she could just leave right now, except Niomi said not to. They couldn't alert security.

"Can we talk about this in private?" Ari offered a kind smile.

Hailey laughed. "Sure. But you're not leaving the building." She extended an arm. "After you."

"Okay." Ari headed towards the elevator, not sure where she was going. The closer to an exit and past their fire walls the better.

As they rounded a corner, Hailey changed into a security guard. Her new look took less than a second and no one around appeared to notice, everyone busy with their day.

Now a good foot taller than Ari, she looked down and winked at her. "All the better to apprehend a spy with stolen data in her pocket."

"Like you're one to talk." Ari noticed a restroom up ahead and pulled Hailey inside. The room was more of a lounge with mirrors to touch up in, and couches to relax. Ari locked the door or, more specifically, she blocked the door by morphing the code.

Ari turned to Hailey. "What the hell? When did you become so self-righteous?"

Hailey's body shuddered, and she turned back into herself. "I've always been pretty self-righteous, if you ever got to know me."

Point for Hailey. Ari didn't really know her.

"Are you going to let me leave?"

Hailey leaned against a counter. "Of course. But not with the data in your pocket."

"Why does it even matter to you? Are you mad I haven't joined Emil's team?" Frustration started to mount, a tightness gathering in her shoulders. "Just for the record, I asked about the warpers. And they gave me their files. They are willing to give me the information and keep me and my family safe."

Hailey tapped her hand against her leg not appearing to be bothered by Ari's temper. "Huh?"

"Huh? Is that all you got to say? I thought you'd want the files for yourself."

"Nope. Why would we? We know a hell of a lot more warpers than VisionTech has ever hired."

"Then what's the problem?" Ari's voice raised in anger. Her thirty minute window was coming closer to an end.

Hailey picked at her nails. "Do you ever think what

happens to the names on those lists you have? I mean *really* happens to them?"

A dark pit in her stomach tightened. "They just want the names. Nothing else."

She jumped down, facing Ari. "You keep telling yourself those lies and maybe one day you can sleep through the night. Those *names* are real people who will have a huge target painted on their backs once that list is out. Lives ruined, families put at risk and for what? Cryptos? So, you get a comfy bit of paradise."

"Niomi said people don't get hurt." After she said it, Ari realized how naive that sounds. She probably shouldn't have used Niomi's name either, but it wasn't her full name at least.

"You're young but you're not stupid. Don't question my morality when I don't want to play with your little company. I asked nicely. Next time I won't ask. If you're not with us, you're against us. Working for the man, screwing over everyone you can."

Ari struggled to swallow. Before she could gather a reply, an alarm sounded through the building. Her heart picked up. "What did you do?"

"Me?" Hailey pulled back in mock surprise. "I didn't bar an electrical door, changing the structure of a government building. How long did you think you could go unnoticed here?"

Ari pushed past Hailey and searched past the walls into the code beyond. Guards raced towards the bathroom. Ari turned back to Hailey, "Why aren't you worried?"

"I have no reason to be. You're the stranger with stolen data on you."

Ari spun around realizing the truth of the situation. She wasn't getting the data to Niomi. Not that it was the end of the world, if anything this only created more questions and doubts. And even if Hailey was right, Ari wanted to slap the pretty little smirk off her face. She deleted the data.

Hailey obviously noticed the change in code. "Thank you for your cooperation, but remember, next time, there will be no asking. Governments love to find and hang little warpers every now and again, just to make sure they are safe."

Closing her eyes, Ari pulled out of the simulation. She wouldn't forget.

CHAPTER TWENTY-SIX

Gasping for air, Ari woke in Niomi's lab and reached for the plug. Her sweaty hands struggled, and it took a minute longer to unplug. Before she sat up, Niomi loomed over her chair.

"It's bad enough constantly waking up in different worlds. I don't need you watching me," Ari snapped. Heart racing, she averted her gaze, struggling to come up for an explanation of what happened.

"Your vitals were amped. What happened?"

"Your *easy* in and out mission wasn't as simple as you thought." Ari got out of the chair and headed over to get a drink. The cool water quenched her thirst and gave her a much needed minute to calm her shaky hands. Could she really believe Hailey? What would VisionTech do with the names? On the opposite side of the coin, Hailey almost turned her in. She wasn't playing any more. They wanted Ari with them, or Hailey would soon turn into an enemy not an ally.

Standing with arms crossed over her chest, Niomi stood

waiting for more information. Obviously, she wasn't going to read it in the report. "Did you get the data?"

"No." Ari traced a finger around her glass. *It was a lot worse than that.*

"What. Happened?"

"Someone found out that I wasn't Rajit!"

"Someone? What? How?" She didn't even wait for an answer but rushed to her computer. Fingers flew over the keyboard. "Keep talking. We need to let Security know."

No longer under Niomi's intense gaze, the lies poured easily from Ari's mouth. "A co-worker noticed I wasn't Rajit. They must have had some relationship or something."

Niomi's pounding fingers ceased and she turned to Ari. "What exactly happened? Word for word?" She hit another switch and a red light flashed from her screen. "I'll record it, so you don't ever have to write the report."

Ari rubbed the back of her neck around her port, her clammy skin wet under her hand. "It was a pretty girl, woman actually. She approached as I was working on his computer. I didn't see her behind me."

"How long was she standing there?"

"I'm not sure. She was *behind me.*" Ari let the sarcasm highlight her words. How much should she tell her? And would telling Niomi the truth help Ari get the information she needed?

"Okay." Niomi swallowed, obviously trying to get her own emotions in check. "What did she say?"

After weighing the consequences, she made her decision. "She told me to give her the list in my pocket."

Niomi pulled back, her eyes darting around as she computed what Ari didn't say.

"You told me I couldn't leave the program with the list, so once security was approaching, I left," Ari continued.

"Whoa, whoa, whoa." Niomi raised a hand. "Let's go back. How did she know the list was in your pocket? It's not like you use a computer so anyone can see you. Did you?"

"No."

"She read the data on the chip you kept in your pocket? That could only mean..."

Ari waited, for once it was nice to not be the person in the dark.

"The woman was a warper..." Niomi turned back to the computer.

Ari assumed she would have to report that to Security as well, but Niomi's fingers hung heavy over her keyboard. She turned back to Ari, "Did she hurt you or restrain you in any way?"

Ari swallowed. "No. She just wanted the data I stole. Told me that we had no right to spy on and hurt any of the candidates on the list."

"And just like that, she let you go?" There was a hint of disbelief in her voice.

This part was the truth, though. "Yes. She was more interested in the data than me. Granted the security guards didn't appear to have the same belief."

"Hmmm..." She turned back to the computer. "Come have a seat. I want you to start again from the beginning. Losing the list was unfortunate but finding another warper working for the UN throws a whole other kink in this. Right before session breaks too." She trailed off and took an incoming call.

Ari turned back to the water dispenser and filled up her glass again. Fear prickled along her spine and she wondered why she had to do her report in person. Could the computer tell she was lying? She had heard of that kind of software before. She stuck close to the truth and that would help her.

Taking another drink, she mentally prepped herself. Maybe it was good that she had so much practice lying lately, because her gut told her these lies would be some of the most important lies she had ever told.

———

Her digital reports took the whole morning, leaving her back aching with every step. Maybe she'd take the company up on the massages they always offered her. After a nap... and a bite to eat.

She plopped down in the kitchen with a large variety of food, enough for probably a family of four. Guilt nibbled on her, thinking back to the days when her mom couldn't afford to feed them this well. She resolved to talk to her mother this week. Whether through Tess or Niomi, she needed to see them. It had been too long.

Before she even made it through a third of her courses, her AI announced Vinh. Soon appearing in the doorway of the kitchen, his gaze traveled to the food in front of her. "Did Niomi make you skip breakfast and lunch all week, or something?"

Ari shrugged. "Starving and not sure what I felt like. Don't worry, I eat leftovers."

"I guess you'll be set for the week then." He plopped down and grabbed a nearby fry.

"You here to hang out or do you have to run some reports? You may have to do them in my sleep. After this morning, I'm not going to last long."

He cocked an eyebrow. "What happened?"

Letting out a low moan, she dipped her fry in a nearby shake. "I've told this story a million times. Can't you just read the report?"

"Reading is overrated. I'd rather have the firsthand account."

She watched him for a moment, his finger drumming on the table. Rarely even twitching, Vinh exuded an awkward energy with his eyes flashing away and back to Ari. Shaking off her paranoia, she pulled her hair band out and began re-braiding it. "Okay. Pass over the strawberry pie. I'll need some stamina for this."

After she retold her story, her stomach ached from all the food.

"What did this Hailey look like?" He kept the question light with a slight cock of his head.

She still found it unsettling. "Already told you. Pretty girl with brown eyes and hair. Unfortunately, pretty generic, nothing too unique. Why do you ask?"

He leaned back in the chair. "Just curious. It's huge, you know. A warper that infiltrated the UN. Bigger than anything we've seen before."

"I suppose, but isn't that what we were doing, or trying to do, until I got caught?" Ari stood and began putting the food in the fridge.

"Did you remember any of the names on the list?"

Ari slammed the unit and turned to him. "I've answered these questions about twenty times for Niomi and whoever else she shows the recording to. You can access it if you want."

He stood, lifting hands in the air. "Sorry. I'm just trying to wrap my brain around all of this."

With an exhale, she tried to rein her temper in. "Don't worry about it."

He helped her with the food. The few moments of peaceful silence were short lived. "Have you ever seen another warper in there before? Maybe even a friendly one?"

The hair on the back of her neck prickled. This wasn't her friend Vinh coming over to hang out and chat. His awkward behavior had a motivation, one that Niomi probably put him up to. Her chest ached at the betrayal. Her time on the island had been lonely, isolated. Vinh had been one of the few people she called a friend. She bit her lip as her emotions flew from anger to hurt, not wanting to deal with him right now.

She turned to face him, knowing she didn't answer his last question. He didn't deserve it. Her eyes burned with the threat of tears. "I'm really tired right now. I'm going to head to bed. Maybe we can talk another time."

He nodded, color flooding his cheeks as he glanced away. He reached forward to hug her, which wasn't usual for Vinh. Clinging to her tight, he turned his mouth near her ear. "You're messing in bigger things, more dangerous things, than both of us know. Be careful."

CHAPTER TWENTY-SEVEN

The next morning, she woke to the rain still splattering against her windows. She could always electronically change her view but never did. The glass wall was the only contact with the outside world she had. The constant fear of becoming like her father, of losing the touch she had with reality, never left her.

Rolling over, she looked at the large screen in front of her bed. A message from Niomi flashed. She told Ari to sleep in. Trips to the VLEX were canceled. Ari was to report in after a late breakfast for training and an appointment.

Appointment?

Vinh usually dealt with her health diagnostics and other concerns. What could this appointment be? Staring at her ceiling, which was currently programmed to match the night sky outside, she failed to go back to sleep. How could she? Obviously, there were repercussions from her encounter with Hailey, but it wasn't her fault. Or at least they didn't know that.

Finally, she got up with hours to go until she was supposed to report. The rain still pounded, getting harder by the minute. Between the storm and Niomi's message, the walls felt more substantial, trapping her inside. Back home, anytime it rained they would run outside and play in the street. What happened to the old Ari?

Determined to get out and do something with her free time despite the weather, she headed outside and jumped in one of the cars. She pushed the ignition, and nothing happened. She tried a couple times before Niomi's voice sounded through the speakers.

"There is a hurricane in the area, and you think it's time for a joy ride. What happened to sleeping in? I heard teenagers tend to do that?"

"I couldn't sleep. And the rain's not that bad." At that moment, thunder shook the small car.

"It's not safe for you to be out. Where are you going? Reed's?"

Ari didn't think Reed would be available. Since he got into the Art Department, he'd been putting in more hours. She wasn't sure where she was headed, but that didn't sound good. "The community center to chat with some friends."

"Friends?" Niomi's voice raised in question. Unfortunately, her trainer had the ability to review all her correspondence and knew that friends was a stretch.

"Some of the islanders, maybe Vinh if he's around. The only reason I don't have many friends is because I'm stuck on this side of the island all by myself. I may start searching for dolphins or mermaids as friends soon if we don't watch it."

Niomi gave an audible sigh over the line.

"Come on. I'll only be gone for a minute, I'm sure you have some goons, or tracking devices to keep an eye on me."

"You know they are all security measures to keep you safe."

"You know I can't be kept in a glass bowl forever. I need a life and some sanity. Talking to mermaids isn't considered sane." Ari knew she'd fall for the sanity line.

VisionTech main concern was Ari's mental and physical wellbeing. A tool can't be useful if it doesn't do its job. She wasn't under the illusion she was anything more to the company than that.

"Okay," Niomi caved. "I'll have some security out in a bigger terrain vehicle to go with you in case the storm worsens. You have two hours and don't be late for your appointment."

"Deal." Ari pushed the button again, but it still didn't start. "What—"

"Give me a minute to get security. Once they are en route, I'll release the lock on your car."

"Oh, gracious," Ari murmured, hoping her trainer didn't hear it.

It took ten minutes before she could start the car, but Ari didn't mind too much. The trip to the community center was rough and she was glad she had backup. As much as she enjoyed the storm, she didn't want to be lost in the jungle during it.

The community center was quiet this morning. As she headed over to grab a drink, she noticed Tamar talking at the vacant gambling tables with his sister.

He leaned back and laughed, his eyes jovial. His sister turned away from him, acting annoyed but struggling to not smile. Ari missed that sibling rivalry with her own brother, even missed how he would frustrate her.

As she approached, Tamar finally noticed her. "There's our desert girl. Surprised you made it out in this, you might have drowned."

"Desert girl?"

"Yeah, Jewels told us how enchanted you are with all this green. You must be from the desert."

"She's right. But it doesn't mean I don't know how to swim."

He appraised her, looking her up and down like an analyst. "Not bad for a desert rat, but do you know how to surf?"

"No." Reed tried to teach her, but it wasn't her favorite. Flipping upside down with water up her nose wasn't her idea of fun.

"Don't let him give you crap. Not all of us run away to surf instead of working."

Ari chuckled and asked Oliana, "Tamar ditches to surf?"

"Since he was three."

"Three? Impressive."

A smile lit up his face as he took a seat nearby and kicked off his shoes.

Oliana turned a disappointed look at Ari. "Haven't you learned not to complement him yet?"

"Sorry. I'll restrain myself in the future." Ari fell into a nearby plush chair as well. "So, Oliana, what do you do for fun? Are you a surfer?"

"No." She shook her head dismissively. "I'd rather dance."

"That was pretty impressive." Ari remembered the islanders at the party with their rhythm dancing.

Keeping her smile to a minimum, Ari could still see the pride in her eyes. Going back to work, Oliana stood on a stool that raised her up to the large gaming screens. These screens showed inside the VR where people competed and gambled. It surprised Ari that the islanders, who worked with the gaming and electronics so closely, seemed to shun it at the same time. Maybe they didn't?

"Do you guys ever play in the games?" Ari asked.

Oliana turned, the scathing look on her face spoke plenty. "No," she said, before returning to her cleaning the screens.

"Sorry... I didn't mean..." Ari turned to Tamar for help.

He reclined in the chair, obviously not as bothered as his sister. "Don't worry. VRs are a sensitive subject among our people."

"Not that I blame them, but why?" Ari asked.

He shrugged. "The usual stuff. Many of the islanders became addicted. The elders banned them. There is still a battle as each generation grows."

"Can't say I blame the elders." Visions of her father trapped in a VR coma flooded her mind. Struggling to keep composure, she stuffed that back into its neat little box in her mind. There was nothing she could do about that now.

"You too?" He leaned forward. "You have loved ones that are lost as well?"

"Yeah." She must not have hidden it as well as she thought.

"Then why are you here?"

"Money. Safety. I could ask you the same thing."

With a small tilt to his smile he replied. "Sometimes the only way to survive the devil is dance with him."

"Huh?" Ari leaned back in the chair.

"Idiot." His sister mumbled under her breath and he smiled.

"So, you've never gone in?"

He cocked an eye.

"You don't have to lie on my account. I know you do occasionally." Oliana finished cleaning the screens and hit the button to lower the stand.

"Many islanders try them now and again, but for the majority of the time, I try to steer clear."

"I wish I could." And normally, Ari did, but right now she wanted to get inside to check on her family. She didn't feel like she could trust Vinh to relay messages to Tessa and was sick of going through ten channels to get a hold of her family. But what about other channels?

Tamar stood and got a drink for his sister. With a steaming cup of coffee in her hand, she took a seat next to Ari. "What are you up to?" Oliana asked, snapping Ari out of her thoughts.

"What do you mean?"

"I can tell your wheels are turning. What's going on?" Oliana sipped her drink.

Glancing around, Ari leaned forward a bit. "Do you have a way to contact people off the island?"

"Why would we need that?" Oliana had a tension to her words.

When Ari turned to her brother, he shook his head. Obviously, it wasn't something they could talk about here.

"You should come dancing again." Oliana gently sipped her coffee. "You really are horrible. Practice may help."

Ari's gaze flashed in between the two siblings trying to read what they didn't say. "Sure, I'd love that."

Oliana set down her drink and stood, signaling the end to the conversation. "Good. We'll let you know when."

As Ari headed back into the stormy weather to her unknown appointment, an inkling of hope stirred. Could the islanders help her talk to Marco and her mother? Maybe, maybe not. But it'd be better than sitting in an empty room like a grounded little girl.

CHAPTER TWENTY-EIGHT

Making it back through the rain with her guards close behind, Ari had time to grab lunch before hurrying down to her appointment. She wore her normal clothes, jeans and a shirt, to the appointment. She didn't want to give Niomi anymore of an advantage with her smart suit by letting Niomi know just how nervous she was.

Heading down the hall, she passed Niomi's offices and stopped at conference room C. Standing at the door, she waited for it to open and resisted the impulse to bite her lip. Finally, with a swoosh, the door slid open.

A long smooth white table stood in the middle of the room. Along one side, Niomi sat next to the director and another woman Ari didn't recognize. The woman had pitch black hair, a feature perfected to a fine edge. Ari reminded herself this wasn't her fault—maybe if she really believed that the knots in her stomach would ease.

"Welcome, dear Arianna." The director stood, motioning with a hand to the seat across the table from them. His appearance was perfect, not a strand of hair out of place.

Ari slid into the seat, trying to paste on an innocent, totally relaxed smile. "Hi."

"Relax, Ari," Niomi said. "We're here to help you."

"Yes," the director replied. "Also, here with us today is Dr. Davis."

The word 'doctor' pulled Ari up short. With the machines today able to function better than any human doctor, it was rare to meet one in person. Usually there were just nurses to help administer treatments. "Is there a reason I need a doctor?"

"Dr. Davis is a psychiatrist that specializes in... well, in you."

The doctor was what Ari and her old friends from school would call a plastic. A very expensive one at that. Some people's plastic surgery was so good, they looked flawless. But humans aren't flawless. So, their perfected bodies almost looked plastic to Ari, who grew up in a neighborhood where nobody even bothered with cosmetic surgery.

The woman gave a light laugh. "The director means to say I specialize in people with your ability, commonly known as warpers, as well as holding advanced degrees in neuro-psychology. I heard you've been having headaches, and I came to help you."

Looking between the three adults on the other side of the table, Ari couldn't help but wonder what they weren't saying. "Why now?"

Doctor Davis pulled back a second, but then asked, "What do you mean?"

"Well, the headaches have been happening for a while, but you show up after my first failed mission." She left out meeting another warper. Maybe they didn't buy Ari's story as much as she thought.

The director lifted a hand. "Let me, Doctor." He

focused on Ari. "You are a highly intelligent young woman, but you're still young. After recent events on assignment, we decided it would be best for us to ensure your mental and physical health by recruiting the best in the business. It took us a while to hire Dr. Davis, but she is worth it.

"We're hoping she can help you process things like being away from your mother and brother, and give you the tools you need on assignment as well. Being young, others can influence you, especially people inside VLEX that can appear as friends. And after certain self-destructive behavior in the VR, we want to make sure you are getting everything you need."

So, it does come around to the assignment. "Okay."

"Does that mean you're willing to work with me?" Doctor Davis's grin was a tad too large for Ari's taste.

"Yes." *What could it hurt?*

"Also, we want you to take a break from work for a week." The director motioned to Niomi who had remained quiet for most of the meeting. "Exercise with Niomi and spend time with Dr. Davis."

Her stomach dropped. Not that Ari wanted to go into VLEX, but how else could she contact Tessa or her family? The islanders may be able to help but she doubted they had that kind of access unnoticed or unmonitored. "I'd be willing to participate in the required therapy, but I want to go back in to check on my family."

"I'm sorry. It's too dangerous right now. We need to do what's best for your health." The smug smile on the director's face burrowed under Ari's skin.

"You mean what's best for you and your investment." Ari knew she was a tool for this company and nothing more. It came down to money and she was worth a lot.

Niomi leaned forward, elbows on the table. "Ari, we

both want you healthy and strong. Don't be stubborn about this. You get a week off to hang out with Reed and go to the beach. This isn't that bad."

"Is my assignment with Kari closed?"

The director answered in his condescending tone. "Let us worry about that."

Ari gritted her teeth. Of course, she's just the dumb teenager. Forget about the fact that Kari had a life, a boyfriend and a job, that's just silly responsibility. Niomi narrowed her eyes at Ari, like when they'd fight, and Ari would lose her temper. She forced herself to calm down and remain silent. If she learned anything here at VisionTech, Niomi taught her the best fighters kept their temper, and Ari felt like this battle had just begun.

CHAPTER TWENTY-NINE

Seething as she returned to her rooms, Ari couldn't figure out why she was mad at first. Given an opportunity to not work or go into VLEX was a true vacation. She could spend more time with Reed, at the beach, or even with Tamar and Oliana. Yet, this was a punishment. Not going inside the VLEX or a VR meant she couldn't reach out to her family. Yes, being grounded on a tropical paradise was nice, but she was still grounded.

She headed to the cafeteria to grab a bite before her next meeting but stopped short. What about Antoine? He and Kari were supposed to go on vacation at the end of the week. She still needed to end things with him. If Kari failed to show up, that may be more suspicious than safe.

Turning around, Ari headed to Niomi's office. After a brief scan the door opened for her. Niomi and the director stood near the door, in what appeared a heated discussion that they promptly stopped once she walked in.

"Sorry to bother you, but I needed to talk to Niomi." Ari touched the necklace Reed gave her, which was becoming a nervous habit.

"I'll be with you in a moment. Wait over there." Niomi waved Ari away.

Not one to revel in awkward conversations, Ari headed over to Niomi's long work bench. It held several stools in front of her array of computers.

When she sat down, she saw one of Niomi's computers was still logged in. The argument behind her vanished as Ari read the file in front of her, her file. Niomi must have left it open by accident or maybe they had been talking about her.

Ari didn't have time to read the lengthy file, especially where Niomi and the director would quickly notice. Glancing at the two still arguing, she pulled out the small drive in the necklace and slid it in Niomi's computer. The file would have been protected for outside copying or trans-ferring the file, but hopefully not her old school hardware. Adrenaline raced through her veins as she quickly shifted over to copy the files. Nervous fingers flew over the keyboard as she tried to silence the keystrokes.

"She's only seventeen!" Niomi's voice raised to a new level.

Yanking her hands back she turned to find them looking at her. She tightened them in the lap, unable to think up anything plausible to say in the moment. "Want me to come back?"

"No," The director's lips were drawn into a tight line. "I'm done here."

As he walked out, Ari glanced at the screen. The file had copied. She turned back to find Niomi facing the door and pulling a hand through her hair. Ari yanked out the drive and jammed it in in her pocket before standing up.

"I'll head out of here, Niomi. I'm sorry, my timing sucks." The drive felt heavy in her pocket. She itched to race out of here and read through it. But on what? Vision-Tech watched everything she did. She'd worry about that later as she headed out. "We can talk later."

"No. Stop." Composure returned, Niomi faced Ari. "You have a right to know what we were talking about, or some of it at least."

Truly curious, Ari paused. "What happened?"

"I recommended a longer suspension."

"What?" Niomi always seemed to push the mission, the goal before all else. "Why?"

"Because of what I just told the director. You're seventeen years old."

"Oh..." Ari didn't know how to take that.

"Don't get me wrong, Ari. I think you're intelligent, capable, and talented beyond belief, but you're still a kid. You need to be dating your own boyfriend, not figuring out how to break up with Kari's lover."

Ari let out a breath. She never saw Niomi as the protector, just the person who pushed her to constantly be better. Thoughts spun together in Ari's mind.

"Didn't you ever wonder why we worked on self-defense so much?"

"I thought you loved to torture me?"

A sly smile pulled up on Niomi's bright red lips. "At times, yes. But for the most part I wanted you to be able to protect yourself in and out of the program. Growing up alone as a woman in this world is tough. And a major thing you lacked when you came to me was confidence.

"You may be able to do all the missions VisionTech asked of you, but it doesn't mean you should have to. I asked them to extend your suspension, but they denied. They gave you a week, and then they want you back inside."

The strong stone statue, that Ari always viewed Niomi

as, started to soften a little. Maybe there was more to her trainer than Ari thought. The data sat heavy in her pocket, burning with her betrayal. As much as she wanted to race out of there to look at the file, Ari did come here for a reason. "I need to get a message to Antoine, by the way."

"Really? Why?" Exasperation heavy in her voice.

"He's expecting to go on vacation with Kari by the end of the week."

"That's even more stupid. I told you to break up with him and instead you plan a vacation with him."

"Kari planned it," Ari said. "And if Kari returned, I didn't want to ruin her plans. When is Kari coming back?"

Niomi's eyes flickered down before meeting Ari's gaze. "We should operate under the assumption that she isn't coming back."

A flood of emotion tightened her throat. "Is she dead?" She wasn't sure how or why she got so attached to a woman she never met, but somehow living her life connected them.

"Honestly, I don't know. Maybe. Or maybe she took a sweet payout and is off vacationing on her own."

'I don't know' wasn't good enough for Ari. Burying the guilt, anger reared its head for a moment. "Guess it doesn't matter if we work for murderers, does it?"

Niomi's shoulders tightened, the muscles in her neck standing out. "It matters. But every major company has dirt under its nails, Ari. Don't be naive. Let's focus on the task at hand."

Dread bubbled at what Ari had to do next.

"I'll authorize a short trip inside the VR. We can't send a message to Antoine from here. It can't be traced back to us. Break up with Antoine or cancel the trip, I don't care which. Just be quick. You'll go in for lunch and then head out. We already contacted your boss to let him know you'll be out. It won't be a surprise to check in with a boyfriend."

Forcing herself to uncurl her fist, she concentrated on slowing her breath. Angry, Ari didn't always think straight, and she needed to concentrate if she was going back in. "Okay. If I plug in now, I can catch him before he heads off for the day."

"No, not today. Tomorrow at lunch, okay?"

Ari hated not being able to get this over with. It was one thing to have to end things with Antoine but having to dread it for the next day would be even worse. He deserved better, but didn't they all? Ari headed to the door.

"Ari?" Niomi called.

She turned back around, "What?"

"Do you understand what needs to happen? You can no longer afford to be emotionally attached to these people. Tell me you understand."

"I get it." Her body felt cold and empty. "Break up with Antoine because that's easier than knowing I stole his girl-friend's life, and she may be dead."

Niomi and Ari watched each other for a moment, a room full of secrets between them. Without another word, Ari turned and left. If Niomi couldn't be honest with her, she would find her own answers, starting with the file in her pocket.

CHAPTER THIRTY

Unable to read the drive without notifying VisionTech, she stashed it in her room for now. Yet being so close to a file full of answers made it difficult to stay asleep. Awake before six, Niomi had messaged Ari to call her when she woke. Her trainer must have had her own problems sleeping because they ended up outside at their exercise area just as the sun was rising.

They ran several miles along the beach. Niomi even took it slow. Not that she had anything to say, but it calmed Ari to run beside the endless waves, then they finished their run with light sparring. Light sparring still ended with Ari sweaty and breathing hard.

"You ready to go in to meet Antoine?" Niomi asked. "It won't be lunch, but a quick trip at the end of their day. About two our time. You can leave him a message to clean up this mess."

Ari bristled at the casual reference to this man whose heart Ari was about to trample on. "I'll be there. I wanted to go to the community center for some late breakfast. Catch up with Vinh."

"He may be busy."

"If so, I can eat alone." Ari realized during that long run that the only place that she could look at her file without alerting VisionTech may be Vinh's, since he was assigned to treat her.

Getting him to agree to it, or look the other way, may be the problem, but she'd get to that when she needed.

"Okay. Don't be late."

"I won't."

Ari hurried to shower and drove down to the center, continuing to mull over the plans in her mind. Vinh was the first person she considered going to. If he helped her contact her family once, he may be able to give her a device that was offline. But did she really trust him not to say anything? Or did she want to be the kind of friend to put him in that position?

Then Reed flashed in her mind, and she felt guilty for not thinking of him first. Even though he was in the Art Department now, he specialized in security and hacking. If anyone could get her a private connection, it was him. Granted, he hadn't been able to figure a way to contact their family, but that involved getting off the island. She had to try.

Not exactly sure where she was going, it took a good thirty minutes and a few stops with the interactive maps to find where he worked now. On the third floor, or top floor, of this building, the Art Department held amazing views of the islands. The curved clear walls showed off the luscious jungle beyond and the ocean as far as she could see.

"Can I help you?" a man asked.

She turned, a bit startled. "Yes. I'm looking for Reed. He started last month."

"Oh, yeah. The new kid. He's down the hall. Let me show you."

She followed the tall man. He didn't wear a uniform either, just khakis and sandals. The relaxed atmosphere of the Art Department looked appealing to Ari.

They entered a nearby door, which opened up to a large workspace littered with cubicles.

"Reed," the man hollered. "Someone here to see you. Cute too." He sent a wink in her direction.

Reed stood, his head sticking up among the cubicles. When he gazed at Ari, a warm excitement colored his eyes. Ari wished this was only a social call. After saying something to a co-worker, he headed over to her.

"What brings you to my neck of the woods?" He leaned over to lightly kiss Ari's cheek.

"I was hoping you could help me out with something."

"Of course. I told them I was taking a break." He patted the bag at his side. "I have ten minutes or so."

"Great."

He took her hand as they walked down to the common area. "I'm glad you stopped by. I've wanted to talk to you for a while."

"About what?"

"Not that quick. You first?"

Noticing all the people around them, she worried about others hearing. "How about we grab a drink and go outside?"

He raised a brow but didn't ask any questions. "Of course."

With warm drinks in each hand, they headed outside and found a small table in the courtyard. The weather had been overcast and windy. The threatening of a storm that hadn't materialized. She sipped her coffee and took a seat.

"Did I ever tell you how cute you look when you're cold?"

She laughed mid drink almost spitting coffee all over him. "Nope. Where did that come from?"

"It's so hot at home, and don't get me wrong, I thoroughly enjoy you in shorts and tank tops. But when it's a bit chilly, your nose gets pink and you huddle more against the weather. It's adorable."

Her cheeks pulled up in a smile, and she realized just how much she loved Reed. After being caught up in the drama of her job, it was easy to forget what was important. Moving her drink out of the way, she leaned over and kissed Reed. Losing herself in those soft lips that hinted at the hot chocolate he was drinking.

"What was that for?" He asked after she sat down.

"Because you're pretty adorable too."

He grinned and took another drink. "Before we get sidetracked and make out for the next ten minutes, which by the way, I'm totally okay with, what did you want to talk about?"

Like a splash of cold water, her real purpose in being there, killed her Reed-high. Tracing the lip of her coffee, she spoke quietly into her cup. "I need to read a file without VisionTech knowing anything about it."

His body tensed as worry creased his forehead. "What's going on?"

"I can't say right now, but... I have a file about me. I want to read it without them knowing in case that creates more problems. I figure since it is about me, I have a right to read it."

After a deep breath, the tension in his shoulders relaxed. "I agree, you do have that right." Leaning over he pulled out a pad and a screwdriver from his bag. He flipped it over, unsnapped the edge of the cover, and with a flick of his small tool, popped a wire out of place.

After putting it quickly back together, he handed it to her. "If anyone catches you, play dumb. The wire must have accidentally broke, severing the connection to the network. You were just trying to admire your boyfriend's artwork."

Relief loosened the tension in her shoulders. "This means a lot to me."

"One condition."

"Name it."

"I get to take you out and you'll fill me in on what's going on, soon."

"Definitely." Nodding, she looked forward to that. Then she reminded him what he said earlier. "What did you want to tell me?"

"It can wait."

"Really?" Curiosity and patience never went well together for her.

"Yeah. You need to deal with this first."

"Thanks." She checked the time on the electronic pad he just handed her. "By my calculations we have three more minutes to make out before you have to go back to work."

"Does that include walking back there?"

"We can't kiss and walk?"

"I can learn." He laughed, his gorgeous smile lightening up her spirits. The worry about her file lessened as she soaked him up for the three minutes they had left.

———

Ari didn't head back right away as the increased security in her room could make even opening the document in her dorms chancy. Instead, she paid for a private VR room and didn't plug in. After locking the door, she sat down on the reclined chair, feet crossed, and opened the file on the electronic pad.

The amount of data she found on herself was overwhelming. Every public record, every test, school report, on not only Ari but every member of her family. Her heart tore as she flipped through the information about her father. Surprisingly they didn't have much information about his past work with the government. His files were sealed. Huh? Once he married Ari's mother, her father worked at odd jobs to sustain his VR habit.

It looked like they even went over her brother's life with a fine-tooth comb, which didn't look great under magnification. But when Ari opened her file, pictures, charts and lengthy documents opened on the small screen. The first picture came from the weekend away at Tessa's parents vacation home. The first time she used her abilities, by accident. She didn't even know what she was. So, how did they already start tracking her?

She thumbed through charts from her smart suit. Medical data to track her health. Who would find how often she slept or had a bowel movement relevant? It felt like overkill. Checking the time, she hurried through the file. Time raced by, and she couldn't be late to meet with Antoine.

In the back of her health files, she found a document titled Shelf Life. It grabbed her attention, and she opened it for further inspection. The document was long and complex, but at the end has a SUMMARY heading.

· · ·

Ariana continues to excel in cardiovascular activity and complex physical training. The migraines only occur when she pushes her abilities inside the program, which has been reduced with environmental manipulation. Her blood pressure, blood tests, and neurological testing predicts a healthy future for the subject and shelf life of five years or more given the continuation of optimal conditions.

A knock sounded at the door.

She jumped, the pad tumbling to the ground. "This room is taken."

"Ariana Mendez?" A deep voice sounded on the other side of the door.

They found me. She swept up the pad on the ground. "What?"

"You need to get back to your wing. I noticed you were out of the VR. Is anything wrong?"

A myriad of swear words flew through her mind. "Nothing's wrong. I'll be right out."

"Please hurry. We need to escort you back right away."

"Okay." Ignoring his request, she looked at the file one more time. 'A shelf life of five years or more.'

Her chest tightened as she realized what exactly that meant. She had a shelf life, like a tool or a fresh vegetable. In five years or less she'll expire. Not exactly sure what that meant, she assumed the worst. If it wasn't bad, then they would have told her from the beginning.

But why would a company mention that the one thing that will bring them millions of dollars might cause someone to die? They aren't stupid. And that's probably one reason there aren't many warpers around to tell the tale afterwards.

She remembered Hailey and the other warpers inside the VLEX. Why would they continue to do it when they had a choice?

"Ms. Mendez." The man now banged on the door. "We have security here and will be opening the door."

Her hand trembled as she replaced the drive into her necklace and hurried to open the door. "Sorry."

The two towering guards didn't look happy.

Ari forced a smile and pushed by them. "We better hurry."

Driving back to meet Niomi, her mind spun out in every direction. How could Niomi, who she considered friends, continue to put Ari in the VR knowing it was slowing killing her? How could Vinh? Does he know? Does everyone here know but her? Slamming on her brakes, she almost crashed into a small monkey, skittering across the path. Her breath escaped in short pants filling the otherwise silent car.

Pull it together. Don't jump to conclusions. Knowledge about warpers was as rare as warpers were. Shrouded in rumors, not many people knew about them. And any available information was heavily guarded. But what she did know was when she used her powers, she got sick. Thinking back to the few times she was pushed inside the VR, she remembered the hallucinations, the confusion of voices and noise. Would she go insane before she died?

She bit back the sob that threatened to erupt. She noticed one of the guards in the car behind her stepped out and approached her vehicle. Rolling down the window, she waved him back and started to pull forward. Fighting every instinct to run back to Reed to find comfort in those arms that provided so much of it, she drove forward for her appointment in VLEX—back to the one thing that would kill her.

If she was going to totally freak out, and she knew she would at some point, this wasn't the time or place. Ari needed more information, needed the truth, and there was only one place to get it: VLEX.

CHAPTER THIRTY-ONE

Running behind, Ari hurried to her rooms, changed into her smart suit, and managed to skid inside Niomi's lab right on the dot.

"You're cutting it a bit close." Niomi stood in front of her screen.

Not trusting herself to speak without a flood of anger and resentment pouring out of her, Ari shrugged. Her trainer glanced in her direction but said nothing. Ari reclined on the chair and reached for the cable.

Niomi turned around to face her. "You were suspended for health reasons and have only been given a chance to go and collect your messages. Answer anything urgent with work as to not arouse suspicion with Kari's absence, though I doubt there's much to do this late in the season. Then message Antoine. Make it quick."

"I don't think he's the type to settle with short." Her words were sharp, Ari's hurt and betrayal seeping through.

Her dark eyes narrowed. "We don't know the warper in there and now isn't the time to hang out. Watch your back and run at the first sign of trouble. Okay?"

"Okay." Ari wished she heeded those words long ago, and she would have never trusted Niomi or anyone at VisionTech. Leaning back, she closed her eyes and entered VLEX.

She found herself in Kari's office and wondered if this would be the last time she saw it. God, she hoped so. She was tired of living someone else's life, of being a chameleon in someone else's game. After hurrying through the emails, she messaged Antoine as soon as she was inside. "Can you meet real quick before you head home for the day? It's important."

It took a few minutes for the reply.

I can get away. What has been going on? You haven't said a word to me in days. This distance makes me wonder if you really want to go away with me.

You have no idea, she thought. Instead she kept her reply simple and sent it off.

Hurrying down to the market, she grabbed a table in the corner for privacy. She twisted the cloth napkin in her hands trying to figure out how to explain this to him. Would he even believe her? Maybe she had more options than she thought. Thinking of her shelf life, ideas began to grow.

His tall frame maneuvered through the tables. She greeted Antoine with a hug, as he kissed her cheek softly, she didn't even bother pulling back to watch the interaction in code. She owed it to him to be here, to be present.

Once they sat, he ordered a drink and swiped the screen aside. Looking into her eyes, Ari could see the pain and worry.

"What's been going on, Kari? You don't return my calls, you miss work all the time. I'm surprised you still have a job."

Ari was too sometimes, but she didn't know what was

going on behind the scenes. "I'm sorry." Struggling to swallow, she realized she wanted to tell him the truth. To be honest about everything and release the heavy burden she'd been carrying around. She couldn't do that... now, but it didn't mean she couldn't do it one day.

"I need more than sorry." Antoine's brow tightened as he watched her.

"There is only so much I'm allowed to tell you," then, leaning forward, she added, "here."

"What are you talking about?" He lowered his voice as well.

Adrenaline raced as she thought about what she was going to do next. It was crazy, but right now, she didn't know what was up from down. But a nugget of an idea sprouted, and she had to keep her options open.

Keeping her voice low, she reached for his hands. "It's stuff with the government, outside of the VLEX. Nothing I can talk about inside here, but I'll tell you later. When we meet outside."

He searched her eyes, looking for something more. Something she couldn't give him. Not now.

"We're still meeting?"

Ari prayed she was doing the right thing, not that the right thing was clear anymore. She could feel the emotion burn the back of her eyes. "Yes. Just... be there, okay? If you want the whole truth."

"Don't be nervous." He squeezed her hands. "I've wanted you in person, to really touch you, look at you through my real eyes, not this dusted over computerized version. I love you for you, not this program. I hope you remember to feel the same when you see me."

It dawned on her that he may not look like this in the real life. Normal people couldn't just change how they look, but they could buy skins. Diplomats and officials didn't bother, since they were well known, but the lesser staff probably would.

"How will I know it's you?"

"I'll be holding your favorite flowers, waiting for you."

Thinking back to the file on Kari, Ari remembered the lilacs and smiled. "Okay. I'll see you then."

He leaned forward and placed a sweet kiss on her lips, then walked out. A pain tugged at her gut, realizing however much she did this for Kari, part of her cared for Antoine. She had grown to care for Antione. He was a good boyfriend to Kari and obviously kind and loving. She didn't love him, but she cared for him.

This may be something she needed to tell Reed about. He deserved to know, yet it hurt to think about it. Maybe hearing the real reason why she was doing all this would help Reed move on, because dating a warper with a shelf life wouldn't end well for him either.

———

Since her meeting with Antoine went smoothly, she had time for one more visit. Down a couple blocks was Emil's office, where she'd met him before. This may be her last visit inside here for a while, she had to know the truth.

Standing in front of the coffee shop, she wondered how to get in. Hailey had entered a code. Focusing intently on the characters within the code, she couldn't see anything beyond the coffee shop. Beneath it was nothing. A blank sheet of some sort. Ideas of yelling came to her mind, but she quickly dismissed them. She didn't need any unwanted attention right now.

When she was about to give up, Hailey opened the

door. "Did you want coffee or to see my gorgeous face?" She ushered Ari inside.

The two girls stood inside the long black and white corridor, empty except for them. Ari couldn't help but wonder why, and at what cost, Hailey remained here. "I want to talk to Emil."

The smile vanished from Hailey's face. "He doesn't keep regular office hours."

"I don't care. I have about five minutes until I'm off the radar for a bit. Tell me how to contact him on the outside or let me talk to him now."

She bit her lip and glanced down the hall. "Give me one minute." She disappeared in one of the many doors.

Shivering, Ari rubbed her arms. She'd never felt cold inside the VR before, unless in a snowscape. She could only wonder about the coding to make a place like this. Invisible to the others in the program yet connected in so many ways. As she started to stare at the coding surrounding her, Hailey reappeared.

"This way." Hailey led the way down the hall and opened a door for Ari, remaining outside. "Here you go."

Inside, a simple room held two chairs, Emil in one. "Have a seat. I assume this isn't a social call."

"No, it isn't." Ari sat in the other seat, perched on the edge. "I need to know if warping will kill me. Do I have a shelf life?"

A hint of amusement glinted in his eyes. "You read your file?"

"This isn't funny. I want to know the truth. And if so, why is your team still here?"

He leaned forward, elbows on his knees. "This will kill you, Ari. Companies will try to use up your shelf life for their profit. Because even a couple years of your talent is worth more than most other people's whole lives."

She slumped back his words echoing in her mind. *This will kill you.* He gave her a minute to absorb the truth. Part of her wished shelf life was code for something else. One year or ten years did it really matter? Niomi, who worked so hard to keep her healthy, was just fattening her up for the slaughter.

"Is that where the headaches come from? The hallucinations?" Ari knew they were connected but never dreamed of the extent of the damage. No wonder Niomi was mad from before.

"Yes. This ability takes a toll on our mind. Our brains slowly deteriorate until we don't know what is real or not."

"Then why do you do it? Can't you make enough money to retire for the rest of your life?"

"We think our lives are for more than just making money." He cocked a brow as if daring her to challenge that statement.

Ari didn't reply.

"Our team helps to shape humanity, when humanity delves into things they shouldn't. So many people spend their lives doing nothing of real importance. With this gift, we can topple governments, free a whole generation from slavery, the options are limitless."

A small knock sounded on the door, and Hailey stuck her head in. "They are pushing at our wall."

Emil turned to Ari. "I'm sorry, but I'm needed elsewhere. Can you see yourself out?"

"Wait, is there a way to find you on the outside?"

"I told you. Meet us in the game Gaia. And the next time I see you remember to bring your file."

Before she could say anything else, Ari found herself

outside the coffee shop, staring at the door. *That's one way of seeing people out.* Walking down the street, a strange numbness traveled through her body as she processed what he said. So many people do nothing of real importance. It struck her as true. How often do we run around putting work, money or overall busyness as the priority in life? She had this gift that while costly, could do a lot. Hailey worked on the UN inside of VLEX. Changes that affect the world, while Ari was slowly killing herself so that the VisionTech could make more cryptos this year.

CHAPTER THIRTY-TWO

Pulling out of VLEX, Ari's mind spun in different directions while her body waded through reality. Pull out the plug. Turn off the connection.

"What happened?" Niomi asked, snapping Ari awake.

"What?"

"How did things go with Antoine?"

"Good."

"You ended things with him?" Her gaze bore into Ari. They had worked closely together for some time and Niomi could read her too easily.

"He won't be a problem anymore." Ari tried to stick as close to the truth as possible to keep her suit calm.

"Good." Niomi turned back to her screen.

Ari stepped up to her desk. "Niomi?"

"Yeah." Her eyes stayed forward.

"I want to quit."

Niomi's hands froze over the keyboard, and then she turned. "What happened?"

"Nothing," Ari lied. "Well, maybe everything. I'm tired of living other people's lives. I want out of my contract."

"It's not as easy as that. You signed a contract for five years. If you back out now, you don't have the money to pay back all the money they invested in you. You don't have enough money to get off the island."

"What about my salary? I've kept some."

"That would be taken away from you. It's not yours if you quit." Niomi brushed a hand through her short hair. "Look. I know they are asking a lot from you."

Yes, they are. My whole life. Ari kept her mouth shut.

"But put in your time, and you'll have enough money to retire after this. Trust me, if you want to do what's best for you, don't push this issue. It won't end well. If you don't believe me, bring it up in therapy."

Biting her lip, Ari nodded. How could she ever trust the words coming out of Niomi's mouth? She lied to her day in and day out. They wanted her for five years, but after that, what? Would she even be able to function or get off the island?

Niomi reached forward and took her hand. "Do you understand me?"

Repulsion rolled around Ari's stomach. It took everything she had, not to yank it back. "Yes, I understand." For the first time, she really understood what this job meant.

———

Walking out of Niomi's office, Ari's eyes burned, heavy with unshed tears. One of the worst feelings in the world was being stuck, trapped in a world where her voice wasn't hers, where the institutions rule your life. Tired of feeling like a rat in a cage, she gritted her teeth. She wasn't helpless, and she was tired of everyone else directing her life. Between her skills and connections, she began to formulate a plan. She needed to talk to Reed right away.

He beat her to it as his call rang through when she entered her room. His smile lit up the large screen in her sitting room. She forced a pleasant look, despite her inner turmoil. He had a way of doing that to her.

"You won't guess my news."

Ari plopped down on the couch anxious to talk to him as well, though it would have to be off line. "You've been assigned project manager?"

"I said you couldn't guess." He enthusiasm was contagious.

"Okay, I give."

"My mom's coming here."

Pausing in the middle of reaching for a drink, her gaze lashed back to the screen. "What?"

"They said since I have earned an official position, they are able to review family requests."

That sounded great. Almost too great. "Did you request it?"

"No. I guess there was something about it on paperwork when we first came." His eyes looked so happy. He looked like... he was finally getting something he'd wanted for a long time. Despite what he said about leaving his mother behind to accompany Ari, she knew it bothered him. "I just can't believe it. It's all coming together. She'll work an administrative job with a decent wage and an apartment. This is a dream come true."

Her stomach dropped. A cold feeling traveled down her body. Her plans, her ideas of being free of all this, and then VisionTech offers Reed the one thing he's always wanted. She forced a mask in place, a guard to the truth going on inside.

"When is she coming?" Ari hoped maybe they could change plans. Get her out of the country another way, another time.

"I still have to convince her to come, which may be the hardest part. They have to schedule a meeting. My mom doesn't even like VRs so it may be a little bit."

Swallowing, Ari blinked back tears. They did this on purpose. VisionTech knew she wasn't happy, so they brought more people here to keep her here. They probably would have sent her family here if they hadn't gone underground with Tessa.

"What's wrong?" Reed leaned forward.

"Nothing," Ari responded fast. "I'm just not feeling too great. Tired."

"I'm sorry. I wish I could be there, to help. Which actually brings me to my next point."

"Which is?"

"Niomi said I was also approved to get a room next to yours."

Even though Ari knew this was another ploy on the part of VisionTech, she couldn't help the happiness spreading in her chest. She'd been so lonely lately. "That would be great."

"Now that I have an official position, I can request co-habitation status. I have to be careful of what I tell others is the only thing, really. I didn't want to assume you'd want to live with me, but they said I could have a room in your wing."

"That'd be great." Ari had asked for this several times when they first arrived on the island. She didn't want to tell him the real reason for VisionTech's decision. How could she? How could she ruin this dream of his? On the island, he can have a future and career he only dreamed about. His mother could have this too. And in time they could move wherever they wanted. Even then, why would they? Working here was as close to paradise as one could get.

It may be a death sentence for Ari, but it would be a great life here for Reed. She had derailed Reed's life for long enough. Though it felt like her heart was tearing apart, she found happiness in Reed's future and joy. With so much practice lately living other people's lives and detaching from her true emotions, Ari had no problem exhibiting the joy she should feel.

"Are you okay?" He leaned forward, his brow creased. "Is it my mom? I'm sure we can get Marco and your mom here too."

She forced herself to act happy. "It'd be great if you two could be together." It wasn't a lie. She always admired his mom's loving attitude despite her hardships. "Promise."

"Good, should we go out and celebrate?"

"Definitely. How about that place up high in the trees? Could you snag us another reservation?"

"Probably. I'll give them a call and get back to you."

"Message me. I'm going to head to bed." Ari watched him on the screen, memorizing every aspect of his imperfectly perfect face. "And Reed?"

"Yeah."

"I love you."

He paused, the declaration not new, but must be surprising. His soft lips curled up in a smile. "I love you, too."

"Goodnight," she said and clicked off the screen.

That was how Ari wanted to remember him, blissfully happy and obtaining everything he deserved in life. Vision-

Tech wasn't a bad company as blood-sucking companies go. Hailey had said the same thing. Ari loved Reed enough to give him the life he deserved. Even if that life meant she was not a part of it.

CHAPTER THIRTY-THREE

New messages pinged on her screen, telling her she'd slept in. Slices of sunlight cut into her room behind heavy clouds. It looked like another storm was coming. They weren't kidding about the rainy season here.

Rolling over, she opened her messages. The first one was from Niomi reminding her of her therapist appoint at ten today followed by a workout. Ari groaned, not looking forward to it either. A week off didn't feel like time off with this crap.

Next one was Reed telling her that if they wanted to go back to the tree top restaurant, they would have to go tonight. Another storm was due to come in and expected to last the rest of the week. At least she had something to look forward to after her therapist and Niomi.

Getting out of bed, she lost herself in thoughts of Reed. Realizing that this may be the last date she got to have with him. Realizing she no longer had an appetite, she didn't bother going out to the kitchen but grabbed something in her room. When she reached for a juice from the small fridge, a note fluttered to the ground.

It wasn't Jewels' handwriting, but looked sloppy, probably Tamar's.

Meet us by the beach at 5:15 if you can. We're calling in the storm.

Calling in a storm? Ari wondered what that all included and how one called in a storm. The idea intrigued her until she remembered her date. Maybe she could meet with Tamar and Oliana first then meet Reed. It may be a good cover as well. She sent Reed a quick message confirming plans and telling him she'd meet him there at 6pm.

The idea of a date tonight kept her mind busy all morning, until her therapy appointment. Walking down the hall, Ari wondered what therapy meant. Granted people had psychologists, but most used the VR for that. Simulations geared to heal people of phobias, psychological disorders, and for anything the programs couldn't fix then surgery could help. When one could have all the great doctors in the world in one program, why would one doctor on the outside be so special? She had never heard of talking to a person face to face.

She stood in front of the white door in her smart suit—which she was instructed to wear—waiting to be let in. Doctor Davis's name ran across the electronic panel. After a few moments, the door hissed open and the therapist greeted her. Her skin was flawless like expensive china, and up close, her bright green eyes looked ever more manufactured—definitely a plastic. "So good to see you again, Ariana."

"You can call me Ari, everyone else does."

"Okay, Ari, please take a seat." She motioned to the long blue couch against the wall. The small office was decorated in neutral tones, calming tones with sparse furniture.

"Do you know why you're here?"

Ari shrugged thinking that was really a good question. Granted, what she knew and what she was supposed to know were two different things. "I messed up on my last mission."

Doctor Davis laughed lightly. "You didn't mess up, dear. There were circumstances beyond your control."

Ari stiffened as the doctor called her dear but didn't say anything. Instead she renamed her Doctor Plastic. Tessa would find that fitting.

The doctor didn't seem to notice and continued to talk. "Niomi and your supervisors called me in to make sure you're happy here."

How kind of them. "I'm fine," she said instead.

"You look great. But being so young without your family can be hard on a teenager. I heard Reed and his mother may move into your wing. I suggested that. Having a community and support system is important for your health, especially when dealing with stressful situations."

It didn't seem like the woman wanted an answer, so Ari remained silent.

"Why don't we start by how you are doing with your work and social life?"

This wedged right under Ari's patience. This doctor, perfect as a woman can be, who must come from a different universe, wants to know about Ari's life. This doctor must be paid a lot. Granted Ari didn't want to create unnecessary problems not with everything else going on. So, Ari shared, just a little, trying to stick to the truth as much as possible. There was a reason Niomi wanted Ari to wear her smart suit. It traced her blood pressure and other vitals that could read her better than some therapist.

Everything continued along with Doctor Plastic being so supportive and kind nearly made Ari puke. Then, just when Ari was ready to leave with five minutes left of her appointment, the real question came out.

"Tell me about the other warper in the VLEX?"

Ari swallowed. "I told Niomi all that I know and put it on the report."

"Yes, I've read the report, but I'm curious. Have you ever met her before?"

Breathing slowly to get her vitals back to normal, Ari replied, "She looked familiar. I probably saw her before at lunch or something. How do I really know if she is a warper?"

Doctor Plastic glanced down at Ari's hands twisting in her lap. "You know you need to tell us if you meet another warper?"

"Why? So, you can recruit them?" Track them down, manipulate them, and work them to death was what Ari really wanted to say.

"No, for your protection. We want to keep you safe in and out of the VLEX. And surprise guests can cause a lot of problems for you."

And a lot of problems for you too. "I understand."

"Do you? Do you understand how important you are to VisionTech? Niomi and Vinh consider you family. Our goal is to make you content as possible."

Anger rose, bristling at the lies that poured so easily from this woman's mouth. How many years would this have gone on? Until Ari's brain snapped? This company lying over and over until there was nothing left of her. Ari leaned forward this time to make herself perfectly clear. "I. Understand."

CHAPTER THIRTY-FOUR

Blocking, striking, and pushing herself to the limit physically, distracted Ari's mind. Harder and harder she struck out at Niomi with the staff, pressing her trainer to retreat. The clash of wood on wood echoed through the forest, scattering the nearby wildlife. It gave a rhythmic steady beat that calmed her nerves as Ari's heart pounded along.

For the first time, she found she had the upper hand. Instinct and training kicked in, and when an opening presented itself, she thrust the staff forward, hitting Niomi in the thigh. Her trainer crumbled to the ground, while Ari stepped forward pausing the staff an inch before it hit Niomi's throat.

Looking into her eyes, Ari realized the haunting shadows under Niomi's eyes were guilt. She let Ari get this close because of her remorse. Ari didn't want this woman's pity. Niomi must have known all this time what would happen to Ari if she pushed herself too much in the VR. All the rules, the exercising, the overprotectiveness wasn't for Ari, it was to keep a million dollar asset alive.

Niomi's silent gaze told Ari more than Niomi knew. Ari stepped back lowering her staff. "I'm going to go shower."

"Wait, Ari—"

"No. Not today, not right now. Someone I know said there are no excuses." Quoting Niomi's words back to her, Ari tossed the staff on the ground. Part of her knew she should be grateful for everything Niomi taught her, but she couldn't. Niomi kept her alive as part of a job—it was only a job. "I'm taking a night off. We can talk tomorrow."

———

When she stepped out of the shower, the afternoon light had faded behind dark heavy clouds. No rain yet, but it was on its way. Why would islanders think this would be a good time to have a beach party? This storm didn't need calling in, it was well on its way without an invite.

Grabbing a plush jacket, she headed outside to meet her two security guards. She had to give them credit, they didn't even cower against the gushing wind. "Ready?"

"Are you sure you want to go out in this weather, Miss? It's going to hit hard soon."

Just then a message pinged. *Storm coming in sooner than expected. They're closing the restaurant early because of it.*

Ari wasn't ready to call it a night. She'd made it through this in a car before, she could do it again. Hitting a button, she spoke a message back to Reed. "Let's meet at the community center in an hour instead."

Out of the corner of her eye, she noticed the guard roll his eyes. *Good.* She hated being spiteful, but due to recent events, it was hard for her not to detest anyone who played a part in her employment.

"Ready guys?"

"We're heading to the community center?"

"I still have to make a stop at the islander's beach party. They are calling a storm."

"I would recommend against that." The tall one with dark features stared down at her.

Smiling back, she responded, "Good thing I don't take recommendations from you. And aren't you curious what a calling entails?"

"No." His stone face didn't move an inch.

"I bet he is." She motioned to the other guard then headed to her car. Her anger gave way to indifference. What could VisionTech do to her that they weren't already? Granted, she supposed they could step to some seedy methods, but that wasn't their style. She gave them credit for that. Adviser William would have probably tortured Reed or her family slowly until Ari conceded. But just because they wore a nice face didn't mean that it was alright that they were slowly killing her.

She entered the vehicle, started it, and turned off automatic driver. There wasn't an address where she was headed. Several miles down the beach, it would be easier to drive on the sand even if it was longer instead of navigating thru dense forest. The vehicle was made for an island though, and the wheels pushed through the sand easily.

Heavy waves crashed against the shore, anxious, like her, of the upcoming storm. Lightning struck off in the distance, causing her to jump. She had lived through several storms, this was just another one. Calm down. Oliana and Jewels must be doing one hell of a dance.

Despite the wind, a fire roared in the distance, like a beacon calling to her, and Ari pointed the car towards it.

The idea of a warm fire and safety in numbers held that anxiousness at bay.

She parked on the outskirts of the party and walked into the crowd. As the security followed, she turned over her shoulder. "You guys can stay in the car."

They glanced at each other, obviously hoping for that same thing. "We need to keep an eye on you."

"Don't you have my electronic tracker?" She rubbed a hand under her VR port. "You can watch my movements. It's not like I plan on moving far from that fire, and I'll be back in the car before the storm hits."

He pulled out an electronic pad and flashed it at her. "We'll keep an eye on you from the car."

As they turned back, the shorter guard with lighter hair, mumbled, "Can't see why she wants to hang out with these cavemen."

Ari snorted and continued to the fire. Maybe these people were cavemen compared to the technology the world currently had, but that's what made them real. In a world where the lines of reality blurred, the basics of humanity became the most important.

The women and men danced around the fire and chanted, their arms lifting while they turned in a circle. Ari spotted Oliana in the midst, her beautiful black hair spinning behind her.

Ari got lost in the mesmerizing dance, until Jewels brushed up beside her, long silvery hair let down and flowing in the wind. She leaned close to be heard over the singing. "I hear you want to contact the mainland."

"Yes," Ari nodded.

"You want to leave?" Jewels watched Ari as if the old woman knew everything without Ari saying a word. "Did they finally tell you the truth?"

The question stabbed at Ari. She didn't want to believe everyone knew but her, like an idiot. "How did you know that my job would kill me?"

"I didn't. Just guessed. I'm an old woman and have been around through the last warper. But like most white men seeking to make money, they don't always tell the whole truth."

Ari choked on her next word, fighting the instinct to bury herself in this woman's embrace. This madness called VisionTech had to stop now. She had to talk to Tessa and get off this bloody island.

"Come with me." Jewels motioned to someone in the crowd and walked away from the group. In the midst of a few palm trees, the wind lessened with their protection.

Tamar joined behind them, sweat dripping down his temple and glistening on his bare chest. "Hey, Ari."

"Hi."

"I talked to Jewels about your situation. We can send a message to the mainland with a ship that leaves tonight. They have to make it out before the storm."

"How long until we hear back?"

"A few days. And you'll have to pay him." He ran a hand through his damp hair, getting it out of his eyes.

Glancing at Jewels, who just confirmed what she already knew, Ari's thoughts spun with what type of message to send. She could just tell Tessa to come get them. By where was she? The islanders would know. But could Tessa actually bail her out?

Jewels stepped forward, placing a hand on Ari's arm, but speaking to Tamar. "She needs to leave tonight."

Startled Ari pulled back. "What?" Granted, it may be just what Ari was thinking, but not so soon.

Tamar must have been as equally puzzled. "Why, Grandmother?"

"The work they have her doing is killing her. If she stays, she will die."

He turned to Ari. "Is that true?"

Ari's chest tightened as everything in her world spun out of her control. "Yes, it is. I want to leave, but don't have everything set up. Could we do it later? Maybe in a few days?" At the end of the week, Kari was supposed to meet Antoine for vacation. If she could get her information together, she could pose as Kari and move between countries. She'd been playing with idea since her last meeting with Antoine.

"The next boat won't be going out for two weeks," Tamar told her. "The good thing is if you get out in front of the storm, no one will be able to come after you for several days."

"Do you think they'll send someone after me?"

"You are an expensive commodity. If you leave, I assume you will be breaking contract and owe them quite a bit of money. They will come after you to prosecute you. I don't believe they will hurt you. You are worth too much."

If she was ever going to leave, it had to be tonight. Right now. What about Reed?

"My boyfriend, he came here with me."

Tamar shoulders sagged. "It will be harder with him. Getting new identities, traveling as a pair you will be more conspicuous. The new identities will be expensive, and you will have no money."

"But I've been paid—"

"In electronic traceable currency. You have to go off-grid to truly get away."

"I can't leave him without telling him." Was that the

right choice or would it just guilt him into coming along? Remorse ate at her that she was about to destroy his life again. Maybe he would choose to stay, and part of her hoped he would for his sake.

Tamar nodded. "Let's go then."

"Wait—my tracker." She motioned to the back of her neck. "The guards are watching me from the car."

"I can hold that for you for a while. Give you a head start," Jewels said.

That's all fine and dandy, except getting it to Jewels involved cutting it out of her neck. "Do either of you have a knife?"

"I do." Tamar said. "You're not a man if you don't carry one."

Ari let a nervous laugh escape. "Never heard that one yet." Turning around, she pulled up her thick braid. "Don't cut deep. It's right under the skin and hopefully should slide out."

"Don't worry. I can gut a fish with precision."

The wind wiped through the trees, the skin on her neck raising. "Great. Just think of me as an oversized fish."

A small sting bit into her skin. Then his cold hands added pressure to her neck. "Here." He dropped the tracker onto Ari's hand, a bit of blood along with it. Staring at the small silver device she realized it was all over. Her dreams of a better life, or starting over with Reed, they were all gone before they even got a chance to begin.

She forced herself not to go down that dark train of thought. Now she had a chance at a real life, a life away from fake skins, electronic dangers, and people who wished to use her like a tool. It may not be the way she wanted, but this may be the best way for things to play out. Her heart tugged at the thought of Reed and the Islanders and everything they have done for her.

Glancing between Tamar and Jewels, she said, "Thanks for everything. Really. I hope nothing happens to you because you helped me."

Jewels shook her head and pulled her into a hug. "Don't worry about us. We've been dealing with these city folk for years now. They're not as smart as they think." She took the tracker from Ari and held her hand for another moment. "Be strong, Ariana. It's a big world out there with a lot of paths. Find yours and find the courage to take it."

Tears fell from Ari's face, a mixture of the wind and emotion, as she nodded. She found solace in the old woman's words. "Thank you."

The woman turned to her grandson. "Take her to find her boy. Then hurry to the boat. The storm is angry, and they'll be safer out at sea." Jewels walked out of the safety of the trees and headed to the fire.

Tamar reached for Ari, and they ran.

CHAPTER THIRTY-FIVE

Running fast through the dark night, the wind howled through the trees. Ari remained right behind Tamar, often grabbing onto his shirt for guidance to not get lost. Only someone who grew up on these paths could take them so fast. He maneuvered with a swift coordination that even Niomi would be impressed by.

He slowed once the dorms came into view and turned to Ari. "Go in and grab your boy." He motioned to his bare chest and tied skirt. "It'd attract more attention the way I'm dressed, which we don't need right now."

"Okay."

As she walked off, he added, "You don't have time to convince him. The boat will not wait for you if their shipment is loaded."

Nice to know. Jogging upstairs, she tried to gather her thoughts of what she'd say to Reed. By the time she arrived at his room panting from exertion, she still didn't have a clue.

Opening the door, Reed looked surprised as he took her jagged appearance in.

He had no idea what was about to hit him.

"Am I late?" he checked his HUB.

"Do you trust me?" Standing up, she met his gaze and prayed this was the best thing for him.

"Of course."

"I don't have time to explain. I'm leaving the island right now. I have to." She gulped knowing this was the hard part. "If you want to stay, I totally get it. You have a great life, with a chance of being reunited with your mom. I can't promise you any of that. I just have to leave and couldn't without telling you goodbye first."

He blinked and with a brief nod said, "I'm coming."

It was Ari's time to be reassured. Despite the hell of the situation, she smiled, reaching forward and kissed him. He reached out, but she pushed back. "No time. We have to go, now."

"Should I grab anything? Clothes, food?"

"No time... except do you have any money or stuff to trade."

"Yeah." Keeping the door open, he rushed to his dresser. A bag lay on top, which he grabbed, and opening his top drawer threw stuff in it. It took all of thirty seconds before he turned. "Let's go."

Ignoring the looks of others, they ran through the halls and outside to the outdoor patio, the same one in which they often shared several conversations, meals, and kisses. Standing in the middle of two tables was Vinh.

His hands fisted by his sides, almost shaking. "Where are you going, Ari?"

Her jagged breath did nothing to help hide her guilt, thankfully Reed was thinking straighter.

"On a date." Reed ran a hand through his hair. "We're

hoping to make it back to her rooms before the storm hits. You know, nice cozy night during a storm."

"Then why is her tracker on a beach dancing right now? I thought it funny when I saw her sprinting to your room, a bit over eager." Vinh's chest puffed up in an aggressive pose that didn't suit him. Unlike his easygoing temperament, it appeared to take effort for him to be this confrontational.

The wind picked up, and it was accompanied now by a light rain. She didn't have time to waste. "Step aside, Vinh." Ari moved forward, not willing to let him ruin this for them.

"I can't. I will lose my job." He remained still, hands clenched at his side.

"I trusted you," she spit at him, her voice raising as drops of rain fell on her face. "I thought you were my friend."

"I am." His earnest face showed that he actually believed the lie.

"Friends don't let friends kill themselves."

"What are you talking about?" Reed said next to her.

Vinh gulped and glanced down. "I was doing everything to keep you healthy and safe."

"You didn't tell me the truth, so I could decide for myself if it was a risk I wanted to take."

"I couldn't. I would lose my job and not be able to help you at all."

"Maybe. But it's still my life to gamble, not yours." A tinge of sympathy tugged at Ari. She knew about tough situations that life can put you in. She may be able to forgive him one day for this betrayal, but she couldn't stay here.

She started forward to forcibly move him, but Reed beat her to the chase. Storming forward, he punched Vinh in the face. He fell backward on the ground and didn't move.

Looking back and forth between them, Ari was surprised and impressed.

Tamar emerged from out of the foliage. "About time," he motioned to Vinh sprawled out on the ground. "We have to run. I just got a call from the boat. They will be gone in ten, fifteen minutes tops, and can't wait."

"Okay." Ari took a step before remembering one last thing. "Reed's tracker."

"Right?" Tamar pulled out his knife.

Reed didn't blanch but turned around, which said a lot given he didn't know Tamar well.

"It'll be quick. I already did mine."

"I know." He flinched slightly as Tamar made the incision. "I saw your neck in my dorm. I figured it was pretty serious if you cut it out."

"Let's go." Tamar placed the tracker in Vinh's pocket which was next to him.

Reed turned to Ari, "You have a lot to explain."

"I will, later. Promise."

For the first time since her arrival at the island, Ari was grateful for Niomi's obsession with running. Once they made it deeper into the jungle, Tamar pulled out a light to help speed up their trip. Her heart pounded in her chest, but every step took her closer to freedom and survival.

With her legs rubber and numb and her hair sopping wet, the dock came into view. Ari had never been to this part of the island, and its dated and industrial structures were out of place in comparison. *Guess VisionTech hides away the gritty side of life in more than one way.*

A tall light pole illuminated a portion of the massive boat, bigger than her apartment building growing up. It was large and dark but teeming with life. Men shouted on the deck, working against the rain now falling in a heavy sheet.

They raced up the ramp, a man on top greeting Tamar with a hand on his shoulder. "Cutting it close, cousin."

"Keep safe on the waters." Even Tamar appeared slightly out of breath.

"We always do." He motioned Ari and Reed on top of the massive boat.

Hand in hand they stepped on to the boat, and the large metal gate shut after them. Ari turned back to tell Tamar just how much all this meant, for being a friend and caring for her when she really needed it.

Tamar just shook his head. His kind eyes peering through wet clumps of hair that hung down his face. "No time. Be safe."

She nodded, knowing he was right. Emotion flooded through her, washed away by the rain splattering her face. There on the ship, she promised herself if she ever had the means, one day she'd return to the island, where beautiful people gave her a gift she could never repay.

CHAPTER THIRTY-SIX

Being stowaways, Reed and Ari were led to a small mop closet for their lodging. Tamar's cousin, Manu, handed them some water and a couple of blankets. "Sorry I can't do much better. If we give you a room, then I have to log you in as passengers or crew. Both have a record I think you'd be better off avoiding."

"Don't worry. I appreciate what you're doing for us." Ari squeezed the water out of the ends of her hair, straight into a drain. Practical at least.

Manu shook out his short curly hair. His tall and wide build barely fit inside the room. "The crew knows you're here, but it's best if you keep to yourself and only deal with me. The bathroom is down the hall if you need it. Hunker down for the night as we sail ahead of the storm, and I'll come bring you breakfast in the morning."

Reed reached a hand out and clasped hands with Manu. "Thanks again."

"Night." Manu turned down the hall.

For the next few minutes, Reed and Ari took off extra wet layers, squeezing out the water. In an undershirt, Ari wrapped the blanket around her. Reed, in a pair of boxers, did the same.

They picked the corner without the drain and cuddled next to each other. Reed placed an arm around her. "Let's hope our clothes dry by morning."

"It'd be nice."

"Since we have time now, can you tell me what happened? And why you didn't tell me until tonight?" Reed didn't yell or even sound angry for Ari flipping his world upside down.

With guilt heavy on her shoulders, Ari explained the mess she found herself in and how the restrictions in her contract forced her to not tell him. Even though he knew that, he agreed the separation between them was just another ploy by VisionTech. He didn't argue, just listened.

Then when she began explaining about her mission, the hardest part came—explaining about Antoine. "I should have just broken up with him. Niomi told me too, but I thought the mission would end soon and Kari would have her life back. I didn't want to ruin her life more than I already did."

"That makes sense." He remained composed, his face not giving anything away.

"And there's more."

"What?"

Ari pulled back, not willing to let herself be comforted. She didn't deserve it. "I kissed him. At first, I pulled back. Only watching their interaction within the data. Like a director moving Kari's body to react positively to her boyfriend. Keeping everything normal until..."

"Until what?"

"The last time I kissed him." Tears fell silently down her cheeks. "I can't really explain it. I don't care for Antoine like that. I just... I felt bad for stealing his girlfriend, for destroying her life, maybe even being the cause for her death. I caused him so much sorrow that I wanted to say goodbye and have it be as real as possible for once."

Reed stood up, fists clenched, he looked like a trapped animal. With a loud exhale, he stepped forward and slammed his fist into the wall. Ari flinched, but he didn't seem to notice.

The punch dented the drywall, but probably hurt him more. Shaking his hand out, he then slapped the wall with such force. With both palms on the wall, he lowered his head. The muscles on his back strained.

Ari gave him time. He deserved it with the bomb she just dropped on him. And now he was unemployed and on the run to a foreign country. He could have all the time he needed.

"Do you love him?" He spoke softly, still looking down.

"No. I care for him, mostly out of guilt. I love you." She prayed he believed her. "I'm sorry I didn't tell you on the island, before you came with me."

He spun around. "Do you think that really would have mattered?"

"I don't know." She lowered her eyes to her lap.

After slowly exhaling, he kneeled in front of her and lifted her chin with a finger. His anger appeared to melt off him, his face softening. "I don't regret being here with you. I'm furious at VisionTech for putting you in an impossible situation, and even more furious that I couldn't do anything about it."

"It's not your job."

"But I want it to be." He cupped her cheek with a soft hand. "I know how you feel about the VR, and after Garrett last year I know how you feel about romance in the VR. I don't think for a minute you did it because you had some virtual fantasy. We're real, together, and that's what matters."

The pressure of shame and guilt that had been bogging her down finally lightened as she reached for Reed.

He sat back down and pulled her next to him. "What ended up happening with Antoine? Did you break up?"

She bit her lip, hoping he wasn't going to hate this next part. Her story just kept getting worse and worse. "No, I told him to plan on their vacation."

Reed turned to look at her. "Isn't that worse? Leaving the poor guy stood up on vacation by himself?"

"Well, I thought we could meet him there?"

A short laughed erupted from Reed. "That's what a guy wants. Instead of a romantic getaway, two strangers show up. One who has been pretending to be his girlfriend."

"Not too far from home, but it should offer the privacy and freedom we need. I can't think of any other options."

"You've thought this through."

"I've had a lot of time on the last couple runs with Niomi." The mention of her trainer's name pulled on her heart. After the months spent together, the betrayal hurt.

"I suppose you did. Tell me about this vacation? And how you found your file?"

She continued her story, letting him know everything she had been forced to keep from him. When she talked herself out, silence fell upon them. It was several minutes before he spoke. "Did you really think I would have chosen to stay on the island without you?"

She shrugged. "You finally got your dream job, using your art."

"I only got that job because of you."

"But you're so talented."

"Thanks, but apparently I was under qualified. My boss hinted more than once at that fact. Yet Niomi would always check in on me to make sure things were good between us. If I ever needed something, it was taken care of."

"Really, why didn't you say anything?" It hurt to know that maybe he wasn't as happy as he was pretending either.

"I know you would feel guilty that we ended up here, even though you didn't need to. I may not have chosen to move to an island or end up in the closet of a boat, but I chose you and all that entails. Every moment since, I have chosen you."

Her heart pooled around her feet as she leaned forward. "I love you," she whispered before kissing him.

His soft lips and warm taste flooded her mouth and she couldn't get enough. His hand gently cupped her cheek, pulling her close. Her nerve endings in a flurry of delight. Every touch was bliss and with it a desire for more.

Her fingers traced down his bare stomach. He shivered as a moan escaped his lips. "You're killing me, Ari."

"Sorry." Leaning back, she was only partially lying.

He gripped her hand searching her gaze. "You know I love you."

"I know." She could get lost in those eyes. They held the promise of her future, always next to him. "That keeps me going despite all this." She motioned to the small ratty closet they were in.

"Things will settle down one day." He pulled her next to him.

She rested her head on his shoulder. "I hope so. Until then, we'll keep dreaming."

"Yes, but it's nice to dream, isn't it?"

"With you, always."

———

Even with the storm brewing outside, eventually Reed and Ari slept. The next day, true to his word, Manu brought breakfast. He said they outran the storm and should make it to the mainland by nightfall.

When Manu returned sometime later in the day, he had an armful of supplies. Flipping over a bucket, he laid a variety of items on the ground. "Jewels gave me very little notice of you two, and even less money."

Reed straightened. "I have some—"

"Keep it. I can't buy anything now, and you'll have better luck on the mainland. Here, you'll both need these." He handed them translators.

Ari had seen them on the island for those that spoke different languages. She slipped the small ear pieces in her jeans. They would be needed.

"Where are we going exactly?" Not knowing where the island was, had kept Ari very much in the dark, and she could only hope she was headed in the right direction.

"We're in the middle of the Pacific Ocean, heading towards the United Asian Association. We'll take you up as far north as possible."

Asian? Glancing at Reed's worried expression, Ari realized they were both really far from home. How would they ever find their way back? And did they even want to? Now knowing the true nature of a warper, she couldn't go back to a government that would force her into service until she had nothing left.

"Why north?" Reed asked as he picked up a heavy jacket. Neither he nor Ari were used to cold climates.

"With the fallout of the war, most people moved south."

Manu looked between them, with a lifted brow. "Do you not know what happened?"

"We're not from here," Ari said. "We only got the history and education our government saw fit." It had taken Ari the first couple months to learn the truth of world history on the island.

He nodded. "Well, the land up north is bad. From the poison there is no farming, no grass, just desolation. Left for the poor and the beggars."

"We aren't going there." Reed pushed back the gas mask.

"Okay," Manu replied. "It's just where most of the transients go."

Reed and Ari had spent most of the morning discussing their options. Granted, ending up across an ocean from where they wanted to be presented a few more challenges. Ari agreed that hiding out in a wasteland didn't sound like a plan.

Pulling something out from his pocket, Reed laid a simple gold ring with a decent stone in his palm. "We need connections for new identities. We can pay."

Manu eyed the ring with an envy he couldn't hide. "You better put that away. I wouldn't be able to look Tamar in the face again if anything happened to you."

Ari looked at Reed and wondered where the ring came from. They spoke of the future the other night. Did Reed plan more of it than he let on? A warm chill lifted the hair on her neck, but she tried to focus at the plan on hand.

Turning her attention to Manu, she put the ring out of her mind. "We need an island or city that won't require identification. Then a chance to buy new names and faces for ourselves."

Manu drug a hand through his dark wavy hair. "That's

going to be tricky, but I have a connection that can help. It's dangerous, staying off-grid is the safest route."

"We know." Reed didn't seem happy about that but didn't want to live out their days in a wasteland.

Ari knew if she could get online, they would have more resources.

"I'll come get you when we're near the major Asian Islands," Manu said. "They are a major trafficking port for black market items around the world. Be careful though. You'll need weapons more than masks."

"We appreciate your help."

"Don't thank me until you get off at the Land of Smiles."

"Wait, what? The Land of Smiles?" Ari asked.

"Well, the real name is," Manu said a long name that Ari couldn't understand at all. "But it is a land of pleasure or sin however you consider it. It's the land where you can even die smiling, they say."

Ari's mouth opened but couldn't think of a response.

"Just don't die," Manu said as he left the room.

Once he left, Reed turned to Ari. "Do you think we're doing the right thing?"

"I do." Ari reached for his hand. "Between your skills with security and mine, we can get what's needed to create ourselves new identities anywhere, and with them, the money and power to get our families back. We may not have much, but what we do have is worth a lot. We just need to find the right people."

"That's what worries me." Reed reached an arm around Ari and held her tight, which was perfect because she had no plans of letting go.

CHAPTER THIRTY-SEVEN

As the boat unloaded supplies in the morning, Ari and Reed left their room with Manu. He gave them directions to someone who could find them identities. They thanked him again and headed off. The storm had passed but not without obvious damage. Tree limbs and debris littered the shoreline, puddles and trash lining the landing.

As they ventured further into town, life looked undisturbed by the storm. Granted, living out here, most people were used to the violent behavior of mother nature. Only damp awnings and wet debris littering doorways showed the presence of a storm last night, along with a scattering of heavy clouds in the distance.

In the light of day, the Land of Smiles sounded creepily close to its name. She imaged some haunted carnival and wasn't far off. Flashing neon lights offered perverse activities for a variety of addictions, sins, and fetishes. And if you couldn't find it here, VR bars lined the streets able to take you anywhere. Even though most of the city spoke an Asian dialect she couldn't understand, the pictures did plenty of the talking.

"Are you okay?" she asked Reed.

It was obvious how uncomfortable he was from his stiff stance. "No, but neither are you. I'm just trying not to look at anything and pretend I'm not really here." He motioned to a man standing at a booth, offering up services of a variety of women. "He deserves to get hit or worse."

"Ugh. Most definitely."

"Let's just get our IDs and off this island as soon as possible." Reed gripped Ari's hand and pulled her close to him.

Her skin crawled with the dirt and sadness that lined the city. It didn't matter what the drunken crowds on the street thought. Their alcohol-induced exuberance was deplorable.

They followed the directions through the streets that Manu had given them. Finally passing the swarm of VR dens and brothels, they found the address on a two story brick building. Vines crawled up the walls as the wet climate gave bravery to Mother Nature. A tall man stood at the door.

"We're looking for Fetu," Ari told the man.

Without even looking at them he pointed to the side of the building. "Take the stairs up."

"Ummm, thanks." Reed led the way around the side of the building into the alley.

They climbed the metal stairs that wound their way to a door. Once above the street, shouts emerged from within. Standing on a shaking metal balcony, they glanced at each other.

"Are we sure about this?" Reed asked, his hand posed to knock when there was no sign of a bell.

"We don't have a lot of options, unless you want to

make a home here," Ari pointed out. "I think I saw a for rent sign next to that den of women."

"Don't joke." Reed knocked on the door, but no one could have heard with the racket inside. So instead of waiting, he opened the door, and they both slipped inside.

An irate woman screamed in a foreign language at a tall man who looked like he had his share of a rough life. He glanced at Reed and Ari briefly, and the woman's pitch increased even more. The room looked like a small apartment but instead of a living room, a desk and a couple chairs had been set up a makeshift office of sorts.

After another minute of trying to talk her down, he finally grabbed her arm and led her to the door. Reed and Ari stepped to the side, and he gently pushed her out. Once shut, he locked it, turned and leaned against it, saying something Ari didn't understand.

She pulled out the translators and placed a set in Reed's hand. Even though they were old tech, they were a much needed tool. While they put in the translators, the man straightened and made his way to his desk.

He clicked a button near his ear, to probably activate his own translator. "I can see you two are not natives. What brings you here?"

Ari straightened. "We need new identities for travel. Are you Fetu?"

"I am." He gave a short chuckle. "So, you want to start over with a fresh digital thumbprint. The dream of everyone here." He motioned for them to sit. "It won't be cheap."

Reed took the chair next to Ari. "We know, and brought something you may be interested in." He pulled out the ring.

Fetu leaned forward in his chair, obviously interested in it. "May I?"

Reed handed it over but didn't take his eyes off it. The rock on top of the gold band was bigger than Ari had ever seen before, but that didn't mean much growing up where they did.

"Where did you get it?" Fetu pulled out a magnifying glass.

Surprised, Ari wondered that as well. There were no stores of that type on the island that she saw. Her thoughts meandered to what could have been.

"A friend got it for me," Reed answered then turned to Ari. "Niomi got it for me a few weeks ago. Sent for it from the mainland. At the time I just thought she was super supportive. Now, I just wonder if they wanted it to keep you there."

"I don't know." Ari had thought back to her relationship with Niomi several times, wondering if VisionTech's motives tainted all the good things that happened to her. "Maybe both."

"The cut is from the Far North, the Russian mines." Fetu set the ring on the desk in between them. "You know I can't give you what you paid for it."

"We need new lives and a ship to cross the ocean to Acadian." They had already picked where they were headed.

Antoine and Kari's vacation destination had the benefit of being a very liberal country with many tourists and was not too far north from their own home. They would have the best chance of getting in without much suspicion and contacting Tessa. She knew that with DNA scans, they could probably never go home again, but somewhere safe was all they needed.

Fetu leaned back, a tattooed hand running over his short beard. "Those are hard to come by and will take some time."

"How long?" Ari knew VisionTech would be sure to look for them soon.

"A couple days at least."

"We need them sooner. We can't stay here long."

Fetu's gaze traveled between the two of them. "The best I can do is tomorrow morning."

Ari and Reed glanced at each other, both probably wondering the same thing. Did they have that much time? Or did they have any other choice? Turning back to Fetu, Reed nodded agreement.

Ari turned back to the man. "Can you recommend a clean place to stay?"

"We do offer a lot, but that may be one of the more difficult amenities to find."

She cringed. "The cleanest and cheapest possible."

He gave them directions to a nearby place with rooms to rent. They closed their business deals, and Ari prayed this man would keep his word.

As they climbed down the stairwell, she voiced her concerns. "How do we know he'll keep his part of the deal? I don't even want to know how many cryptos you spent on that."

"Then I won't tell you." Reed stepped on the stairs and reached for her hand. "Don't worry I had the money even after sending some back to my mom."

"What if he takes off?"

"Then he takes off. I trust Manu and hopefully Fetu will play out too." He started down the street. "But we don't have many options, and we're doing the best with what we have. Nothing else we can do at this point."

"You're right." Ari leaned into him, grateful for him at her side. "By the way, that ring... way too big for me."

"Really?" he glanced down at her. "Niomi said something about three months' salary, and they paid me well on the island."

"In retrospect, I'm glad you did since it was the best way to get money off the island. But for the future, I'll take an old washer if it means I get to be with you forever."

He chuckled. "I'll remember that. Scratch ring, find old tech for a ring."

He wrapped an arm around her as they walked and squeezed. "Let's go find somewhere to rest."

She wrapped an arm around his waist. "With luck we may actually have a bed tonight."

Before he could answer, something sharp poked through her jacket, a breath away from cutting her. A rough voice spoke behind them. "Want to pay me for your girlfriend's kidney before or after I remove it?"

CHAPTER THIRTY-EIGHT

Reed started to turn around and something slammed into the base of his skull. As he fell, Ari started to tumble with him. Without thinking, the countless hours of training with Niomi kicked in.

Grasping for the hand behind her, she spun out of its reach while twisting the man's grip. He pulled back, and instead of fighting against him, she let go, using the momentum to strike out at his throat. Obscenities flew through the night, obviously these two young attackers were not expecting someone to fight back.

Ari tried to focus on the man in front of her, ignoring the struggle with Reed nearby. The faster she eliminated this threat, the faster she could help Reed. She wished for a staff or, hell, even a stick or pipe would help. Instead, this guy, probably not much older than her, with dark greasy hair, held a knife while she had nothing. Well not nothing, she did have a bag.

He stepped towards her, and in a flash, she tossed the bag at him, rushing in right after it. While he fumbled with the bag, she struck repeatedly at his face with her palm and elbow. A sharp crack told her she did some damage.

Pushing back, her attacker held his nose, which now gushed with blood. With a final curse, he turned and ran. Reed and the other guy were locked together in an awkward embrace while they each struggled to get hits in.

Searching the ground, Ari found a piece of twisted metal. Hard to grip, but not impossible. It cut into her hand, but she ignored the bite of the metal and slammed it into the back of the other thug's head. He crumpled into a heap and almost took Reed down as well. She caught Reed's arm and helped him regain his balance.

Reed glanced her way; his battered eye was quickly swelling. "Thanks."

"Anytime." She looked down the empty alleyway. Guess his friend didn't stick around for backup. "We better get out of here before the authorities come."

"If there are authorities here." He wiped at some blood at the corner of his mouth. "Damn, that guy could hit."

"Sorry. You okay?"

He shrugged then winced. "I'll survive, but I have a feeling neither one of us will be fine unless we get off this garbage pit of an island."

———

Next to their hotel, they found a store with food and supplies.

"Why don't you go to the room to rest while I get something to clean you up," Ari offered.

"No. I'm not leaving you alone anywhere on this island. I'll be fine." His eye looked horrible, but at least it wasn't swollen shut.

"If you say so."

They walked in to the store, which smelled heavily of bleach. Tall metal rows of supplies and food filled the store. They roamed up and down the aisles which resembled more a pawn shop with scattered items than proper store. They found a first-aid kit, then continued down the row.

"What do you think of that?" Reed pointed to an old computer. "They can't be asking much for it and if I can get it to work, we can connect with Tessa."

They left in such a hurry that they hadn't had time to grab any of their electronics, though Ari wouldn't have trusted VisionTech's stuff anyway.

"Check it out. It may be worth it. I'll try to find something edible." Ari headed to the next row, while Reed dusted off the computer.

It was slim pickings for healthy recognizable food, but she grabbed a couple of items. Her hand stung from where the broken pipe cut her. She'd need to glue that up so she didn't catch some crazy disease on this island.

On the shelf over, some hair dye caught her eye. She had always loved her long brown hair, especially when her mother would play with it and braid it for her. But she'd be willing to part with it, if it meant she could see her mother again. She grabbed the box and some scissors and went back to Reed.

Reed had the computer in his hands. "Let's see if we can afford it now."

The man sat behind a clear barrier and spoke through a microphone. "That'll be 100 cryptos."

"You have to be kidding me," Reed said. "You couldn't do anything with this old junk."

"Then why do you want it?"

"I said you couldn't, not that I couldn't. I'll give you 50 for everything."

"90," he countered.

"75. We're doing you a favor."

"Deal." During this whole encounter, the man behind the desk appeared completely bored, not even a reaction to Reed's swollen eye. Reed paid the man in island coins. A nearby computer converted Reed's coins to the correct currency, and they left for the hotel.

The word *hotel* was a bit of a stretch. The room held a simple single bed and bathroom, and everything else looked like leftovers from a street sale. The plus side was it had a lock and gave them both a moment to breathe. They had to wait until the following day before they could get their IDs, and it would be a few hours after that before they could catch a ride out of here.

Sitting on the bed, Ari cleaned and sealed the cut on her hand, and counted how much money they had left. They would have to stretch things a bit. They had been lucky Reed had as much as he did. Growing up in the slums, he tended to keep a backup. Ari had grown up in the same neighborhood and would have done the same, but never saw cash on the island. VisionTech never had her wanting for anything. She trusted that sense of luxury like a pig fattening up for the butcher.

Reed exited the bathroom and somehow his face looked worse. His eye had doubled in size and turned to a dark bluish color. He had put his pants back on but left his shirt off. Normally she would have taken a moment to fully enjoy shirtless Reed, except for the colors blossoming on his torso.

"I have a cut on my back I need you to glue." He turned showing a large gash that started on his side and continued around his back.

"My God, Reed." She bit back the urge to cry. Reaching out, she stopped short not wanting to touch him. "When you picked up the first-aid glue, I didn't think we'd use the whole bottle."

He smiled. "Please don't make me laugh. It hurts."

"Deal." Tears swam in her eyes as she reached for the small first- aid kit. She cleaned and sealed the wound on his back, then turned to sit in front of him. She worked on the small cut on his temple. "I'm so sorry, Reed." Her voice hitched as she dabbed ointment on the wound.

He reached for her hand, waiting until she met his gaze. "Don't. They did this, not you. We're in this together, right? From your first day at the academy, I knew if given the chance I'd never leave your side. I don't regret a day of it."

"Really?"

"Really." He tried to grin, but it soon turned into a grimace. "Ouch."

Emotions and warmth flooded her body, and she knew if she didn't do something, she'd end up crying or trying to kiss him. Which would hurt him, with his lip cut up like that.

"You up to contacting Tessa?" Ari turned to the used computer on the table. It was an older computer, older than the stuff they got at home, with a large screen and basic keyboard. An actual keyboard with keys. "If that thing *can* contact Tessa."

"Hey, don't doubt my skills. We may not be playing elves in her game, but I should be able to send her a message." He stood and picked up his shirt. Moving slowly, he put it on.

"You didn't have to put it on for my benefit," Ari said.

"I wanted to make sure my virtue remained intact."

She laughed. "I'd hate to ruin your virtue."

"Truthfully, I don't think I could ruin it right now if I tried. It hurts at a mere touch. Will you hand me the pain relievers?"

"Sure."

After he dissolved a couple of tabs, he moved to the computer. He had to fiddle with the hardware, but soon his hands flew over the keys. At first, she could follow his actions as he hacked a nearby server to get access off the island. Then soon she couldn't keep up. Eventually she hit the bathroom and washed up. By the time she returned, he'd set up an anonymous account to contact their loved ones.

"What should we say?" He turned to Ari. "I don't even know where to begin with my mom." Leaning back, he rubbed his hands over his head and stared at the screen.

"Why don't we start with Tessa? We'll need to be careful in case they are watching her."

"Her system should be secure but since she's still in the country, who knows." He sat up, and they pieced together a message telling Tessa they were on the run. They couldn't afford to tell her any specifics. They did mention in a few cryptic suggestions to check on Reed's mom.

Ari placed a hand on Reed's arm. "When we're set, we'll work on getting your mom out."

"I'm not sure she would want to go, to be honest. She never was much for change."

"You're her only son. She'll come."

Once the message was sent, there wasn't much they could do. They couldn't risk setting up an account to receive messages. VisionTech was probably watching Tessa.

"Ready for the fun part?" Ari asked Reed, thinking to the other supplies they bought.

"Which is?"

"Haven't you always wanted to try dating a blonde?" She picked up the dye and scissors off the end table.

He stood and ran a hand through her hair. "Tried once. It didn't take."

"Good thing I bought red."

They headed into the bathroom where Reed proceeded to cut Ari's long brown hair into a short bob that curved around her chin.

"Sometimes I worry I really don't know what the hell I'm doing," he said, staring at her hair.

"Don't worry, it'll grow back."

"I'm not worried about the hair." His lips pursed together, and a frown crinkled his forehead.

Nerves pricked along her back, and she focused on what they could do. "You're a hacker, a job everyone needs. And I can program by hand if needed. We'll find work and a place to stay. We'll get there. We just need to make sure no one from VisionTech stops us in the meantime."

He picked up the red dye next, and she stood to lean over the sink. Grabbing her hand, he pulled her back and into his arms.

"I don't want to hurt you." She gently laid her palms against his chest, a tingling sensation traveling up her arms and settling into her stomach.

"Doesn't matter." He pulled her close, and she melted into his skin, his touch, and his smell. The kiss was gentle but held an electricity that could have powered the whole island. Separating a couple of inches, their breath echoed throughout the room.

She stared at those dark eyes that saw her for more than she was. "I couldn't do this without you. You know?"

"I was thinking the same thing." Leaning forward, he kissed her softly one more time.

And she decided she could live a happy life as long as there was always one more kiss.

CHAPTER THIRTY-NINE

The next morning Ari opened her eyes to find Reed watching her. Through the night, Ari had ended up next to him, hands entwined. His intense gaze made her self-conscious.

"Do I have some horrible bed head or what?" She covered her mouth with one hand, to spare him from her morning breath.

"No. Just getting used to you as a redhead. It took a bit, but I still see the beautiful Ari in there."

She ran a hand through her short hair, it felt off when her hair came up short. "You sure you don't want to dye your hair too? Who knows, red may be your color."

"Maybe. I'm sure it'd match my face." He touched the side of his mouth.

She cringed as she examined him, the bruises were deepening to an ugly purple. "Let's just go with a hat instead. Are you in a lot of pain?"

He shrugged and got up. "I'll feel better when we get out of here."

"Me too."

Glancing at the clock embedded in the wall, she got up as well. "Let me hit the bathroom, and we can head off. The IDs should be ready soon."

"I'll warm up some of the food from last night."

"Deal." Stopping him at the door, she kissed his cheek, one of the few uninjured spots on his face.

After realizing she had no idea how to style short hair, she just combed through it and left it straight down, hoping to cover her face as much as possible. Reed came back with food, and they packed up. All that they had to their name fit in a small backpack which Ari wore on her back.

Instead of the drama from yesterday, they found Fetu at his desk smoking an unusually long pipe. "Come in, come in," he said, waving them inside. He looked recently show-ered and shaved, displaying the scar on his chin more.

"I like what you've done to your hair." He motioned for Ari to sit. "You know, there would be work for someone like you here on the island."

A cold chill ran up her spine. Did he know who she really was? Maybe he just knew they worked at VisionTech. Either way, it made her uncomfortable. If people on this island really knew how much she was worth, she'd never get away.

Before Ari could reply, Reed stepped in. "No thanks. We just want the IDs."

"I'll just need a photo of both of you. To update your files." Fetu pulled out a small camera. The process took mere minutes.

Yet Ari couldn't stop fidgeting or stop the uneasy feeling that they were being chased and they needed to hurry.

Along with their documents, Fetu handed them new fingerprints. They both had to scrub their fingers as much as they could with a pumice stone, then placed the new silicone fingerprints over theirs.

"How do you know they won't notice these?" Reed asked as he finished putting on the last one.

"Because we use them all the time. Officials know what goes on here, and we pay them to look the other way. They work at the bigger ports too. You can't tell even if you shake someone's hand. Enough hand washing and they will come off, though, so take them off if you expect them to last more than a couple days."

"Okay." The silicone went on smoothly. As Ari rubbed her fingers together, she could barely notice them either. She slung her bag over her shoulder. "Thanks, Fetu."

"I got you on the first ship out of here this morning, the *Jackal*. Don't be late." He picked his pipe back up and waved goodbye. "Safe travels."

Once back on the street, she turned to Reed, who looked just as agitated.

"What's wrong?" she asked.

"Nothing. Or at least nothing I can put a name to." He tugged on his cap. "I didn't like him offering us jobs."

"Me either."

After a moment, he continued, "I just don't feel comfortable here. After the attack last night, I feel like I can't protect you or keep you safe, and that bothers me."

"I get it." She reached for his hand. "But it's not your responsibility to keep me safe."

"That doesn't make me feel a whole lot better." He leaned down and kissed the top of her hair. "Let's just get out of here."

"Deal."

The smell of the port hit them before they saw it. Instead of the fresh seafood Ari regularly ate at VisionTech, it smelled like rotting fish. It didn't look a whole lot better either. Too bad they couldn't afford a plane to get off here.

At least the storm had passed, and clear skies greeted them on their voyage today. A cool breeze brushed against them as they strolled down the port. Keeping to the shops, they aimed for the crowds whenever they could. Ari couldn't help looking back to make sure they weren't being followed. It felt like people were watching them, more than when they first arrived. Maybe it was Reed's bad eye.

At last they found the ship called the *Jackal*, sitting low in the water. Its green paint highlighted the rust on the large tin can. Smaller than their last ship, it sat a couple stories high. Hopefully the important parts of the ships weren't rusty. No use regretting their decision now.

Ari squeezed Reed's hand. "Ready to get back on board?"

"Yeah. I won't be looking back on this place for sure."

There was a line of people lined up on the ramp. Men and woman of all shapes, sizes, and colors. Reed and Ari placed their translators in and stepped in line.

"What's taking so long?" the man in front of them asked the fellow next to him.

"Probably doing a head count for supplies or something. Don't worry."

Ari shivered and shoved her hands into her pockets.

Reed pulled her into a hug. After a moment he stiffened, then spoke in a low voice. "Don't turn around, but I think I recognize someone from before."

She tensed in his arms. They couldn't have come this far only to be caught now. "Who are they? Guards from the island? They won't attack us in public like this. Will they?"

"They looked like they are from here. Thugs really. If they were going to attack us out in the open, they would have done it by now. We need to keep an eye on them." He pulled back, smiling and rubbed her arm like nothing was wrong. "They are the two tall guys, wearing black tees and ball caps."

After a minute, she glanced back to find the men. They quickly averted their eyes, lowering their faces. Obviously, they were watching them, but for who? Did Fetu rat them out?

The line moved forward, and Ari and Reed followed, stepping up on the ramp. Fetu had told them a couple of lazy security guards would check them in. Instead, they found a team of agents in keen blue suits managing the check-in and even searching bags. From the crisp tone of their voices down to the razor-sharp haircuts, something felt off.

The line separated then, one for males and one for females.

Something Fetu didn't warn them about either. She turned to Reed, her chest tightening with fear. Behind them were thugs and in front of them, security obviously on high alert.

"It'll be okay." He gazed into her face as if memorizing it. "It'll be okay." He repeated before they separated, each going into their own line.

Once separated, the lines sped up as they ushered people through. *Maybe it would be better to not be together*, Ari thought. VisionTech would be looking for a couple. Except now the two men in the back were even closer to Reed, and he was outnumbered. She kept them in her peripheral vision, waiting for any sign of attack.

The guard spoke, pulling her focus forward. The computerized translation coming through her ear piece. "Hurry up."

Stepping up, her stomach tightened into a mess of nerves and fear. She slipped off her backpack and handed it over to the guard. While one guard pawed through the backpack, another guard waved her forward.

As she stepped into the metal arch that scanned her entire body, she held her breath. What if the pads on her fingers showed up on the scan? Hands shaking, she jammed them into her pockets. Not until he waved her through, did she finally breathe out.

Someone handed her bag back to her. She avoided their gazes in case they'd seen a picture. She threw the bag over a shoulder and turned to watch Reed go through the scanner.

His ball cap was pulled low to cover the bruises, but it didn't help. His gaze flicked up to Ari and the edge of his mouth pulled up. It helped melt the tension inside of her. The scanner beeped at completion.

Reed stepped forward, but an arm intercepted him. "Excuse me, you're not cleared."

Confusion flash across his face. "What's wrong? I have my—"

Two other guards hurried to the scene, weapons drawn. "Stand down!"

Before Ari could rush to his side, someone grabbed her from behind and lifted her into the air. Struggling against their hold, she screamed. "Re—"

A hand slapped over her mouth as her captor pulled her back away from Reed and the guards. Panic rose up in her as she slammed her head backwards. It hit a rock-hard chest.

"This way," a familiar voice from the island said. It sent a wave of anger through her.

They dragged her into a small room. Her captor loosened the hold on her mouth, and she bit down, hard, until she tasted blood. He swore and threw her to the floor.

Pain shot through her body as she connected with concrete. Looking to the side, she realized she was in a bathroom, inches away from a toilet. Turning she wasn't surprised to find Niomi standing over her. Granted, the familiar bodyguard from the island didn't surprise her either.

For a moment, neither of them spoke but just glared at each other. Ari's eyes focused with all the hate and loathing she could manage, yet Niomi remained a blank slate.

Niomi turned to the man. "Give me a moment."

Holding the bite mark on his arm, he spit on the ground by Ari's feet and left the room.

Ari scrambled up. If it was just Niomi, she may have a chance.

Her trainer must have sensed her plan.

"If you fight me, I'll drag you out and hand you over to the authorities myself. You'll have no chance in hell to save Reed."

Ari blinked and pulled back. *Save Reed?* Her mind played through the last couple minutes. "What are you doing here?"

"You read your file." Compassion showed in Niomi's eyes.

The loathsome compassion of a murderer, Ari reminded herself. Grabbing her bag off the floor, Ari shook with the anger and betrayal. "Must have ruined your dream job. How much do they pay you to slowly drive me insane?"

"It wasn't like that. I—"

Not able to listen to Niomi's lies while Reed was being taken away, Ari charged forward. Niomi side stepped and brushed Ari's attack aside. In mere moments, Niomi had her pressed against a wall, hands pinned behind her back.

"Bury the rage, Arianna." Niomi leaned against her, her words urgent in her ear. "You need to think. VisionTech is crawling all over this island. I'm supposed to be helping them secure you and bring you back. They have Reed and will now be searching the whole boat for you. They want you."

Some part inside of Ari knew she was right. Ari wanted to scream, to fight, to cry that there was nothing she could do. "I won't go back there. I won't be other people until one day I don't know who I am anymore. I can't lose myself for them."

"I don't expect you to."

"What are you doing here then?" Ari assumed her trainer would drag her back to the island, but if so, what are they doing in a bathroom?

"I didn't want to hurt you. Why do you think we trained so much? I put off your trips inside as much as possible. But I knew you were too weak to survive on your own."

"I hate you," Ari spit out between a clenched jaw. It didn't make sense, but she felt so helpless and to be called weak on top of it all stung.

"Fine. Hate me. But don't be stupid. You won't get another chance to escape and you won't get out of your contract for years. You need to leave now and without Reed."

Her heart tore at the thought. "No. I won't. I can't leave him."

"Why? They will keep him well fed and working on the island for another year or two in hopes you'll return. We can reunite him with his mother and they both will be watched carefully. He will at least be safe, unlike you."

"I need him." Tears fell down her face at the selfishness of that statement. She would drag him all over the world because she wanted him by her side.

"If you go to him now, you'll both be trapped on that island until you can't remember him anymore. You're a smart girl. Don't be selfish and for once think of what's best for him. Let him go now, and you can get him later." Niomi stepped back, releasing Ari. "I promise I'll keep an eye on him."

She wiped at her face before turning around. "How can I trust you?"

"Despite what you think, I tried to help you. When they approached me about a young untrained warper, I knew if I didn't take the job, they would just go to the next person who may not feel the way I do. I trained you to fight and to become anyone. Not just inside the system, but out as well."

The hurt inside of Ari wasn't ready to forgive her in the littlest bit, but Ari knew she was right. Joining Reed wouldn't help him at this point. Getting strong enough to rescue him would. She knew what she had to do, but it didn't make the decision any easier. Lowering her eyes, she nodded in defeat.

"Okay." Niomi pulled out a device. "I'll make sure to put you in a section that has already been searched."

Unable to face Niomi, to face herself for abandoning Reed, Ari focused on the floor in front of her.

"Ari."

She lifted her head as Niomi handed over a small bag.

"Take this. The money's untraceable, and with a couple IDs and proper documents you should be able to start over. Keep your head down, okay?"

She felt empty and cold as she accepted the bag, like a traitor for leaving Reed behind.

"Once I leave, I'll empty the hall for you. Count to twenty and go to your right. Room 101 will be yours." Niomi stepped towards the door. "I wish I could have done more for you. I really tried." She left without another word.

Ari stood there, struck dumb for a moment, trying to think back to all her interactions with Niomi. Was she training her for the VLEX or for this? *Move, idiot. Think later.*

Not sure of how long it had been, Ari placed a hand on the door, a manual door which she hadn't seen since she left home. With one more deep breath, she pushed through, heading towards the unknown.

CHAPTER FORTY

The pain of loss hung with Ari through her voyage. She ended up sharing a room with two other women, but early on turned off her translator. The sway of the small boat brought on a new wave of sickness and Ari welcomed it.

Even though Niomi's advice was logical, Ari couldn't help the aching in her chest. Thoughts of Reed, of what he was going through plagued her. Even her own family seemed worlds away. The hope of a normal life had been shattered. Isolation was the only way to keep her family safe. Though the idea brought upon a new wave of darkness and despair.

The journey took three days. She never left her room except to go to the bathroom. The women would bring back food for her, which was probably for the best. By the morning of the last day, the fact she hadn't showered for three days didn't even bother her. Niomi's voice haunted her, shouting that Ari couldn't give up. Keep running, keep fighting, until there was nothing left to give.

She realized she couldn't check out of this life. Not yet. Not until those she loved were safe, and she made amends for those she hurt, if that was even possible. Then after that... well, her life would be hers to do with what she might. Until then, she needed to get off her butt.

Exiting the boat in a small port in Acadian, Ari rubbed her arms as she maneuvered off the docks. The temperature had dropped considerably as they made their way north. She'd need to find some warm clothes.

Walking into town, she rehearsed her identity one more time. *I'm Tara Phillips, running away from my abusive husband, Dan.* At least Ari didn't have to act to much. She was a runaway with a new identity, a new skin, a new life. Pushing away the past, she focused on the task ahead of her.

While the town was large, it held a quaint fairytale feeling with fresh paint, smiling faces, and flowers dotting the storefronts. A night and day difference than where she left Reed. Her heart ached at the thought of him. He would have loved this place.

She found a clothing shop and searched for a warm jacket. Niomi had given her plenty of money, so she also picked up gloves, a hat, and a couple of extras that fit in her bag. The shopkeeper, an older woman, was happy to help Ari check out. Her accent was thick, but they communicated fine through Ari's translator.

As Ari packed her bag, she wondered how much she could trust this woman. With few choices and even less time, she hoped she was making the right decision. "I'm meeting a friend." Ari then repeated the address of the restaurant where she was meeting Antoine.

"It's a day's ride to the north. You'll have to take the tram."

A day. It took a minute to remember what day of the week it was and realized that Antoine was expecting Kari tomorrow. She'd need to move fast.

"How can I get there?"

"The station is two miles down the road. Is he someone special?" The woman smiled and winked at her.

Lowering her eyes as if embarrassed, Ari nodded and thanked the woman before leaving. The station was loud and crowded but offered a lot of different ride times. She ended up purchasing an overnight ticket which would save her from renting a room.

Once bought, she wandered aimlessly, waiting to board. Her movements became robotic and without feeling. If she started thinking about what she left behind, she couldn't do what she was about to do.

The growling of her stomach awakened her for her need to eat. She grabbed a small meal and boarded the tram. The countryside flew by as the sun set behind mountains of glistening snow. Exhaustion set in and she slept sitting up.

She woke to the sun rising on similar mountains yet now more grandiose. The morning flew by as she stared out the window, only getting up to take care of her body's needs. She fell into numb trance as the tram raced towards what came next: Antoine. The idea filled her stomach with ice cold dread.

In the afternoon, the overhead speaker announced her stop. She freshened up in the small bathroom, trying not to look as ragged as she felt. Her brown eyes looked lifeless accompanied by dark circles hanging underneath. The red hair still bothered her, like a stranger staring back at her. She finished brushing her teeth, spat in the sink and left the room.

Back in her seat, tall heavy trees flashed by, growing in number. The view opened, and the tram slowed. A mountain resort sat nestled in a small valley.

Zipping up her coat, she exited the tram and headed to

the wood fashioned building. It looked like it was constructed from the nearby trees. Ari had never seen anything like it before.

A pretty woman greeted her at the door. "How can I help you?"

"I'm meeting a friend, Antoine, for dinner." She bit her lip as she scanned the room.

"Of course, let me take your coat." The attendant helped her out of her coat and led her into the dining area.

Ari spotted the table first, the one with a large bouquet of lilacs. A bottle of wine with two glasses also waited for her. No, not for her, for Kari.

As they approached, Antoine pushed up from the table, dressed in black pants and a nice button-up blue shirt. He looked similar to his VLEX profile. An extra ten pounds or so rested in his middle section and face. His jaw wasn't as chiseled as inside VLEX, but he was still attractive. His kind gray eyes greeted her with excitement.

Her stomach ached with dread and guilt. She had hurt this man maybe more than anyone. Would her next step help or hurt him more?

Reaching for her, he wrapped her up in a big hug. "You look nothing like I imaged but still so beautiful." His heavy accent laced his words, but he spoke in English.

Uncomfortable with his embrace and not able to hide in the program, she stepped back. Even though he felt like a good friend after all the time they spent together, he was still under the notion she was someone else.

She motioned to the table. "Sit, please. We need to talk."

His brow furrowed in confusion. "What's wrong, Kari?"

Guilt felt heavy in her stomach, and Ari didn't want to answer to that name.

"You are Kari, aren't you?" His confusion turned to apparent concern quickly.

She was surprised he connected the dots so quickly, but also grateful. Motioning to his seat, she waited until he was seated. "I'm not Kari. I'm sorry, but I thought you would want to know about her."

Bewilderment flash across his face. "What about her?"

Glancing down, Ari noticed his restless fingers picking at a napkin on the table. "There's no easy way to say this. Kari hasn't been inside VLEX for months." Before he could react, she continued with her story of how she was hired by a company to impersonate Kari, and how Ari didn't know where Kari was or what happened to her.

By the time she finished, Antoine strangled the napkin in his hands, staring at Ari with a strange mix of rage and concern. Finally, he poured himself a tall glass of wine and drank half of it. Looking up at her, his expression was hard to read. "Did they kill her?"

"I was told that she was alive, but I don't know if that is true. I had a friend check Kari's house, and she was no longer living there."

He glanced away, quiet. Ari recognized that painful ache deep in his eyes, because it mirrored just how she felt. Maybe she did deserve to be alone after all the pain she caused this man.

"Why?" His words came out as a whisper barely heard over the roar of nearby conversation.

"Why what?"

"Why are you here telling me this? Why did you keep up the whole character with dating me inside the VLEX? And how did you pull it off? The skins are permanent inside VLEX."

"Not for someone like me." For the first time, she wasn't

afraid of what she was, but ashamed. "I'm telling you now because I wanted to make it right."

"The only way to make it right is to bring me Kari."

The thoughts that had been swirling in her mind formed into the start of a plan of how to find Kari and take care of what she needed for Emil. "I don't know if I can, but I'm willing to try."

She gave him a moment and resisted the urge to comfort him. Hugging him would be natural as she thought of him as a friend at this point. But he didn't know Ari, he only knew Kari.

His gaze turned steely. "How can you fix this? If she's not home, where would she be? She may be dead."

"I'm hoping I can find someone else that knows her, family, friends that would know where she would be. Thing is, I don't have a way to get back inside."

He glared at her under his long lashes. "Is this some sick joke? You tell me my girlfriend's possibly dead, and the only way you can save her is by using my credentials to get inside."

"No." Looking back at the conversation, she had to admit he had a point. It didn't look good. But getting inside would give her the resources she needed. "I just... look." She leaned forward, elbows on the table. "I don't need your credentials, I just need a way inside. I left the company I worked for. They, along with a government or two, are searching for me. My skill set is... very unique inside. Give me twenty minutes, that's all I need."

He finished off his glass of wine. "How dumb do you think I am?"

"I'm sorry. I'm trying to make this right. I'm caught up in something bigger than I imagined. But believe it or not, I care about her. Always wondered about her. That's why, I couldn't break you two up. I have access to her files and hope they have some information on her family and loved ones. If you want to find her, I will help. I will do whatever I need to make this right. And I can give you my personal information or whatever you need to trust me."

He stared at the empty wine glass in his hands for a minute, the heavy silence full of unspoken pain and emotion. Shame ate at her as she watched his empty expression.

"Okay." He finally lifted his gaze. "I'll give you twenty minutes. If you get caught, I'm saying you broke in and stole access. I won't go down for this."

"Of course. Antoine," she waited until he met her eyes, her own emotion fighting to get free, "I'm so sorry. I want you to know that."

He shook off her hand. "No. You don't deserve any sympathy or forgiveness until I have her back."

"That's fair." She couldn't deny the mistakes she made, which were many. "The sooner we get in, the sooner we get her back."

CHAPTER FORTY-ONE

The sun had settled behind the mountains and darkness settled in the valley as they boarded the tram. They needed to get to Antoine's office back in town. Only a few silent passengers littered the car, making for a quiet ride through the dark of night.

Buried deep in thought, Ari wondered exactly where Kari was. Did she have some type of illness, or maybe Niomi was right and she sold out? Ari wasn't sure what to hope for.

And what would the cost be of going back in? Was her life like an hour glass? Every trip or manipulation ticked off a few more days or weeks of her life?

Antoine offered her a drink of the large wine bottle he'd taken from the restaurant. "You look like you could need a drink, too."

"No thanks."

"Do you have someone here with you? Family nearby?"

Ari turned to him, wondering why he asked. "No."

"I'm just surprised you came all the way here to tell me this."

"Me too."

They rode the rest of the way in silence, interrupted only by him finishing off the bottle of wine. They stepped off the tram, and the cold slammed into them full force. She burrowed deep in her jacket, but the cold still penetrated.

"Up this way." He motioned to the right, then watched as she put on her thick gloves. "You really aren't from here are you?"

"No. I can't say I care for it."

"People wonder why we drink so much." He buttoned up his thin coat and headed into the wind.

Tall old buildings lined the street, and he motioned to the brick one on the corner. "Keep your head down. I can erase the security feed, but in case they beat me to it, we don't need our mugs pasted everywhere."

Surprised at his ability to erase the security feed, she pulled her hoodie up and focused on her steps in front of her. Every step felt surreal, like she was back in VLEX living someone else's life. Someone who escaped off islands, stowed away on boats, and went with tall dark strangers in the middle of the night to break into buildings. Kari's life almost felt normal in comparison to her own.

He quickly got them inside the building, bypassing the security with ease.

"What do you do for work?" Surprised at his ability, Ari didn't think most diplomats or aids could hack a system like Reed or Marco.

"I started here as IT. After a few years, I got assigned to provide technical help inside the VLEX."

That's convenient.

Heading upstairs, she pulled off her gloves, rubbing her hands together to warm them. Then she pulled out the small drive from her necklace. "I'll need you to upload this to the server when I get in."

"Why?" He took the miniature drive and turned it in his fingers. "What's on this? Codes for stolen cryptos?"

"Nothing that exciting. It's just me." Files and characters that boiled down to be the story of her life. Sad to think everything she had and was could be hidden on something so small. That was all she had left. Yes, inside a program she may have vast possibilities, but out in the real world, it felt insignificant.

"Okay. Have a seat." He powered up a nearby station. "Now, I warned you. Twenty minutes is all I can give you before security is alerted and is on their way down. I want Kari's real address, her physical location. If not, I turn you over to the authorities. I have enough proof even now to throw you away for a while. Do you get me?"

Mouth dry, Ari nodded. "The drive has everything you need on me to help you put me away for a while. I'll put Kari's information on the drive I gave you. If things get bad, take it and run." If things went bad, jail time for breaking into here would be her least concern.

Pushing her hair aside, she plugged into the machine and leaned back. The cold leather chair sent a shiver down her spine. Closing her eyes to the real world, she wondered if reality would look the same when she woke.

CHAPTER FORTY-TWO

Since she was signing in under an unfamiliar account, she was careful how she entered the VLEX. Keeping her presence a secret was imperative. As she entered the VLEX, she awoke to the code surrounding her. Antoine put her outside his office building. Because of the time zone change, she barely beat the rush hour. Checking the code for time in VLEX she realized she had a few minutes until most offices opened. For now, mostly security and overzealous employees roamed the open streets.

She thought of just stealing the data from Kari's old office without even appearing in the program, but the mass amount of data to sift through was too much, even for her. She didn't need Kari's real address. Tessa already searched that out and didn't find Kari. Ari would have to locate her family home or some other connection to find her.

So, between one second and the next, Ari donned Kari's familiar skin and stepped out from the shadows of a nearby building. She followed the familiar cobblestone street to the building where she had spent so many hours. It was quiet as she took the elevator up to her office. They had changed the access codes from those she previously knew, but a quick hack of the code and she was inside.

She dug through files wondering where someone would put their own childhood address. It's not like she'd be writing a personal plan for a visit. Despite Antoine's threats, Ari really did want to find the address, to find out for herself whether she killed Kari by being willing to take over her life.

File after file and she couldn't find anything. Ten minutes had passed, and she still had a lot to do besides this. Ari turned to Kari's email in hopes maybe she found a meeting with someone for coffee or something. Then she remembered she wouldn't contact outside people or at least she shouldn't. Ari had been reading her emails for weeks now and would have seen something. When else would someone refer to something personal at work? Then it came to her. School.

Ari searched for any mention of schools, colleges, and then resumes. She found it. A message from a college six months ago that mentioned an upcoming reunion. It wasn't an address, but it would have to be enough. She saved the information to the drive Antoine could access. At least she found the school Kari had gone to, and who knows, maybe she grew up nearby. Ari closed the computer then stood to leave when President Higgins walked in.

"Good morning, sir." She stiffened slightly, realizing she had no idea what VisionTech told him when she left. They oversaw the real life deception of this program.

Pausing mid-step, he looked at her with bewilderment. "What are you doing here?"

"Just finishing up a few things. I'm all set, so I'll be heading out though. Have a great day." She walked past him, eyes focused on the door behind him.

He reached out and grabbed her arm. "You should not have access to this floor anymore. You shouldn't be here."

"I'm leaving now." She pulled on her arm, but he didn't loosen his grip.

"Security," he yelled. He didn't have to yell, since inside the VLEX calling for security notified them electronically. They would be here in mere seconds.

"I wish you wouldn't have done that." She considered fighting him. He was tall, but with his age, she'd have the advantage. She couldn't chance though that she couldn't be gone before security arrived. They could track her electronic signature and possibly track her down physically.

As he started to drag her outside, she focused on the code around her. In mere seconds, President Higgins was left grasping on to thin air. She poured through the code enough to find herself outside nearby the fountain. A small pain throbbed behind her eyes. She pinched the bridge of her nose until it passed, not dwelling on what it meant.

Instead of donning Kari's appearance, which may now be linked to security. She chose another of the skins she memorized, Stacee. Her dark skin blended with the variety of ethnicities found in VLEX. Ari kept the clothes and hair simple focusing more on getting through the shops undetected.

When she arrived at Emil's offices, she waited impatiently at the door. A few passersby gave her awkward glances as she waited in front of a door that was obviously open. Finally, an unfamiliar man opened the unseen door to Emil's rooms and without a word he escorted her in.

Once inside Ari spoke, "I need to see Emil right away."

"He's been waiting for you."

They entered the room, where Emil stood to the side of

his desks staring at an empty screen. Empty to her at least. Who knew what Emil saw in this place.

"You shouldn't have alerted security." He remained focused on the screen. "The place is on high alert."

"I have my file," she told him, uncertainty tightening her stomach.

"I know. I found it when I realized you were here. You'll need to learn how to hide your information better in here." His calm demeanor infuriated her.

"I need help and I need money. I'm no longer with VisionTech."

"Good girl." He turned with a smile. "Go to worldwide game Gaia and search out Bacchus. He will set you up with what you need."

Ari recognized the reference to Greek mythology but had no clue where to find this Gaia. "Don't you get it. I'll be homeless by the end of the week, stranded in some foreign country."

Emil stepped towards her. "You're smart and more than capable if you got away from VisionTech. We can only do so much inside the VLEX. We have connections all over the world. You're part of the team now and will be taken care of, but it's not for free. You have to do your part."

Ari swallowed, wishing for damn water, as she wondered what exactly she'd have to do. She'd do what she had to, to get by and then get those she loved and get the hell out of here. "Okay. I'll talk to you in Gaia."

"Not yet. I have a task for you before you leave."

"A task?" He made it sound as simple as getting coffee, but she knew better than that.

"Yes."

"I have now," she checked the time on her HUB, "eight minutes before I need to leave."

"Then we better not waste time debating this."

"And if I don't?"

"Then I won't be able to help you financially." His smile vanished, an icy demeanor chilling her to the bone.

"So that's it, huh?" Ari didn't have much to bargain with, but at the same time, it's not like she could really hurt anyone in here. If Emil wanted money or something of the sort, he could get it himself.

He waited for an answer.

"Okay. I'll give you five minutes, then I'm gone."

"Good choice. We're ready to announce to the world that we are watching them. Hints and rumors have flown through the years. It's time the world leaders know that they are being watched and will be held responsible for all their actions."

"And you want me to say that to who?"

"To everyone." His chagrined smile returned, full force. "I assume you can figure that out. I uploaded the short speech to your drive."

"Everyone." The magnitude hit her, but she couldn't dwell on it. On the physical cost it would take and how it would be painting a target right on her. "You have four minutes."

Without thinking too hard on it, she focused on what she had to do. As she fled his office, she realized she had wanted to do this for some time. Tired of the hiding and the lies, people needed to know warpers were real. Presidents and those in power already knew as they used them for the tools and weapons they could become, but everyone else should know. Parents raising their kids, and people whose lives were run by their oppressors.

Ari knew exactly where she needed to be. As she worked the code through her mind, a code she learned back at school which felt like an eon ago, she rushed to the main fountain. The morning rush was heading in. People appearing outside buildings, some headed for a morning coffee. Was she really going to do this?

Don't think. Just do. With that thought she climbed on the edge of the fountain and turned to face the crowd. A few people glanced her way, but no one stopped. A quick glance on her HUB and she realized she had two minutes. Taking a deep breath, she put the code in place, pulled up the speaker, and exhaled.

"To the people of VLEX." Her voice boomed through the courtyard, startling her for a moment before she continued. People in the square now stopped with confused expressions. Ignoring their shocked faces, she stared at the building in the distance. "This is a warning. Warpers are rising up. We're taking off the chains you want to bind us with. We'll no longer be slaves to the highest bidder, no longer doing your dirty work. We'll fight for the world we want to create. Starting now!"

A firm hand gripped her arm as she finished the sentence. A tall guard pulled her to the ground. "You're under arrest." He quickly slapped something metal on her arm.

After pulling back for a moment, she focused on the code, retreating to safety. As the code appeared around her, she realized the guard slapped her with something more than a mere restraining device. It was a tracking device of some sort. She didn't dare take it back with her. If they traced her back to the real world, she didn't have the means to relocate or escape. Anger and frustration boiled under her skin.

More security appeared in the courtyard, surrounding her. A myriad of thoughts colored in panic fled through her mind. The security guard locked her hands behind her, and it pulled her out of the code. Twisting, she kicked at the guard, and it took him by surprise. He stumbled back, and she took that moment to free her hands. She couldn't flee though not until she took off the tracking device.

She saw the tool on the guard's hip. She moved towards him and another pair of hands fell on her. The alarm she'd set on her HUB began beeping. If Antoine pulled her out now, they would know where she was. Rage exploded coloring her vision, and she struck out at the man behind her. Instinct must have flowed through her as the guard flew backwards ten feet or so.

Code flew in and out of her vision, mixing with the images around her. She didn't think, just acted. She took the tool from the guard's belt, some kind of program but made for an idiot. She hit the key which unlocked the tracer on her just as she was tackled to the ground. Others joined him, pressing down on her.

Pain struck at her, clouding her thoughts. *Just leave.* But fuzzy spots blocked her now. Her vision blanked in and out, a sharp pain stabbing in her mind, and fury exploded. She screamed, the sound echoing through the program, blocking out all conscious thought, but it gave her the out she needed to leave.

Soft hands pulled the cable out of the back of her neck as black stars danced in her vision.

Antoine's dark eyes bore down on her.

"I got Kari's information." Her words slurred slightly.

"Wonderful, my dear. Some were surprised you'd go through all of that. They even doubted your power when they saw you dancing with me."

He continued rambling on, and Ari wondered if that

last trip caused some type of brain damage. Why was Antoine talking about dancing? She struggled to sit up.

"Give yourself time, my dear. You've been through a lot. We have time to rest, then I'll take you back to the others. Sarah has a great remedy for our special kind of torturous hangover."

Our? Our special kind of headache. Slowly sitting up, her vision finally cleared, and she struggled to put together the pieces of what was happening.

Looking up into his dark eyes, Ari remembered what happened after her first trip to VLEX and Niomi's surprise that Kari had a boyfriend. A boyfriend who stuck with Kari despite Ari impersonating her, a boyfriend with amazing abilities to hack security feed, and a boyfriend who put her inside VLEX without much resistance.

"Who are you?" she asked.

"I think you know." A familiar smile flashed on Antione's face, or who was also known as Emil. "Welcome to the team."

END OF BOOK TWO

Thank you for reading SYNCHED.

If you're looking for more from DeAnna, keep reading for a peek into her Urban Fantasy, DEMON RISING, the first in her Dark Rising Trilogy.

Don't miss out on the prequel novella, EVIL ETCHED IN GOLD, now available!

Do you want to share your exciting discovery of a new read?

Help others add it to their To Read lists by rating and/or writing a review:
Goodreads
Amazon US
Amazon UK

Sign up for DeAnna's newsletter for the latest news, free releases, and new release information.

Or you're welcome to come for a visit at Deanna's website at:
https://deannabrowne.com

her tattoo? He scanned the crowd with a demon dog at his side, a German shepherd with unnaturally large black eyes.

Turning forward, she let her dark hair fall into her face, not wanting to draw his attention. She stepped past the guard undisturbed. She could handle herself with the guards, but her boss, Nikko, constantly nagged her about keeping a low profile.

The crowds pressed together, and a large man knocked into Becca's side, tripping her. She stumbled, spilling the remains of her coffee all over her black jeans. Someone swore as the crowd surged forward, and she stepped to the side.

At five-foot-five, she was on the small side, but strong enough to cause pain and scrappy enough to avoid it when she could. The crowds weren't her problem, though. That would be the presence behind her, causing her tattoo to burn.

She whipped around and grabbed the small hand, reaching for her hunting knife. A young boy, maybe ten or twelve years old, struggled in her grasp. Blond hair curled around his ears. His face was lined with dirt. Once she glimpsed his eyes, she tightened her grip and shoved him back against a brick storefront.

A hellish black, his eyes revealed the demon residing inside of his body. Becca clamped down on any sympathy she might have had for this child, for he was no longer a child but a Soultorn. Fury rose, fast and fierce. Some wizard had corrupted this boy past repair by summoning a demon and using the boy's body as a host.

She pinned him against the wall with her forearm, her knife pointed at his throat. "Where's your master?"

"It could be you if you want," he lied.

His lips twisted into a wretched smile, revealing broken

Some sacrifices cost more than death...

The tattoo on Becca's neck prickled as she walked the crowded path to work. Searching for the possible source of magic, she continued forward, with coffee in one hand and the other resting by the knife at her waist.

She moved amid a throng of people, shuffling along the worn walkways. Heavy clouds were scattered across the sky, while dilapidated buildings surrounded them, a haunting reminder of what once was. A young man pushed past Becca, dressed in blue coveralls. *He must be heading to the line.*

The warehouse traveled up twenty stories high, the tallest building in town with a large fountain in front. It must have once been a beauty. Now the fountain, covered in graffiti, ran dry and the boarded-up windows could barely keep the wind out.

A familiar, lanky guard stood watch on the side of the road. Could he have been the source of the magic warming and stained teeth. The sour smell of his fetid breath turned her stomach. There could be only one master a Soultorn would ever answer to, and that magician must be an idiot to let a Soultorn roam free. Maybe they wanted someone else to dispose of it.

She should just kill this body. It would be a kind mercy for this poor boy whose body had been stolen. His blond curls and freckles tugged at her gut, reminding her of a past she didn't want to remember.

"Come on, lady. A kid's gotta eat," the demon whined, trying to force his expression into something pathetic.

A black leather jacket and steel toed boots didn't scream "lady." Ladies didn't work as a runner for the local drug lord either, but at twenty-four, it was the best job she could get. "You're a demon. All you eat is other's pain." Becca edged the knife deeper against his neck.

Demons could eat food. The human bodies they stole preferred it, but death and destruction were a demon's main course. The Soultorn in her grip struggled to swallow against the blade's lethal edge.

Her lips pressed into a tight dark smile. "What? Realizing that a lesser spawn of hell like yourself may not have a shot at the afterlife?" Not that she knew much about demon realms, but she'd heard that demons never enjoyed returning.

What idiot summoned this lesser demon? Weak magicians recklessly played with demons in a hopeless attempt to grasp power. Demon pets and Soultorns were not allowed in the Mundane market streets without a leash. The law, weak as it was, helped to keep the Mundanes somewhat safe from being enslaved by every two-bit magician. It wouldn't do any good for the wizards to kill off the work force.

The Soultorn spoke in a foreign tongue. Her tattoo tingled, and dark spots filled her vision. She focused on maintaining her grip. As the Soultorn's dirty fingers dug into her jacket, pain shot up the arm that clutched the knife. Her tattoo protected her against minor magic, but not direct attacks.

Out of time, Becca grabbed its hair and rammed its head into the wall, hoping to weaken it and break the spell. It took several hits before those pitch black eyes rolled back, and it collapsed on the ground.

Her breath left in a rush. Her fingers tingled with the return of feeling. She shook them out and stepped back, knocking into her now empty coffee cup. Dang demons, she'd lost her coffee and had to deal with a minor demon before nine a.m. Yeah, it was a Monday.

The Soultorn fell at an awkward angle, knocked out but still breathing. She didn't have the stomach to kill a child host this morning. Now the magician who created it? That was a different story.

"Are you going to finish it?" Ted, the local coven guard from across the street, appeared behind her, placing a hand on her arm. His vicious grin and long brown hair almost mirrored the look of the possessed German shepherd at his side. The dog's tail wagged high in the air, his teeth sharp and white. Not only could demons reside in humans, but magicians could put them into animals as well—changing the whole meaning of family pet.

Becca shuddered in disgust and backed away from his touch. "Isn't that your job?" It was the one useful thing maggots like Ted did to help the Mundanes.

"Yes, but I like a girl with a little blood on her hands." As if in agreement, the demon dog at his side barked.

The only blood she wanted to spill was his. Wizards

like him caused deaths like this without a second thought. "Just do your job," she said, pushing past him. She might be able to take on a minor demon, but not a wizard. Besides, she had to get to work.

Growls erupted from the possessed German shepherd, and with a single command from its master, the dog pounced on the boy's body. She walked away, the grisly sounds of his attack echoing off the buildings.

She was grateful that she'd skipped breakfast, because there was no way it would have stayed down. Most people avoided the scene, except a couple of onlookers who watched with vacant expressions. Hurrying down the street, she tried to block out the noise. The face of the boy flashed into her mind. Her chest tightened as she mourned the boy— not his body, but his spirit that was stolen too soon.

One more demon vanquished. Hopefully, the creator would be punished, though probably not. And the boy—just more collateral damage.

Something she'd seen all too often with city life. Still, it was better than living outside the city walls, where gangs and demons roamed free. Somehow, that didn't make the boy's death easier to swallow.

She didn't slow her pace until Nikko's building came into view, an old two-story bar with dusty floors, but clean glasses. Its dark frame appeared vacant, but there was a full house. People watched from the darkened windows around the clock. Before she could knock, the door creaked open.

"Hey, sweetie." Tyson welcomed her with a sly smile. His large frame and soft face gave him the appearance of an oversized teddy bear, but she'd seen that teddy bear break a man's neck.

"Nothing sweet here." She strode past.

"Okay," he replied, one hand rose up in defense.

As she continued on, he murmured, "Heard she knifed her last lover."

Her lips lifted in a grim smile. She'd worked hard for that kind of rep—a necessary tool in a business full of men.

The bar reeked of smoke and alcohol. One wall was decorated with a rainbow of colored bottles. Across the floor, two guys played a game of pool. An older man nursed a cup of coffee at one of the many small wooden tables. She'd have to grab a cup later.

She turned down the hallway and maneuvered to the back, to Nikko's office. After a quick knock, Nikko called her in.

He hovered over papers at his desk while a cigarette burned away in the ashtray. He played with one of the metal studs piercing his brow. She studied him while he remained deep in thought, knowing better than to interrupt.

A dark, intricate tattoo decorated one side of his face. Ancient runes she often tried to decipher. Rumors said his family came from Asia, farther away than she could imagine.

Dressed in a fitted navy suit that complimented his short, dark hair, he emanated beauty and terror all at the same time. Long ago she advised him to forget about dressing so nice, since everyone stopped at his face.

"Becca." He didn't bother to look up. "I need this out of here." He finished writing a note and sealed it in an envelope.

"Who in the world needs to get high this early?" She fell into a nearby chair not quite ready to head out. Yes, she ran drugs and other things for a crime lord, but she was never dumb enough to do them. At least with Nikko, she could face the thugs head on, instead of at the factories where they lurked in the shadows.

"What we supply is in constant demand." His brown eyes glimmered with mischief. "That's why we both have jobs. Today, I need you to head out of the city to Mariah's place."

Tension shot through her and she bolted upright, hands fisted on her knees. "Not Mariah's. I'm not going there again."

"Calm down." He dismissed her objection with a wave of his hand. "You're the only one I can trust not to get sucked into her little tricks. Last time, Tobi returned in such a state he couldn't remember how to piss straight. I can't afford that."

"Tell your guys to grow a pair. Or get them tats." She didn't remember even getting her tattoo as a child, but it had saved her hide more than once.

"That would cost more than Tobi." He finished packing the bag. "You know the deal. You want another job, you do this one."

"I may end up killing that witch." She meant it. The best kind of magician was a dead one. She also couldn't ignore the nagging voice in the back of her mind that said she might run into someone she knew, someone she didn't want to see again. The only magician she ever let get close to her, too close.

Nikko ignored her protest. "Just get me my cash first."

"I hate you," she said with no real malice. Lucky to have landed a job outside of the factories, she owed Nikko a lot. He'd helped improve her knife skills and paid her enough so she could afford her own studio apartment. However difficult the job, she'd do it. And he knew it.

"That's why we get along so well." He smiled. "Take the bike. Mariah wants this soon."

"What? Is she sacrificing small puppies?" Becca grumbled as she got to her feet. "Or her own mother this time?" A witch could stew up endless nightmares.

Nikko ignored Becca and tossed her the bag.

Catching it, she sighed. "Don't tell me. I don't want to know." Who knew what dead creatures or bones might be in there? Drugs were easy in comparison.

"I never do." He pushed keys across the table. "Just take good care of my baby. She's worth more than you."

"Telling me that every time I touch Dedra doesn't help my self-esteem."

"Can't believe you named my Ducati like an old mare," he mumbled, standing up. "Just get it done and bring it back tonight."

"Will do." A smile lit up her face. She'd named his bike when she realized the price he paid for it. Guys only do something that stupid or expensive for a broad. With the bag on her shoulder, she turned to leave.

"And, Becca?"

She turned back. "Yeah?"

His dark eyes warmed. "Be safe." Beneath the sarcasm and crappy jobs, Nikko watched her back, maybe because she was his best runner, or maybe he considered her a friend. She never asked.

She winked. "Ain't I always?"

Continue the journey with Becca in DEMON RISING!

DeAnna Browne graduated from Arizona State University with her BS in Psychology. She finds it helps to corral those voices in her mind and put them to paper. An avid reader and writer, she has a soft spot for fantasy with a touch of romance. Despite her love for food and traveling, she always finds her way back to Phoenix, Arizona with her husband, children, and pet dog.

Follow her at:
www.deannabrowne.com

facebook.com/deannabrownebooks

twitter.com/brownebooks

instagram.com/deannabrownebook

amazon.com/DeAnna-Browne/B074L9BH72

goodreads.com/DeAnnaBrowne